Black Water White Fire

Black Water White Fire

Jaspreet Taunque

KALPAZ

ISBN: 978-93-5128-075-0

Price: ₹ 350/-

Third Edition, 2014

Published by

Kalpaz Publications
C-30, Satyawati Nagar,
Delhi – 110052
E-mail: kalpaz@hotmail.com
Ph.: 9212142040

Laser Typesetting: Gyan Print (AB-I)
Printed at: G. Print Process, Delhi

Cataloging in Publication Data—DK
Courtesy: D.K. Agencies (P) Ltd. <docinfo@dkagencies.com>

Taunque, Jaspreet.
Black water white fire / Jaspreet Taunque. — 3rd ed.
p. cm.
Novel.
ISBN 9789351280750

1. Historical fiction, Indic (English). I. Title.

DDC 823.92 23

Dedicated

To my husband and best friend,
Dharam and daughter Zara;
and to all those who believe in love above all else.

Contents

PART–I
THE MAKING OF ZARRAR—WHITE TO BLACK

One

Peshawar, Pakistan, 1977

Music from the rabab wafted through the air and drew him home faster. It was 7 pm and the Sun had relented, signalling them to head home. He had started to walk from *Pepal Mandi* towards *Qissa Khwani*, with his three brothers. It was ritualistic. Like frisky ponies, they would start with a few lazy steps trying to keep pace with each other, dodging people, carts and donkeys. The steps would impetuously turn into a trot, and then a canter.

A walking-race home would gradually pick up pace amid giggles, on the wide street, and turn into a full run as they would enter the last, narrow lane on the left, at the end of *Qissa Khwani* Bazaar, the bustling market place in the city of Peshawar in Pakistan.

On most days, the Bazaar was warm with the high-pitched calls of the hawkers. With idling merchants sitting around a large samovar; a traditional brass urn that doubles up as a tea-brewer; sipping fragrant tea from small teacups, and craftsmen pitching their wares to passers-by, there was hardly ever a dull moment for the boys.

After the afternoon *namaaz*, the song-birds in their cages, waiting to be sold, would offer salubrious twitters as a parting treat to their owners, adding to the pink noise of prayers in the mosque.

Lilting music would greet them each day as they neared the threshold of their ancestral home. That day was no different. Except that the music was accompanied by the ethereal singing of his grandfather. The postcard and a gift had made the day special too. For the first time, *Zarrar* had received a letter from his father. It had been sent to Peshawar with a merchant-companion that his father often travelled with.

"Not for *Babajee* or *Ummi*, or any of your brothers. Only for you," the Uncle had said, with his eyes glinting in the Sun. The little boy's rueful complaining had an effect on his otherwise nonchalant father. Zarrar held the postcard size photo of his father, standing majestically in front of the Taj Mahal in Agra, India. Clutching the small box in one hand and the photo in the other, he had shot through the opposing breeze to be the first one to reach home. Even before he had opened it, he knew what that box contained.

The boys rushed in to greet their old man in the central courtyard of their spacious, ancestral house. He sat there, singing *Baba* Rahman's timeless verse in Pashto:

"Pa sabab da zalimano hakimano, Gore au ore au Peshawar dhray wara yo dee".

(Because of the oppression of tyrants, grave, fire and Peshawar-all three are one).

"Da tse ma-na Babajee?"

"What does that mean, Grandpa", he asked his grandfather, gulping in air as he ventilated and talked at the same time. The old man smiled, gesturing the boys to sit down. They settled around him, on the cotton mattress spread over a large jute mat. Bolsters offered comfort and support as Zarrar spread out on his stomach, listening to him with his chin cupped in his hands, his Taj Mahal postcard placed neatly in front of him.

"Datse ma-na....?" he asked again.

In front of their grandfather, lay the day's newspaper that carried news about the Pakistan Army. General Zia-ul-Haq, in a coup *d'etat*, had overthrown the democratically elected government and gained control at the Centre. It would only add to the unrest at the NWFP (North West Frontier Province) as blood and fire would further consume the vestiges of a bygone era whence the city was known as the city of flowers.

"Oye Rohillay! Let Babajee sing! Ask the meaning later!" One of his brothers had politely told him to shut up. In the old man's absence, he would have been lifted by one of his three brothers and hung upside down. The three of them would laugh at their boyish capers and the shallow smile on their timid, little brother's face. Then pretending to drop him to the floor, they would heave him up and down and down and up till the earth became the sky and the sky became the earth.

He was a tall and well-built boy for his age of seven; just like his brothers who were eleven, twelve and thirteen; but ever since he had been branded the girlish-boy of the family by his grandmother, he had started to brave all such pranks with a sheepish laughter even if the blood in his feet would come rushing to his head and the world would seem to black out around him.

He would sometimes wish to run and take refuge in his mother's long and flowing *abaya* but his grandfather's gaze would follow him and discourage him from falling prey to fear. He envied his brothers for being so fearless and *Pathan*-like. It made him feel like an ill-fitting addition to the family. Yet, they were the collective centre of his universe.

His grandfather however took pride in his well-built youngest grandson and loved to hear him being called Rohillay (which originated from the word 'Roh', meaning 'mountain' in Pashto, and literally meant 'mountain breeze') by the boys. To him, Zarrar was the perfect prototype of the majestic ancestry of which they were the descendants. Of course, it was a fact from the forgotten past; yet, it never took away from the pride and honour that ran through their arteries like oxygenated blood. His family had lived in that house for as long as he could remember and he recalled his mother telling him that their ancestors had come and established themselves on that land a century ago. To express his love and pride for him on certain days, the old man would call his grandson by the name Rohilla Suleimaani.

"*Khanzade, zalimaan* (tyrants) are the people who spread fear, hatred and injustice. And a true Pathan stands up against it! Do you know the story of the *gora* tyrants who once came to *Qissa Khwani*?"

Zarrar shook his head vigorously. His kohl-laden eyes became rounder with intrigue. There was a story coming out of his grandfather.

It had to be something full of adventure and risqué; a tale of a battle of honour.

"So then, let me tell you the story of the story-teller's bazaar," he started in a sing-song manner.

"Once upon a time, some time longer than long ago, there was a land that was called the Golden Bird. Now, you may want to know why it was called *The Golden Bird*. Well, as the name suggests, this land flourished under the wings of a large, magical creature whose colourful plumes were the envy of many a *hukmraan* (rulers) around the world. Under the glorious plumage, there thrived a system which Nature had crafted beautifully and perfectly. Majestic, ice-capped mountains to the North; vast, blue ocean to the South; sun-kissed peaks in the East and rich river-basins on the West; it was Allah's masterpiece. And in His utmost mercy, He gave this land to the most blessed creatures. Many animals of different sizes, shapes and stature, lived here. They communicated with each other in many different ways, ate different things and lived differently. Some were dark and some not so dark, some clever, some plain, but all beautiful in their own right. Some feared the Fire God while a few others believed in the spirits of the forest. Food was in abundance and everyone was content. There was a lot of *melmastia* (camaraderie) and no one ever snatched from the other and ate. The Golden Bird looked after everyone. You know she had magical powers and thus, no one under her wing would go to bed hungry. Do you know where her powers came from?"

Zarrar blinked and tried to think it through.

"Well, nobody knew that but as long as everyone was happy and was living harmoniously, nobody bothered to find out either. But good days, like bad days, have to pass too. Then came to that land, a tyrannous hunter! He was different from all the other hunters in the past. He was white, just like the moon, absolutely! You know what the moon is like, *ho*? Yes, just like the moon. One could never see his face completely; it was always half-hidden and blemished."

Zarrar's attention wandered to the photograph. He noticed his brothers giggling as they exchanged dare glances, preparing ground for a bolster-fight.

"He wanted to not only capture all the animals for their beautiful hide and teeth and claws, but he also wanted to annex the magical powers of the Golden Bird. He was clever. He knew where the magic lay but he could not set his hands on it without help from the inhabitants of the place. So he cooked up a story. Oh what a story-teller he was! Can you imagine what he told those gullible animals?"

Grandfather looked at the boys with smiling eyes.

"Was he just like you, Babajee," Zarrar asked.

"Oye…no, no, no…I'm a poor, old man! He said that he was a messenger of the gods. The animals were completely mesmerised. When he saw their spell-bound faces, he cooked up yet another story about the Rain God and the Fire God.

He told them that the two Gods were very unhappy with the animals as the animals had forgotten about them. Thereafter, they would shower water and provide food to only those animals which would remember them well and did their best to please them. Their progeny would survive only if they demarked and dedicated pieces of land to his Masters. The gullible animals believed him. After all he was a messenger of the gods and he was white.

Then began the fight for territorial rights! That's because the larger the land, the larger would be the offerings for the gods. The push and shove and scrunch for ownership and possessions caused the animals to distrust and deceive each other. Our Golden Bird became my Golden Bird. The Bird became sad and slowly started to lose her resilience. Little did the animals know that the magic came from their unity, which created strong, happy vibes for the Bird's heart to remain strong and pulsating. As mayhem fell upon the land, the hunter grew strong and powerful as many offerings were being made to him to carry to the gods. There were a few animals though, that could see through the hunter's devious plan. Among them were the wise old owl, the alligator and the badger. They met and discussed the state of affairs and decided to bring awareness among their kin.

So they decided to get all the animals together and take them on a march around the Golden Bird and see how her magical powers were leaving her and she was wilting. The badger had questions. "Who will be able to stand up against that powerful hunter? He is strong with his arms and intent! Who will want to risk their lives and bare their chest to the enemy's vile?"

"Do you know what the wise old owl said in response?"

There was a brief pause. The old man now had a vacant look on his face. He was so engrossed in his story-telling that he did not wait for guess-work to happen.

Two of his brothers had already started pulling at each other's *kameez*, making furtive attempts to slip away from there.

"Khudai Khidmatgar" (God will help us), he replied. Then, it was discussed and agreed upon that once the animals could attain an objective view of things, they would then be made to see the destruction brought about by the hunter. It would then be easier to work out a plan to restore the magic to its land and also to find a way to send the hunter packing.

The date was decided and so was the venue—here, right here where we are sitting. This was the place where all the animals had gathered on that fateful day. But the hunter had informers. He learnt of this plan and his evil mind conjured up a counter-plan. He was not about to let his game be ruined so easily. He called his fellow-hunters and hid them in nooks and crannies of *Qissa Khwani*.

The animals arrived, forgetting their differences, of Fire God or Forest Fairy, of dark or not-so-dark. They were all children of their land that day. The Golden Bird lifted its drooping head a bit and smiled. But the hunter came out with a devious scheme and asked all the hunters to slay the animals with arrows dipped in poison and fire. The animals, by now, had an inkling of his evil intention. Instead of running helter-skelter, they braved terror at the hand of the assailants, as they asked the hunter to leave their land and go. They kept chanting for freedom and took death in their stride. The owl screamed 'fire', the crocodile ranted 'death'; and the badger shouted 'Peshawar', all in the same breath."

Grandfather paused to wipe the inner corner of his eye.

"Then what happened, Babajee?" Zarrar's voice quivered as he asked.

Perhaps Baba Rahman, during his celestial promenade, heard these words somewhere. The crocodile, the badger and the owl were overwhelmed to see this carnage and went into shock and grief.

The crocodile's eyes filled with water; such was his sorrow that he remained submerged for days, months and years. The trauma of what he saw made him lose hope in the virtues of mercy and trust. The owl begged and pleaded and cried too but his pleas were drowned in the slaughter. He screamed till his speech was reduced to mere screeches and he cried till light left his eyes.

Thereafter, he spoke only when spoken to and refused to see things in the light of day. He resigned himself to darkness permanently. The badger, even though a brave and fearless animal, stood watching helplessly from a distance. Overcome with despair, he went underground and chose to live digging, trying 'to find a way out'.

"Baba, then did he find a way out? What happened to the Golden Bird?"

"The Golden Bird never recovered from that shock and like a loving mother, agonised over the loss of her sons. The badger kept digging and created another world for himself under the ground. The hunter continued to stay for some more time thereafter till he realised that the new occupants of that land were beginning to get too familiar with his techniques of brute force and were readying themselves to turn the tables on him. Besides, he had plundered enough and was ready to leave for home."

"But time keeps its diurnal pace and things keep changing. Plants grow in cemeteries and flowers blossom out of ashes. It's only memories that find a permanent place, and like thorns and thistles, they keep the pain alive."

"Baba, Baba, why are you crying? It's only a story!" "Just a story now, ho! Do you know what the saddest part of the story is?"

Zarrar shook his head again. Then, he came up with an after-thought.

"That the animals fought with each other?" He wanted to please his grandfather with an insightful answer.

"No. The saddest part is that the story is real. It was the worst day in the history of Qissa Khwani, that ill-fated morning of April 23rd, 1930."

*****

The span of attention had now outgrown its acceptable measure. The brothers were calling out for him from the street at the back of the house. He ran up to them. There was a tattoo-maker doing the rounds and they had made him to sit down at their doorstep. One by one, the brothers got symbols etched in dark-blue ink on their left arms. The eldest one got two crossed-daggers; the second got a falcon and the third's arm decorated with the image of a *markhor*. Zarrar chose to get a scrawl in Pashto. When done, it read:

بيار اژوندي ابن

Body clenched tight with pain, he kept his arm still while the work was being done. Sons of rugged soil were expected to brave pain of any kind with a non-condescending smile on their faces. He was too young but understood. Even their women were never seen shedding tears, publicly. So, he deftly rubbed his eye that was sheltering a tear, pretending to rub out grains of dust. He would never dream of breaking the code of *Pakhtunwali*.

After the job was done, he ran his fingers tenderly over the blood-streaked scrawl, giving his brothers, yet another opportunity to laugh at his effeminate behaviour. However, in his heart he knew that they understood what had brought on the gentle caress.

He had not seen much of his father who, according to his mother, was a merchant and needed to travel to neighbouring countries for trade. Money came by in the form of a decent inheritance and the selling of his grandfather's exquisite collection of brassware. He had enough to last them a lifetime. Till the age of seven he had seen his father only four times. He would bring with him, a few exotic presents for the family, along with sweet and sour tales of his travel. They would huddle around in the courtyard and listen to him in rapt attention, while his mother and grandmother would bring *'kahwah'*, a sweetened green-tea concoction with aromatic herbs, in earthen pots.

Afternoons would blend into evenings and evenings would merge into nights as his grandfather would round off the cheerful banter with music wafting deliciously from his rabab and on special nights, Baba Rahman's poetry. The conversation would then veer towards the political situation between East and West Pakistan and the status of the Awami League. The moonlight, the aroma, the stars and the strumming and the subsequent boredom of political discussion blended together to cast a magical spell on him and he would doze off on the rugs, amidst the bolsters. Then, on one of those fine mornings, he would wake up to find himself inside the house with his brothers and his father gone for another indefinite period.

*****

The day he got the tattoo on his arm was also the day when he rode a donkey for the first time, earlier in the day. It was a hot Friday afternoon and he was hanging about Pepal Mandi with his brothers and their friends. They would often go there to get the flour milled, at the behest of their mother. The area was thronged by people; some of them traders from across the *Khyber*; who would bring in their carts and overloaded donkeys to sell their merchandise in the crowded lanes.

The boys hid themselves in nooks and waited for a donkey with a heavy load on its back. Then, together and very deftly, they would throw darts at the donkey's butt, which would send him hee-hawing and tap-dancing on his hinds. Consequently the load would fall off the animal's back and it would run madly towards the market place creating panic.

Whoever would be the first to run up and catch the donkey by its ears would get to ride it through the long lane and back. By the time the trader would be done cursing and collecting his things along with his composure, they would return the donkey with heroic aplomb and the catcher would be crowned *Khotey Shah* (the king of donkeys) of the day by the amused group.

Now, that day was particularly special, since he had insisted that he wanted to join them in their game. They had warned him of the dangers but did not resist. So, he was initiated into the group. The game started and as usual, the third donkey that got caught in their nexus went squealing down the road. This time, the donkey ran in his direction and he ran after it as directed by the shouts of the older boys. He managed to catch hold of the donkey's ears but this animal was no straight ass.

He jerked his head in retaliation and threw him down, with his hoof scraping against his left cheek. His brother, with the falcon tattoo, came running towards him, scooped him up like a bird and ran after the donkey. Within a matter of minutes, they returned astride the donkey's back, with Zarrar sitting proudly on it, and his brother guiding the animal. His cheek bled and throbbed a little but he was smiling.

The victory made even more glorious by the stoic presence of his brother, tasted twice as sweet.

That day his wish was everyone's command. Nobody ever thought of being non-committal to the rules of the game, even if it was a little boy who had won it. The code of Pakhtunwali did not allow it. The brothers made kites for him, bought him *chapali kebab* (flat and succulent mince dumplings spiced with exotic eastern flavours and smeared with clarified butter while cooking on an earthen girdle), released the song-birds from their cages when the seller wasn't watching and carried him on their shoulders all day long.

He, however, couldn't forbid them from turning him upside down, lest it gave away his fears and made them think that he was a coward.

*****

Later in the night, after the donkey-game, the painful tattoo and the musical story, he lay down beneath the star-spangled sky in the open courtyard, his favourite place in the house. The night was still and the stars spoke to him in characters like a light house to the ships. Holding the photograph in one hand and the miniature Taj in the other, he imagined what the white dome of the most beautiful mausoleum in the world would look like when viewed from the sky. He had heard vague stories about it having been built by an emperor for his beautiful wife.

He saw patterns like the falcon and the markhor and daggers and the rabab in the mysterious open space above him. There were other patterns too but he could not name them. He heard his name being called but he continued to drift in the sea of twinkling patterns.

Far away, the spiralling antlers of the markhor rose high up into the sky, drilling holes, large gaping holes that would close in after them. The goat-faced animal remained unperturbed and continued to drill and drive. It slowly began to take the shape of a large dome, the white changing to red as the antlers drove in deeper. The dome became a large slide and he slipped and slipped and slipped till he fell through the air; and landed on a donkey's back. His brothers cheered for him and sung songs of victory.

As the donkey ran off with him on his back, a voice chased after him shouting out his name, in a weak, laboured monotone. He awoke to his mother calling him to go inside and sleep. He picked up his rug and tottered inside the room where his brothers sat on their haunches and chortled away rather surreptitiously. Bleary-eyed, he quietly slipped into the circle and peered at what they were playing with. There were three matchboxes in the centre, lying side by side and a line drawn by a chalk. One of his brothers opened the match-boxes and out came three adult cockroaches, swishing their antennae wildly.

"What are you doing?" he asked.

"You go and sleep, *kashar ror*."

"First tell me what you are doing!"

"We are making men out of these creeps". And they chuckled again.

Each boy struck a match and brought the fire close to the antennae that were trying to make sense of the activity around them. As the feelers singed, the roaches danced a bit and ran to escape the heat. The only direction available was Twelve o'clock. As the runners crossed the white line, the winner of the race was announced, amid hushed cheer. The race would start all over again, once the roaches were identified and sent back into their containers.

He wanted to ask them to stop but it was useless. He would only end up fortifying his typecast image and yet, wouldn't be able to help the creatures. It was a better idea to pretend to enjoy the game.

Two

Peshawar, 1980

Saturday through Tuesday, at school, were listless days. The only person who made time easy to go by was Zarrar's friend and companion, Shehzaad. He was a well turned-out boy, the only son of a rich business family from *Mohalla Sethian*. The *Sethi Kothis*, an area of plush residences set up by the local, affluent businessmen of Peshawar, was at a distance of a few kilometers from *Qissa Khwani*. Even though it lacked the noise and clamour of the Story Tellers' Bazaar, it bespoke of the many material acquisitions of ambitious *Peshawaris*.

Shehzaad's family could afford an expensive school for him but they wanted their son to retain the values of the old world and allow the true teachings of Islam to complement his gracious upbringing.

Towards the end of an uneventful week, Shehzaad invited Zarrar to visit his house on Friday. It would not only divert his thoughts from the sense of loss that he felt each time his father left quietly in the night, but would also brighten his mood as Shehzaad always had something new and interesting to do. The thought perked up his mood immediately. The next two days passed in sweet anticipation.

On Friday morning, he dressed up in his white *mul* clothing and told his mother about his plan for the day. His mother packed some dry apricots for him to carry to his friend's house. His brother had gotten into a *tonga* (a horse-drawn carriage) with him to drop him off. He would then pick him up after lunch, on his way back home.

Zarrar entered his friend's house with his eyes trying to accommodate the splendour within. A narrow, unassuming passage led to an open courtyard just like his home. The only difference was the opulence.

Shehzaad's home was what grandfather's royal tales were made of. The arched doorways of the passage led to the courtyard, the perimeter of which was adorned with more arched doorways decorated with stained glass. Filigree work on marble and fine embellishments in coloured stone added a classic middle-eastern charm to it. Walls rose up in limestone and *waziri* (a small brick from Kashmir) and were adorned with curtains in fine skill and vibrant colours.

Ten doors led to ten different rooms. He wondered how many people lived in that house. As his eyes wandered upwards, he could see more doors and rooms upstairs with small balconies jutting into the vacant space above the courtyard.

Shehzaad took him straight to the rooftop where Peshawar seemed to become one long, stretched canopy over a city from another era. Little wooden bridges criss-crossed the roofs; thus, connecting the world that thrived below. Under the open sky, all of Peshawar seemed like one big family.

Zarrar's wide-eyed amazement peaked when he saw, in a corner, the most endearing array of kites, small and large, yellow, green, orange, red and many other hues that were unknown to him till now. Some were shaped as birds and butterflies, while others in the shape of strange creatures. He chose a red dragon with yellow trimmings. Shehzaad flew a butterfly. They were still too young to differentiate between bravado and bliss.

Their kites soared into the clear sky very ambitiously. It was an amicable decision not to snip each other's kite when it was air-borne. Any battle in the skies would only be for defence. Barefooted, they ran across several bridges and back, plunging, ducking, swerving and swooning with their kites. Unknowingly, they had become extensions of an inanimate personality, that remote-controlled their spontaneous joys.

Afternoon made a hurried exit and it was evening before they realised that the day had ticked away a little too fast. Throughout the afternoon, servants had been running up and down to provide the children with refreshing drinks and hot, succulent kebabs to eat.

They had spent lunch-hour in Shehzaad's room with silken spreads and mirrors on the wall. Zarrar stood in front of one of the mirrors. A long face with enormous, bulging eyes, stared back at him. He yelped and Shehzaad laughed out loud.

"My *abba* brought these magic mirrors. You can't imagine the funny faces that stare back at you through them. Try this one."

Zarrar went to the one on the other wall. A pot-bellied boy with stubby legs sneered back at him from the mirror. Soon, they were rolling with laughter, with tears flowing down their cheeks.

"My *abba* also brings very nice things for me. See."

Zarrar stretched his hand to reach the pocket inside his *kameez* (a long shirt). He then drew out the photograph of his father standing in front of the Taj, along with a miniature model of the monument.

"Where is this?" his friend asked, admiring the view in the picture.

"Taj Mahal, in *Hind*. He will take me there when he comes home next time." Zarrar looked dreamy and distant.

Zarrar went on to tell him how the tomb had been built by emperor Shah Jehan, as a symbol of undying love. Shehzaad giggled away in disbelief.

"Then you will come back, find a fat *mehbooba* (beloved) and make silly things for her too."

"Don't laugh. I think you will do it first. Your name is also like Shah Jehan. Shehzaad … Shah Jehan … same-same."

The boys squealed and giggled as Shehzaad chased him around the room, trying to punch him. The laughter was augmented each time they stopped short in front of one of the mirrors and saw twisted, distorted images laughing back at them.

It was time to leave when the servant brought a message from his brother, waiting in the courtyard. When Zarrar ran up to him, he was enjoying a milk concoction, rich with dry fruits. A platter of sweets lay in front of him and Shehzaad's mother was instructing the servants to pack some sweets for him to take home.

As the time to leave approached, Zarrar looked at the kite fondly before he put it back where it belonged.

"You can keep it," said his friend with a beatific smile. Zarrar shook his head, too embarrassed to have allowed his emotion to be so readable.

"No really! You can keep it. Consider it as a gift from your best friend. I would feel very happy. I will write something on it for you to remember me by."

Then he scribbled something in Pashto. It read: Shehzaad and Zarrar, the mountain and the sky.

*****

It was soon Monday morning. Zarrar left from home for the *madrasa* (mosque-school), dressed in crisp white *salwar-kameez* made of the softest *mulmul*. His mother used to stitch their clothes herself and would often adorn them with buttons made from tiger-claws.

His white cap sat itself self-assuredly on his head and his thick curls, short and shiny, behaved themselves. He was nearly ten years old and growing up into a handsome young lad. His cheeks were still peachy, though marred by a crescent-shaped scar on the left.

The *madrasa* was a short walk from home but this morning, it took him nearly half-an-hour getting there. He had to modify his route a little as his kite had gone flying into the lane behind the one where he lived. In the morning, he had heard his grandfather talk about some outsiders from across the Khyber, having come to live with a *Peshawari* family there.

He hoped his kite did not fall into the *verandah* of one of those houses, lest they got angry and insulted him. When he reached that lane, he tried to be civil and not to peep straight through the doors.

The appropriate thing would be to use his peripheral vision to look for his red dragon kite. He crossed two houses without a trace of his playmate. The last one was a house with blue doors and windows.

As he walked past, notes of a *Sufi* song, fell upon his ears in broken bits. Drifting in the direction of the musical draught, his eyes fell upon something even more enchanting than what he was hearing. Even though, his kite hung precariously across the wall, he was unable to wet his throat and ask for it. Instead, he looked for something in his bag, adjusted his cap, scratched his neck and walked away, hoping to catch a parting glimpse.

Thereafter, it became a ritual for him to go past the house with blue doors and windows in the next lane, where he would find swinging beside the door each day, the girl with the most beautiful, transparent grey-green eyes.

It was a Herculean task for him to pull his gaze away from those bewitching eyes that stared at him with dilated pupils. She looked older than him, by perhaps a couple of years. Rustic and raw; she was like a vase made of fuller's earth, taken away half-baked from the fire. It was her eyes that proved to be a tool of sweet entrapment.

Whether she was oblivious or aware of a young boy stealing glances at him, was not known to him. Yet, he was sure he would find her each morning on that swing going up and down and down and up touching the earth to the sky and the sky to the earth.

Weekday mornings came and went like clockwork. She never smiled but on certain days he would hear broken bits of a song that she sang in Pashto. One day, he had dared to make a halt to settle the things in his bag, which would give him an extra few minutes, right in front of her door. The fragmented singing was interrupted by the call of her mother. He quickly recovered his step.

She had responded to the call of '*Husna*' (the beautiful one). Had he stayed for another second, he would have seen her walk to her mother like an angel in the dark, with her long braid swinging above her ankles. It was a day of unusual achievement and he had beamed his way through the *maulvi's* caning for not paying attention. His visits to the mosque were now to become sparse and whenever it did happen, his prayers were replete with the desire to find her on the swing the next morning.

"What's her name?" Shehzaad had asked while flying kites after school.

"I don't know," Zarrar replied, hoping that his friend would mistake the blush as a consequence of chasing paper-shapes in the simpering heat of the day.

"Then you should wipe the name 'Husna' from the back-cover of your *kitaab* (book)!"

He had chased Shehzaad's kite and brought it down with a sharp swerve of his string. Their eyes glinted in the Sun as they tore bits of kite-paper and wrote her name on the tail of Zarrar's red kite.

On his way back, he remembered that his brothers had asked him to come straight to *Chowk Yadgar* (The Memorial Square) after school. There was going to be a gathering of some sort, he'd been told. He trudged towards the monumental arch, no more than a kilometer from his *madrasa*, which was the cultural and social centre-point of the city. The government had recently dedicated the historical place to the soldiers of the 1965 Indo-Pak war.

He reached the place and spotted his brothers standing amidst a group of youngsters. It was a rally by the student wing of the local political group that was mobilising the youth to join the *jihad* against certain forces. The evening was mostly uneventful, except that he got to eat some *naan*, followed by *rabri* and got a ride back home on the shoulders of his brother. His eldest brother looked very excited; it appeared to him that he had made up his mind about taking up a career as an officer in the armed forces.

If that was the case, he would set a new precedent in the family. His grandparents would be very proud but mother would probably resist; or maybe not. He wasn't sure. Thinking, and evaluating the possibilities, they arrived home. It was unusually quiet and the music from the rabab had not greeted them around the bend.

They opened the door and found the courtyard thronged by men in white. They stood around a bed, made with thick bamboo and knitted with coarse jute. The bed covered in a white sheet held the body of his grandfather, surrounded by incense, and his *kulla* (turban) lying in its grandest form, on his chest. The rabab lay on a table next to him. The women were inside, shrouded in black and expressing their grief in stifled sobs.

That day too, his father remained a passive figure in the backdrop of the story of their lives.

The old man had passed away peacefully while in soulful communion with his music. The neighbours mentioned after the funereal prayers, how he had sung the most beautiful and profound verses of Baba Rahman during his last moments. He sounded as if he was in direct conversation with the angel that had come to escort his soul to the yonder side. Without meaning to, Zarrar grew up into a slightly older boy that day.

Three

Peshawar, 1982

Weeks and months passed unnoticed and evenings became the dullest part of the day after his grandfather passed away. In due course, his brother left home to join the army and his mother and grandmother would sit in the place formerly occupied by the old man, creating art-work with silken threads and *mulmul* from Dhaka. This would be a part of the bridal *meher* when the eldest one got married, which was not meant to happen too soon, but they continued to stitch, nevertheless.

Zarrar, almost 12 now, had learnt to demystify intense talk and disrobe the code that wrapped fevered discussions between the boys, about neighbouring countries. His awareness caught and held on to a few interesting words and names like insurgents, militants, *Balochistan*, *Hekmatyar*, *Roosi* and *Jihad*. This vocabulary gave form and weight to the word 'tyrant' that he had learnt from his grandfather. The meaning was unimportant. What was important to him was the excited interest of his brothers, their engaging chatter and animated physicality when they were in the throes of discussion. To him, they were the perfect symbols of Pakhtunwali.

Time flew. His brother kept his promise of staying in touch. Arrival of his letters would be the happiest day in the month. That day they would celebrate with a sumptuous spread of food and the three boys would go to *Qissa Khwani* and replay their donkey game with friends, to commemorate their brother's successful stint as a *fauji*. They would then sit in some empty nook of the street, eating kebabs and telling tales of the eldest one's bravery, endowing upon him the status of a local hero. Zarrar's stint at school was nearing its end. Both Shehzaad and he had started to sprout facial hair and pangs of desolation. On one such morning, thinking about ways and means to extend his stay in the *madrasa*, he entered the lane to her house.

It had been four years since he had started each day of learning by trying to read a message in those eyes. To him, they had responded to his gaze in a quiet, yet promising way. On one such day while on his way to school; when he was besieged by a desperate urge to hold her face and kiss her eyes; he had left a precious part of himself by the threshold where the swing was. It was the miniature Taj Mahal that his father had given him.

"Why did you do that?" Shehzaad had asked, almost rebuking him. "If anybody in her family finds out, they'll roast you alive."

"I don't care. I want her to know."

"Know what?"

Zarrar couldn't bring himself to express himself to Shehzaad, who understood anyway.

"I'll take her to the real Taj one day," he said dreamily.

"O.K., Shah-e-Jahan, time to finish this lesson or *maulvi sahib* will build our tombs right here."

The next day, he had found a yellow paper swan, right where he had left his little Taj.

"Do you think she left this there for me?" he asked Shehzaad, looking at the origami gift adoringly.

"It could be any of the street boys. Or it could be her. We'll put something there tomorrow and see what happens."

The next day he had carried two wild, red roses growing outside a few houses. He had pricked his hand, while being careful enough to not let any of the petals drop.

On his way back, he found a sweet candy lying in its place. His heart leaped into his mouth and he craved to see her before going home.

Another ritual added itself to his morning routine and each day, he would leave a token of his love. Some days he would find a sweet reciprocation and on others, he would just be happy with her singing voice floating out of the room beyond the blue door.

He had waited patiently for many days before he saw her smile discreetly as she sung a love song sitting on her swing. Even though, he could-not decipher the cryptic message, his heart had experienced an inexplicable, emotional flurry.

Two weeks later, while on his way to the *madrasa*, he entered the lane to find a changed landscape. Houses on either side of the lane were outlined with streamers in silvery, rainbow colours. The sun shone through the myriad length of the path right till her house and the prismatic effect of the sun took a left turn through her door. Today, the swing was adorned with large red roses, the kind Peshawar was known for once upon a time.

He couldn't understand the goings on. He stood there in vacant admiration of the decorations when he saw people emerging from the rooms inside. He had to turn around and go back as this lane; that merged into the lane to his school; had been cordoned off by the tent that boarded *halwaai* (the sweet-makers) and cooks. As he did, a group of boys ran past him, giggling, laughing and perhaps sneering at him, he felt. One of the boys tripped over his toes and something crashed to the ground, breaking Zarrar's heart into a million pieces. It was his miniature Taj.

The boy got up, brushing himself and looking crookedly at Zarrar, while the other boys squealed with laughter. "hahahaaaa . . . *Miaan Majnoon*," someone rattled as the boys ran off chasing each other. Many days passed and he was unable to catch a glimpse of her, mainly because of the inaccessibility to the lane, which now thronged with people and carriages.

Later, it was from hearsay that he learnt about Husna getting married. And it was from the same sources that he heard how the American diplomat had been kind enough to accept the blind girl in exchange of a grand *meher*. No matter how much his heart wanted to break out into a cry; he twisted his face into a smile, scratched his neck and walked on. It was his last day at school.

That day, time in the *madrasa* went by like a morbid dream. After school, he went to the Mahabbat Khan mosque and sat by the cooling waters of the pond in the middle. The white surrounding him added to his sense of bereavement. He broke out into loud, full-throated sobs. A man, who had just finished his ablution, rested his hand on his shoulder and asked:

"What's the matter, son?"

He looked up and wiped his tears. Speechless, he stared blankly at the man for a few seconds and then replied:

"I lost someone precious."

The man mumbled something about trials and tribulations being God's tests for good souls, asked for Allah's mercy to be with the anguished soul and moved on to offer his prayers. He might have sat down to share the boy's grief, had he not been getting late for a daily appointment with his God.

*****

He had not been able to sleep very well that night. Up at day-break, Zarrar slipped out of the house and walked towards her house, for no particular reason. Perhaps a last glimpse of that threshold might soothe his aching heart, he thought.

He stopped in his tracks when he saw men in white, walking hurriedly in the same direction. What he overheard from the murmurs of a group standing in a corner, made his heart wrench itself into a tight, tight knot.

The *jihadi* forces have a way of tracking local news. An incident of such stature, that involved the giving away of a local girl to a fair-skinned man, drew immediate attention as well as wrath. For the tribal, it was yet another attempt of the western forces to overpower and marginalise their culture and tradition. It was blasphemy to accept the liaison; and driven by the tenet of '*badal*' (justice by revenge), a group of rancorous tribesmen had intercepted the bridal procession as it was headed towards the groom's residence in University Town, near the airport. Later in the evening, two bodies in wedding attire were found hanging from a tree. People clicked their tongues and spent time relating the incident to the activities of the Taliban, in hushed tones. Zarrar cursed the dead man with unforgiving might for bringing him anguish of such magnitude.

Four

July, 1986

His third brother was now preparing to go to the University. With the passing of the Student Union Ordinance in 1974, student politics on the University campus had gained significant momentum and most hot-blooded youngsters were drawn into it by one party or the other. He often talked about the *Islami-Jamiat-Taleba* and its mission to conserve the sanctity of Islamic learning and teaching. There would be reports of clashes between the left wing and right wing students and it was a perfect opportunity for the youth wings of political parties to scout for promising leaders. The *markhor-khanzaada* always came home with juicy nuggets of student activities and the weapons used in University brawls, which were usually chains, sticks and fists; and in extreme situations, *nunchakus* were used.

One day, his brother with the falcon tattoo stayed back home and the other one went to the campus. Mid-afternoon, he came back excitedly and summoned the two outside in a hurry. He could barely contain his excitement. He ushered the two towards the bazaar and elbowed them into a quiet alley that led to a dilapidating house. Inside, they were greeted by a man who took them into a dark room, lit only by a candle. He opened a chest that contained hay. Zarrar hoped that the dry straw would reveal something exquisite. It didn't disappoint him. As the hay gave way to something long and dark, his brothers gasped as the handler held up the AK-47 in his hands. Nervous excitement shook their bodies, as his brothers held the killer-machine in their hands, one by one. He had seen a transformed look in their eyes and he suddenly felt distant. They passed the gun to him. He remembered the upside-down swinging, and did not let the hesitation show.

It was a strange feeling holding on to something, so clandestine, yet so revealing. But he was good at the art of camouflage. He joined his brother in the quiet revelry of the moment. They spent half an hour eyeing the pieces of ammunition that the handler was carrying with him. The voyeuristic delight was compounded by snuffs of white powder offered to them by the seller.

It was his first experience of orgasmic pleasure; and then, they left after five minutes. Or it may have been five hours; he wasn't sure. The next meeting had been fixed and messages would be exchanged through a chain of communication in the refugee camp on the outskirts of Peshawar.

That night too, Zarrar was unable to sleep uninterruptedly even after his older brother played his favourite songs on his grandfather's *rabab*. Husna's eyes kept chasing him through the night and he kept chasing a white moon-faced man with a *Klashni* in his hand.

*****

Within the next few years, his second brother was also recruited in the army and left home with great pride and amidst much fanfare. For both the valiant sons, the farewell had been ritualistic. His grandmother had touched his grandfather's *kulla* to their head and given them blessings for a long and glorious life. His mother had prepared special sweets for each of them before they embarked on a new journey. Promises of staying in touch through letters had been exchanged and the brothers were given a musical farewell, with songs of valour, honour and pride for the homeland. His grandmother reiterated her husband's words as she sent them off: "Remember, you are a Pathan first, then a Muslim and after that a Pakistani. Do what lies in the best interest of the three but in the correct order."

The following year in 1990, he started to prepare himself to go to the University. He was the only one to have chosen Islamic Studies as his course programme. The third-in-line had dropped out of the Defence Studies Programme a couple of years ago. All three brothers were now enrolled in the Pakistan Army and had legal access to the ammunition they had always mused over in their adolescence. Their initial letters would almost always carry descriptive detail of their rigorous training.

He often wondered why they never sent him any photographs in uniform. He had made several requests and it seemed all the letters carrying such photographs would get lost in transit. One of his brothers had come home in uniform once but something appeared amiss. He couldn't put his finger to it though. His initiation into the IJT during his university years had already been ascertained even though he did not show as much promise as a rebellious leader as his brothers.

However, it was his duty towards his land to continue in the spirit of patriotism and make some contribution towards *jihad*. Even though, it still wasn't clear to him as to what this *jihad* was for and how it would help him or his family. When too many questions criss-crossed his brow, answers were provided by the white powder supplied generously by one of the nomadic merchants who now thronged the *Qissa Khwani Bazaar*.

Life at the University was fraught with adrenaline pumping rumours about the *Klashni* doing the rounds inside the campus. The talk had sprouted in the campus of Lahore and Karachi Universities and had spread unchecked to Peshawar, where student politics was beginning to catch up. He would often be a part of anti-establishment rallies and sit for protests and sometimes unwillingly get drawn into violent demonstrations.

It was during one of these rallies that he saw her again. He couldn't believe his luck. Like a mirage in the desert, she made an appearance and was gone in a blink. He couldn't have mistaken those eyes but she looked different. The fuller's earth complexion was now replaced by a brick-red. But that was just a flash. Or it could be the sun playing tricks on him; or the powder?

*****

It was a Sunday evening when his third brother made a surprise visit home. He had undergone a tremendous change in two years. He didn't speak much or laugh or crack jokes anymore. His enthusiasm about every moment of the day seemed to have vaporised. Heavy stubble now distinguished his face prominently from the brothers, and his body had become leaner. His healthy and ruddy complexion was replaced by a sallow and sun-burnt look. He refused to play the rabab or talk to Zarrar about life at the army base. His mother and grandmother had failed to notice the change, or perhaps not, and continued to pamper him with an assortment of foods and sweets. It was when he refused to eat or drink that Zarrar asked him:

"Pasha, something's wrong. You're not the same as before. What is it?"

"Oye Rohillay, you're talking like a grown up; just like Baba!"

"I can see it. You're keeping something secretly in your heart. There is something…. I know for sure."

His brother looked away.

"You stop your pain from surfacing but you can't prevent me from seeing it. Tell me brother, what is wrong? I have the same blood as you. I can handle it!"

"Rohillay! They are gone," he broke down, first into controlled sobs which gradually ballooned into stifled, yet full-bodied anguish. "Caught by the Indian army at the border and shot in the head. Our brothers; gone forever. Didn't even get to see their corpses! I wasn't there myself or I would have brought down hell on them. What do I do, Roh'ay? From where do I bring them back? What do I tell our mother and grandmother who have been stitching clothes for befitting grooms in the house? I am not going to spare those bastards. They will pay with…." And he continued to vent his grief. Zarrar hadn't heard anything after 'gone forever'.

It rained all night. Zarrar and his brother lay outside in the courtyard, soaking up the flood.

Five

1990, Zarrar's Home

The next morning, they got ready to go to the Mahabbat Khan Mosque. It would bring some peace to the departed and their anguished souls. Neither of them was sure what, when and how to inform the women in the house. They decided to return from the mosque and break the news.

Zarrar and his brother reached the mosque. The whiteness of the place seemed to add a ghastly hue to their grief. The beautiful fluted domes had acquired a new face. They haunted the corridors of the mosque for a few hours and then sat near the *Aiwan*, staring into blankness.

Zarrar looked at the building and asked his brother:

"Pasha, people say the mosque was white when Mahabbat Khan made it. But it looks pink to me and the hue changes with the passing hour. Have you noticed?"

"White can never retain its whiteness. It is too weak a colour. In fact, white's not a colour but the absence of it. Time, weather, people, sunlight, just about anything can taint it. This mosque has the blood of people standing in its foundations. It's that colour that has been running up the cracks. Have you ever seen spotless white ever being drawn from the womb of the earth? It cannot exist."

Even though Zarrar knew that it was the red bricks and marble slabs used beneath the lime mortar that dispersed the pink hue; he chose not to comment. His brother was right about the colour white.

They returned home feeling none-the-better. Both of them tried to avoid eye-contact with the women, as it was difficult to retain a fake expression for a long duration. At twilight, they walked down the *Qissa Khwani*, looking at things and remembering their boyish games. The shop where they always bought their *chapali kebab* was doing brisk business. There were faces furrowed by deep thought and very few with none at all. Each one was part of a journey and each had a tale to tell, mostly of fire and grave and another Peshawar far away. They sat near the man preparing the kebabs.

There was meat on the skewers and meat on the fire.

"Pasha, what was the last thing that Ror said to you?" His brother looked at him.

"Never mind."

"No, I want to know. What were their last words; any desire, wish or anything?"

The meat on the skewers and in the fire seared; as smoke started to hiss its way out.

"A blow for a pinch! They were with me that morning. Our morning exercise had gotten over when we were discussing some of the men having strayed accidentally across the LOC. They were murdered brutally. A blow for a pinch was what they had said!"

The words found their way into the innermost recesses of his waking hours. When sleep intruded, he put up strong resistance by snuffing some powder. It had a contrary effect and sent him into deep sleep for an indeterminate period.

*****

The next day, his brother woke up early; and started his preparation to leave. Zarrar wanted him to stay back for a few days so that they could find an opportune moment to break the news to their mother and grandmother. He possibly couldn't do it by himself. His brother, however, was in a hurry to go. He said that he wanted to show him something before he went away for a really long time. His brother looked like a different man in his uniform. Once everything was in place, he brought out his maroon beret and placed it neatly on his head. It added a touch of credibility to his attire.

Zarrar looked at him unbelievingly. He wished he could turn back the clock by twenty-four hours and regain his sanity.

"Mashar Ror, you said you were in the army's infantry." "Yes, Rohillay! Why do you ask?"

"Then why are you wearing the SSG cap and that too, without a badge?"

His brother stared at him through the mirror for a few seconds. Then, continued with his preening. When he was done, he was ready to talk.

"Rohay, you will get your answer once I've shown you what I wanted to."

*****

They footed it to the destination. There was no communication between them. Anxiety and curiosity turned the space between them into a colloidal suspension, which made it difficult for words to get through. As they approached the government school, about a kilometre and a half away from their home, Zarrar felt a knot building up in his stomach. There was a strange calm that enveloped his brother but he could see a storm in his eyes.

They walked through the school gate and quietly walked up the steps of the building which had been in unfinished stages of construction since the past several years. His brother pushed open the door and they entered. Boys in the age group of six to ten years were engaged in the learning process. Except that they were not learning from books. The room was full of dirks, daggers and dart guns. They had just begun their training in mortal combat.

Zarrar did not need an explanation. Everything fell in place. All questions found their answers and all motives were revealed. His brothers' long absences, the talk about *jihad*, the casual straying across enemy lines and the unceremonious termination; everything stared at him like a painting on the classroom walls. He wanted to turn around and run but his feet refused to move.

"Rohillay! Do you remember the story of the Golden Bird that *Baba* used to tell us?

The hunter never really went away. He kept crouching around our land in different forms. Hindustan on the East, Roos in the North and the Army on the Western frontier; our only ally remains the Arabian Sea on the South. To top it all, the enemy in the far West is lurking in the wings, waiting to pounce upon us in our weakest moment. Fire and water are our only friends.

The world calls us *jihadis* but our land will remember us as martyrs. Is our country, really ours? We are treated as fundamentalists by the world and as *Afghani* insurgents by our own homeland. Where do we belong? We only belong to our *Pakhtunkhwah*, and we seek no other mother. We may lose our brothers, beheaded in front of our eyes but we will fight, but we are not ready to die like those gullible animals of *Qissa Khwani*!"

Zarrar sat down, listening quietly. Something in his temples throbbed and clamped, then started to throb again. Once again, he wanted to go home and hide in the folds of his mother's *abaya*. His brother could see him at war with himself. He drew him by his elbow and embraced him.

"Rohillay! It's for the pride that *Baba* had. It's for the love of our mother. It is for the love for our brothers, who we couldn't put in a decent grave. Allah-hafiz!"

And he walked away from him, to a destination unknown to the wiser world. Zarrar wished he had held him a little longer.

*****

There was an impregnable silence in the house. His mother had slumped and now sat rock-like against the wall. His grandmother kneeled down to pray. Zarrar sat beside them, groping his inner space for justification. None came by.

Caught between acceptance and denial, grief was shredded into invisible slivers.

Days came and went without an identity. He had started to see that pair of transparent grey-green eyes more often now, amid crowds and in his plangent solitude. The more he saw, the lesser he wanted to see of the world. It was one of those days of dark sunlight that his father came home. This time his absence had been the longest and least felt. After greetings and *kahwa*, the news was served to him. He consoled his family without shedding a tear, and played his role rather befittingly.

Despite his grandmother's best efforts, he had adamantly refused to interact with the man who called himself their father. He had crawled through twenty long years with splenetic feelings, keeping his questions buried deep inside and not allowing them to head out.

His life was now like a rudderless ship, sailing dangerously at the behest of a wild tide. The University years had left in him, an illusion of a beautiful, comprehensible world, which had popped sooner than he was prepared for. It held neither of the promises anymore. This time his father stayed on for longer than usual. Each day he would wake up and expect to find him gone but he would be there, sipping his tea in the courtyard. He had never seen him kneel down in prayer. One morning, he made an attempt at conversation.

"Why didn't you ever stay with us?"

His father was not prepared for a discussion, let alone a question as direct as that. He continued to sip his tea.

"Had you thought of being here with us, all this may not have happened."

"It was the will of Allah!"

Zarrar wanted to scream. He clenched his fists.

"It was not the will of Allah. It was your lack of responsibility that led us all to darkness. You are responsible for this. You brought us to this world and then left us to the winds. Who was to tell us which road to take and why?"

His father held his hand and pressed it reassuringly.

"Believe me, my son! It is because I was away, you became a Pathan strong enough to brave such a loss and here you stand like a man to confront me. You are ready for the world."

His father's philosophical reply to disguise his escapism did not go down well with him. He was now writhing like a fish out of water. The only place where the storm within him found a wall of calm was the Mahabbat Khan Mosque. It had been his asylum since many years and he sought refuge in the echoing silence of the long corridors. The domes reminded him of eternal love epitomised by the famous Taj Mahal and the minarets looked as if they were fingering the sky to let heavenly mercies come pouring down. The thought brought back the face of his brother on the horizon. He wished the sky would become the earth and the earth, sky once again. He wanted to hug him again. He sat beside the ablution pond. This time he couldn't find any tears or a reason to produce them. It was Allah's will, and hereafter everything that happened in his life would happen at His bidding. As if in response to his inner chatter, a hand rested on his shoulder:

"Sahat mo tsanga day?" (Are you in good health?)

It was the *Klashni*-man who he had met with his brothers years ago. Zarrar straightened his twisted expression and looked away towards the pond. "How's your family?" He felt like holding him by the neck and drowning him in the water.

"Do you want to meet your third brother?"

Zarrar was startled. He gave him a sharp look for the first time during the one-sided conversation.

"I can take you to meet him tomorrow. Meet me here after *maghrib*." He was about to turn and go when Zarrar caught his arm.

"Where is my brother? Is he well?"

"He is in safe hands and working for his motherland, *Pakhtunkhwah*. You'll get to see him tomorrow."

"How did you know that you'd find me here? And why do you want to take me to him?"

"I just perform tasks. I don't question them. You can save your questions for tomorrow. You'll meet the man with the answers."

*****

The night went by restlessly. Sleep came to him in disrupted quanta and he was up at the break of dawn, with the call of *azaan*. Wild cockroaches had infested his dreams all night, with their antennae burning and heads swinging wildly. He prayed all morning like a hermit. Then, without breaking his morning fast, he headed towards the mosque.

Even though there were many hours to go before *Maghrib*, he wanted to spend his time inside the mosque. In order to while away the long hours, without feral thoughts consuming him, he studied the architecture of the mosque and observed people while in prayer. He waited all day for the *Klashni*-man to reappear. It was futile.

As the Sun sunk into a slumberous state; he gathered himself to go back home, only to come again the next day. He was sure that the *Klashni*-man would turn up one of those days and take him to his brother. He stepped out into the street and walked through the ebb and flow of life around him. In the distance, he saw a group of four men running in his direction. They looked as if they were thwarting a chase. When they rolled into decent view, his senses perked up when he identified two of them as his friends from the JIT days in the University.

A few uniformed men were taking aim to shoot. He shouted out to the third one; who was within his reach now; to duck and take cover but the bullet reached the boy first and he fell straight into Zarrar's arms. It was Shehzaad. Streaks of warm blood splashed across his crisp, white mulmul kameez.

*****

He had reached home late at night, after ensuring that the lifeless piece of his childhood reached the grieving kin. After he got home, he went straight to the cabinet where he kept some white powder, stashed away in a wooden box. He did not want to change his clothes, or sleep, both of which were a rich man's commodity now. Poor are the ones, who carry the blood of their brothers on their sleeve. His mother had heard him come in and came into the room to ask if he needed anything. She couldn't see his face in the dark.

"No Ummi. Go and sleep!"

His mother turned around like an obedient child.

"And mother, do not stitch white garments for me anymore. I want to wear black. It's easier to keep clean."

*****

He continued his visits to the mosque at *Maghrib* everyday, dressed in spotless black. He did not lose hope, or the will to see that man again. He saw people coming and praying everyday and felt sorry for them. They reminded him of the animals of the land of the Golden Bird. One evening, as he completed his wait without a sigh or a whimper, he saw the Klashni-man walk towards him from the *hujra* (prayer room). The day to embrace his brother and bring him home had arrived.

The two of them walked quietly towards the place where the meeting was to take place.

He had never visited that part of the city before. It was a slightly rocky terrain and bore a deserted look. Housing was sparse and reminded him of the lands that his father spoke of when they were young. His accomplice was alert and suspicious of movement ahead or behind them.

They had not crossed any army posts so they must have been within the Pakistan border; or so he thought.

It was a few arduous miles, interspersed with a bit of hitch-hiking from cart-loaders on the way, before they arrived at a walled enclosure which was heavily guarded at the entrance. After a thorough check, they were ushered in. There were extremely low-lying roofs, which could not allow one Pathan to stand up straight. Zarrar observed without thinking.

They were led to one such low-lying roof and that's when he realised that they were entrances to staircases leading underground. They walked down a flight of mud-paved steps that spiralled their way into the earth. Half-baked bricks and mud made up that establishment. The smell of damp earth made it refreshingly cool inside.

When he entered the room, generously lit by lanterns, he came face to face with a man who looked as handsome as his brothers, or nearly.

"*Mullahjaan*, Zarrar Suleiman!" And the *Klashni*-man bowed, kissed his hand and touched them to both his eyes. This was followed by a long silence, which no one dared to adulterate.

*****

The deep, ponderous silence was broken abruptly by the man who had been addressed as *Mullahjaan*.

"Are you a *Pathan*?" "Yes"

"What makes you one?" "My parents. My lineage."

"Why should I believe you?

What is it that you have that proves to me that you are not a disguised ISI agent?"

"My brother, I've been told, is in association with you." "That's not reason enough for me to believe you."

"What proof are you looking for? And why are you looking for it? I am here to meet my brother. Do I need proof for that? Ask him, if he's here. He'll verify my antecedents."

"What if I told you that your brother's head was blown off in an air-raid? How would you then prove that you are a *Pathan*?"

Zarrar's jaw tightened and he wanted to deliver a blow to that face. His impulsive step towards the militant leader was checked by his men.

"Oh, so you do show signs of young blood that boils at a presumption. What happened to the blood of a *Pathan* that is supposed to boil at every injustice and act of cruelty done towards his brethren? Has that blood turned to water?"

"What do you mean? I don't know what you're driving at and I don't want to understand. Just bring my brother to me please. I'll do whatever you want me to do for you, in lieu of that."

I have not had you brought here as a hostage. Allah's will brings you here and you are here as part of the *biradari*. I'm glad to see your love and yearning for your kin. But did you not love your older brothers enough? Those who were killed without thought, for having made the mistake of not carrying a map on them? Do you think their death is a coincidence or a brutal attempt to wipe away valour, grace and trust from the face of the earth?"

"You knew my brothers?" Zarrar's eyes moistened a little. The pain was still simmering inside.

"I not only knew them but they were the true sons of our land, our soil, our Pakhtunkhwah. Roosi, *Hindostaani*, *Amreeki*, *Bartanny*; even supposed brothers of the land we belong to; everyone is an enemy. Their intent is *haraam* and their ways cunning. They all have their eyes set on usurping our land and identity, corrupt and convert it into a money-minting market of the so called commercial era, and create many more displaced generations. Are you then, *Pathan* enough to stand up and refuse to let that happen?"

Zarrar was still thinking about his brother.

Mullah gestured to one of his men. In a few minutes, his brother was chaperoned into the room.

"Oye, Rohillay! How did you reach here? Oye, I'm so glad to see you! *Mullahjaan*, this is my brother, I told you about. He's got the looks of a village-belle and the heart of the wildest lion!"

"Everyone laughed. *Mullah* spoke again. So, Rohillay, now that I've seen your love for your brother, I have no doubt about you being a true *Pathan*. Pasha, make him comfortable ... we'll talk to him a little later."

*****

The two brothers sat on a paved, raised platform that served as a table, seat or bed, as required. In one corner of the room, Zarrar could see from the corner of his eyes, there lay a cache of weapons, including the ones that the brothers had handled with divine enchantment. As they talked, someone brought them sherbet in earthen pots.

"Come home with me. There is no life in the house, only sadness and quietude."

"I know Rohay, but our cause is much bigger than the love of family. I cannot live like a rat and call myself a *Pathan* with pride. I have to avenge the killing of my brothers and many others like him. This is for the honour of Pakhtunwali."

He could never argue with his brother's reasoning. His brother was always superbly convincing. Besides, the loss of his most-loved people had caused a gash on his conscience that refused to heal. Their interaction continued for over an hour which was interrupted by some commotion in the room outside. Men rushed in to pick up the guns that lay in the corner. They were told to take position. His brother told him to stay inside as he jumped into action and rushed out with a *Klashni* in his hands. Within minutes, thunderous sound enveloped the area.

The drone of aircrafts waxed and waned, and was punctuated with the sound of missile hitting targets.

He ran after his brother but the door was secured in place. He looked around. There was no time for hesitation. He picked up one of the assault rifles and spattered the door with bullets. It made way for him. He ran out and up the steps. From under the roof, he could already see a few bodies lying mangled in the open space within the compound's wall. On the horizon, he could see a plane zooming rapidly into view. There was intermittent firing from a few of the other shelters inside the compound, as a block of iron left the plane.

Zarrar had never seen a missile before. The *Klashni*-man, on their way to the hideout, had mentioned something about drone strikes by the U.S. spy planes but they usually occurred during the day.

The heavily armed men on the ground were a much-lesser match to the sophisticated missiles being used by the fighter-pilots. The carnage lasted for about thirty minutes. The planes flew out of sight when the firing from the ground came to a halt. The face of terror had been given a face-off.

*****

Several minutes later, Zarrar sat in the open compound with the head of his third brother in his lap. Markhor had been done to death. He had been unable to trace the strong limbs. Only the lifeless torso remained.

The black of his attire had only become a few shades more impelling. Black consumes everything and cradles every colour inside its darkness.

*****

He did not go home after that. He couldn't have carried his brother's mauled body to his mother. The remains found a respectful burial among the jagged peaks and hot soil; along with the fears within him.

A quiet resolve and an implosion of grief led him to *Mullah*. After a resentful prayer meeting and initiation into a new life, Zarrar, along with a few survivors, started their journey towards Islamabad, where they were to meet *Zaki Chacha*. The time had come, to make some pink noise, just like that of the prayers.

*****

Zaki Ch'cha was a short man with strong hands that held an entire terrorist outfit together. He was known to speak in monosyllables and short phrases, thus maintaining an aura of mystery and colossal intrigue around him. There had been stories about him having shot a couple of his own sons when they had refused to partake in the jihad against the anti-Islamic forces.

Nobody in the training camp knew where he lived or came from. He would often come on Fridays and charge the atmosphere with feelings of hatred, ruthlessness and malice. Young men who dared to ask questions were put through rigorous training sessions and relentless prayer. The tiniest spark of defiance was snubbed by gifts in cash and kind to the family or a bullet in the man's chest.

Zarrar was now ready for a new life, with no strings attached. He knew his mother and grandmother were capable of coping with grief and loss by now.

As weeks changed to months and months changed to years, a cocoon started to spin itself around Zarrar, inside which began the process of his metamorphosis, like a blob of white fire encased in an oyester and buried in deep, black waters.

PART–II
HANSA AND THE FIRE

Six

26th November, 2008, Apollo Bunder, Mumbai

It seemed unreal; as unreal as the moment itself. Or perhaps, as the infinite time within that moment; the kind that writes and rewrites histories. Histories that many a placid times, have gone under the surging sea of moments; unwrecked, and unrealised. But that moment stood still, unwilling to move and make way for the next. They gazed at each other with moistened eyes; each a poem for the other, sailing on the winds and water.

"Try and remember me, my beloved, as the flower you plucked and not the flower you tread upon...," she whispered Ruttie's words to the shadows.

A pale prismatic glow rose with the salty murmur of the sea and merged seamlessly with the ivory and peach of her face; then rose further to lend a blushing hue to the moon above the majestic spires. The yacht danced like a dauntless sea-bird on the Arabian Sea that traipsed away into the darkening twilight. Curly wisps on her forehead frolicked about noiselessly as the waves shushed themselves to catch a sound.

The air and the waterfront played a quiet melody, imitating the clear notes of a clarinet and sporadic strains of the piano. The jasmine in her hair, were only too eager to take a tipsy step forward and kiss the glowing waters. It was a dateless, timeless night; a night of *poesy*.

"Cut!" someone shouted from a distance that seemed immeasurably far away. The word was lost on the echoless landscape. The Diva and the Grand Dame continued their lyrical communion; unstirred. Then in a snap, the water swallowed the reflection and it was gone.

The chord was cut and something snapped within her too. She looked up. From the luxury yacht, the dark silhouette of the imperial structure of the *Taj Mahal* Palace Hotel appeared like a seer calling out the prognosis of an unpropitious moment: just like the kind that erases and rewrites something in history; and she, like a querent, looked on, transfixed. The lights flickered and came back to life almost as soon as they had gone; it was infinite time within a finite moment.

*****

On the esplanade facing the *Taj*, a scraggly old man slept with his slippers under his head who probably had an experience earlier when during his sleep, someone had run away with them. The flies, the dirt, even the honk and rumble of seasoned tyres or the harried sounds of a busy tourist spot did not disrupt his slumber. But, he was going to wake up in a way he had never woken up before. Just that he did not know it yet. The flies buzzed around his scruffy head in discontinuous circles, creating an aural halo around it.

His hand stirred, slumped and then, stirred again. Mosquitoes had agreed to feast quietly on him and leave, without making a fuss.

Bugs fail to bother those who have nothing to lose. He had been up since four in the morning, working at the harbour, and sleep had come without much haggling with the demons of the day.

*****

Back in her suite inside the Taj, Hansa Noorie Walia inhaled the calmness of the rose-scented bath. Even though the *Rajput* Suite in the heritage wing of the hotel was her preferred choice for an overnight stay; this time however, she had insisted on the Dolphin Suite for its calming white decor. Moreover, she had gathered from bits of hearsay that the young and beautiful wife of President Jinnah had breathed her last somewhere in and about there. She had wanted to touch, feel and absorb the same negotiations between life and death that the Flower of Bombay, Ruttie Jinnah, might have experienced in her last moments.

Dwelling upon the ambience carrying phantasms from a bygone era, she wondered if that flicker was merely a flicker of her consciousness or a message from yonder. She had lost track of time, day or date. Not that dates were significant; moments were. It is moments that fill up the hollowness of minutes, hours and years; and give them tangible form.

Her mind ran a rapid course through the passage of the evening. The yacht, the tranquil sea, the resplendent façade of the historical monument gazing at her from below the silent waters, her transformation into Mrs. *Mariam 'Ruttiebai' Jinnah* and a pirouetting, inexplicable sorrow that twined her brow.

Hansa had acquired her mother's Persian complexion, grey-green eyes and coal black, wavy tresses. From her vagrant Muslim father, she had inherited tall dreams and a royal lineage. The love-child of an abusive relationship; she had been given a head-start in the world of responsibility. Ever since her father had left her mother; never to be seen or heard again; she had never looked back and cried over anything that was lost. Consequently, she raised herself to a stature where all material things seemed immaterial and the desirable, left too far behind.

The day's shoot had been more of an emotional taxation than physical. Embodying a character from history and bringing her to life again in full form and blood was something that Hansa had been subjected to many a time in the twelve prolific years of her career as an actor. However, Ruttie Jinnah's tumultuous relationship with her husband and the symbiotic association with the hotel where she spent her last moments had somehow wrapped Hansa in a quagmire of battling emotions that left her feeling vulnerable and exposed.

She had been reading about this remarkable lady for a month now. The more she read about her, the possibilities that lay within a woman's heart and mind, slowly unfurled before her. She had not only started to admire the spunk in Rattanbai Petit but had also started to draw courage to deal with the intricacies of her own life, from hers. Yes, it seemed possible to be in love with more than one.

There was still an hour and a half to go before she had to make her presence at the grand wedding in the Crystal Room.

With a deep amniotic sigh, she picked up *Ruttie Jinnah* by Khwaja Razi Haider and turned to page 107. From the day of narration of the script, she had felt an inexplicable empathy with Ruttie, which was getting stronger as she approached the end of the book.

Before she realised, sleep had overtaken her willingness to read, and ran feather-stroked dreams over her consciousness. She dreamt that she is clad in a silver backless gown and a middle-aged man with seasoned grey in his hair, is escorting her through the ivory-white corridors of a palace with a dome that seems to grow into the skies. His face is always a shadow. She swirls and swirls till the temple flowers in her hair are strewn all over and fill the whites of the marble floors with more whiteness. The place fills up with the scent of a religious ceremony; like it does in a funereal gathering. People with green scarves tied on their heads, chanting the *Ashem Vohu*.

As the crowd turns into a mob and slowly advances towards her, she observes that the procession is readying a place for her in the most beautiful mausoleum of the world.

The whiteness of the marble floors is beginning to get tinged with red. Her own eyes seem to be seeking someone but the person refuses to reveal an identity. Soon, her tall and handsome escort steps in and takes her by the arm. Unwillingly, she starts to run with him. As she looks back, she finds the crowd advancing at an unchanging pace. They run through corridors and staircases and lobbies and doors and in the blink of a moment, are flying through the air; the water below them rising up rapidly to greet them. Through her fall, she realises that she is alone. She hits the water like a bullet, and sits up with a start.

She had slipped a few inches into the bath. But she was not sure if that was what had alarmed her. Something was not right and the air seemed a bit stifling. Perhaps, it was the disconcerting thought of not being at home and in her room that overlooked the city and the goings-about. The bell rang again. She had not called for room-service and she certainly did not want to step out of the bath right now. It could be someone from the production crew. She chose to ignore it.

*****

The grand entrance of the hotel was unusually bright and heavily fragrant that day. *Hussain*'s angels, on the wall behind the reception desk, extended a benign smile to every person within eye-shot. The horses too, seemed to display extra verve and vigour. The receptionists, in their beige and blue, stood like porcelain statuettes against the flaming red and yellow in the background.

Two corridors, running almost parallel to each other on either side of the reception desk, led the guests and tourists to the various restaurants, shops and the heritage wing of the hotel.

A high-profile wedding and an international conference on the following morning, made the air heavy with responsibility.

Staff on duty had been primed weeks in advance. Shoulders were upped and gaits, crisp. The six feet two inch frame of the door attendant appeared even more opulent because of the royal turban that fanned out three inches above his head. Long black sedans were rolling in like bees, stopping and then rolling out of the drive, as the occupants alighted shimmering and dazzling in silks, brocades and magnificent diamonds.

One could not hear the click of the well-heeled gentlemen's stride in the thickly carpeted lobby. As heavy bottoms sunk into paisleys woven in silk and stilettos click-clacked their way about on the shiny marbled floor, the atmosphere exuded cordial warmth of a busy winter evening at the Taj made even warmer by the scent of incense and marigold leis being used to welcome the guests in the hotel. Late check-outs were routine too, as a couple of guests waited at the reception desk for their dues to be cleared.

Buffed by routine, the doormen smiled at the men with black, over-stuffed haversacks as they did at the madams with the *Gucci* and *Versace* clutches. People with black, brown and blond heads of hair added to the fairy-tale charm of the space. The ambience was that of firm and unshakeable opulence made delicate with pink lilies and Belgian crystal suspended in yellow light from the ceiling. Several thought-balloons, as coloured as the heads that owned them, filled up the vertical space and floated about casually, just like their masters. Their jaywalking was soon to find a purpose.

"Please inform Ms. Noorie that her visitors are here. She is expecting us. I shall wait for her by the poolside. Her cell phone seems to be ringing without an answer," someone told the lady at the reception while placing a business card on the desk.

Two men in spotless thoubs and bright shumaggs made their way out of Shamiana, the coffee shop, situated along the corridor on the right side of the reception desk. They approached the welcome desk in front of the poolside lounge and turned right to head towards the hotel's pool. The ornate surroundings and flamboyant cheer in the air seemed to do little to impress them as their facial contours continued to abide by the code of Nazi law.

The pool's sparkling waters shimmered in blue and yellow from the lights gazing at it from three sides. Guests, lounging on the deck chairs, chatted briskly about Indian politics, grand weddings and 101 ways to make millions from the slums. The evening here was pleasantly cool and dry; and the mood, relaxed.

Simone and Ricci were exhausted after a long day of sight-seeing and walked through the lobby, towards Masala Kraft, the Indian Restaurant, to enjoy an authentic Indian meal. This one was situated along the left corridor, ahead of Harbour Bar. They were to leave for Agra, the next morning.

"How about a jump in the pool, before dinner?" asked Ricci.

"Awwh, don't even think about it! I'm sweaty, and tired, and hungry. I could do with a shot right now! Let's hit the bar first", replied Simone, rolling her olive-green eyes. And she tugged him along to take the first left to Harbour Bar instead of going down the corridor and turning right.

*****

The men dressed in Middle-Eastern attire took a good view of the pool and were now headed out of the lounge, towards the grand staircase. They noticed people going up and down the narrow corridor that roomed high-end boutique shops along its length.

At the far end, a sharp turn to the left led the guests to one of the smallest, yet most famous bakeries of South Mumbai. From this bakery, a little blonde boy walked out, with his blonde father, eyeing his carry-bag with a twinkle and a smile and justifying the enviable reputation of the place.

Back at the central atrium, activity was now gaining speed as an array of V.I.P. guests was expected to stream in over the next two hours. A few members of the wedding party were already floating about in the lobby, trying to coordinate arrivals and other arrangements over loud conversations on the phone.

The liftman across the east end of the lobby looked at his watch. His evening shift was about to get over. It was 9:45. Down the eastern corridor, three stiff-spined gentlemen were headed towards the elevator that would take them to the rooftop private club Chambers in the Tower wing.

*****

Simone and Ricci were just finishing their first round of martinis. Simone particularly favoured this drink as it gave her a sense of connection with the Italian artist with the same name. She never confessed though, that it also stirred the Gothic streak within her, which she enjoyed. Ricci, on the other hand, preferred it Bradford style: shaken-not-stirred, made popular by the legendary Bond. But what's the difference between the after-effect of bruised and beaten drinks; who could tell by the end of the third round!

Perched atop the toadstool at the bar, Ricci ordered another round of drinks. Once inside, he had taken a good look around and had decided to modify their plan for dinner, as the crowd had started to catch his attention as well as his fancy. Convincing Simone after a drink or two had been as easy as cream on caramel. She had given her approval with a tipsy nod; she always downed her drinks a tad too fast.

Even when drunk, the girl had a way of finding her way about, thought Ricci. They had now changed their mind about going to the restaurant. Instead, they would try the shrimp tempura at the sushi bar in Wasabi by Morimoto. A red, spiral staircase from inside the bar, led to the Japanese restaurant on the first floor that overlooked the harbour. Destiny had different plans for them tonight.

As the bartender placed his drink before him, a loud explosion resounded in the area. Before he could decipher and understand the turn of events, there was the sound of a spray of gunshots that seemed to be getting closer to where he was sitting. A similar stupor fell over *Shamiana*; which had guests lingering over their cappuccinos and lattes; as they heard the deafening sound of fire-works growing in intensity. With a menacing undertone, the fire-works briskly swallowed the repose of the place.

Moments were now crocheted together, one into the other, forming an intricate web of satanic design. In the lobby, the scent of lilies was slowly turning into a morbid stench of smoke and blood. It was as if a vengeful witch had descended upon a fairytale and taken everything under her spell. There were inexplicable explosions and bullets rattled off one after the other.

The water sprinklers went off in an unstoppable frenzy; sloshing the carpets, that were now streaked with another red, quite different from the one in its weave.

Hands shielding heads, people ducked for cover which was quite scant in the hall. They ran helter-skelter trying to miss the slew of gunshots flying in to meet them from random directions. Screams of people in panic could barely be heard above the din of incessant gunfire. Forty seconds seemed like an eternity to those who were still alive as they tried to raise their heads after the gunfire ceased momentarily.

Heavy bottoms were now lying upturned on the floor and cell-phones rang in lifeless hands. The hands on the watch, like the liftman's own, refused to move. Running feet and animated shouts foretold that the drama had only just begun. In the face of death, dimming eyes tried to capture the face of their executors. All they managed to behold were blurry rat-like movements in an aberrant smokescreen.

*****

Over the next two minutes, the door of Shamiana, the coffee shop, opened but the smiling attendant on duty didn't get an opportunity to ask “How may I assist you?” Bullets cut through the air, ricocheting off brass and metal. Reaction time was little and people huddled under tables and used chairs as shields.

Those who couldn't think on their feet now lay on the floor, face down. The two assailants stood fixed in the passage; one firing away inside and the other gunning people down in the corridor that extended along the line of fire. Ahead of the bakery, the father lay plastered to the floor, with his blood asphyxiating the boy, who lay still with fright. The man with the gun gave a hollow, cold look to the boy and briskly averted his gaze.

The duty manager inside *Shamiana* caught the poolside view from the window on the left end of the coffee shop. In the evening, while they stood beside the pool, he had been describing to his colleague, how the Taj changed colours through the day.

On most days, daybreak saw a deep grey stone-structure withholding a red dome. As the day then progressed, the grey gave off indigo hues as the shadows of the trees ducked and darted in the crimson warmth of the sun and pigeons flew over the white crystals of the pool. By evening, the palace would start to twinkle into yellowness and the pool would be waving its blue at the windows overlooking it. Now, it was an unprecedented red with the blackness of a gory night.

As the manager tried desperately to recall disaster management techniques to be used in an emergency, a waiter attempted to make a dash towards the service door which, he knew, led to an emergency exit. He could only make it halfway to it, as his body collapsed in a pool of blood, like a street lamp in a raging thunder storm.

*****

They were everywhere, like an army of red ants, ravaging everything that got in its way. The carnage had only just begun. They had swarmed upon the Taj in perfect timing and precision. Their entry had been smooth and hassle-free. After a thunderous six minutes, they rattled their way towards the grand staircase, where Jamshetji Tata stood, looking imperial in a befittingly grandiose landing. The mirrored wall behind his bust was about to be frescoed as beleaguered staff members and guests scurried up and down the stairs. The minute-hand on the clock above continued to move dutifully. The tower wing in the South had already been taken over by men dressed in black *salwar-suits*, moving about like bloodhounds, sniffing for the breaths of live men and women. As six men advanced towards the cantilevered staircase of the heritage wing, the emergency lines in police control rooms and newsrooms began to come alive at a frenetic pace.

*****

Hansa's phone rang. She had not answered any calls all evening. It interfered with her getting into the skin of the character. She had especially asked to be put up in the room where Ruttiebai had spent her last days. That suite was on the sixth floor and was unavailable. She had been a guest at the hotel very often but had never had this strange grief take over her.

The phone rang again and she allowed it its impudence while she completed her beauty regime. However, the phone was too close for her to shut herself out from the sound. Rajeev's name flashed on the screen.

"Hi", she murmured huskily into the phone.

"Are you O.K.?" the voice in the phone asked impatiently.

"I am what you want me to be!"

"Can you ever give straight answers? Anyway, just listen carefully…"

"I'm tired of listening to you, Rajeev. Why do you bother to call when we can't have a conversation?"

She heard him inhale deeply at the other end. It was usual.

"Where are you?"

"In the bath. And alone too. Want to come and check?" she smiled, her seductive sarcasm hitting a dead-end.

"Shut up and listen to me! Don't panic! Stay calm. There's some trouble at Taj. Switch off all your lights and stay inside. Don't open the door to anybody.…Ok? And don't do anything stupid … I'm on my way to get you. See if you can catch the news on TV. Actually, don't. In fact, you'll need to keep all sound off. Keep your phone on silent mode and in your hand. I'll call you again. Be calm. I'm coming for you."

She stared at the phone, waiting for words to find her. The doorbell rang again. Startled, she drew herself out of the bathtub and slipped into the bathrobe as quietly as possible, her throat drying up. Water and fear had a disturbingly cold effect, as they found their way down her peachy back. As she tucked in the toga, her cell phone slipped from her hand and fell into the rose-scented bath.

The doorbell rang for the third time. She groped inside the bathtub, searching frantically for her phone. As she did, gunfire peppered the solid teakwood door. Stupefied, she stood with bated breath for a few moments, when she heard voices walking through the now doorless room. Desperate to save her life and dignity, she stepped into the closet, as light-footed as a terrified doe.

Her heart pounded in her head as she heard the intruders talk in a language that sounded like a mix of Sindhi and Pashto. She had heard her mother Noorie talk to her grandmother in a dialect that sounded similar. Even though, she could not comprehend much, she could catch traces of the conversation that told her that the worst was yet to come. She was least prepared for her wish to be granted in this manner.

"The water is still warm!"

"Somebody has to be in. Check under the bed and in the mini bar. In panic, a *kaphir* can get in anywhere. Get the rats out."

"Nothing here."

"If there's no one, set the room on fire."

A cell phone tittered.

"Yes, *Ch'cha*. All is well. Will celebrate *Eid* soon."

The voice on the other end sailed in with the static.

"Just rounding them up. They're scrambling around like rats. We're shooting anything that moves. What doesn't; burns. The boys have spread out like sea-water!"

The voice crackled again and the conversation stopped. She noticed that the light inside the closet was on. Any movement now could prove fatal. Footsteps moved about cautiously checking every nook and cranny of the room, interspersed with amused exclamation on the opulence of the place. Talk was also punctuated with expletives that expressed a clear disgust with all things that were inaccessible in their world. Then, there was a predatory pause. Footsteps now approached her hideout.

Would the next few moments be, Hansa wondered, the most intense moments of her life, or the excruciating end of it? Before she could sort out the fleeting thoughts in her head, the closet door flew back with brute force. She now stood face to face with a pair of eyes glowering through a scarf that covered the head and face in several layers. The eyes searched and scrutinised her white toga, part by part, as she began to cower in fright. It was like embers of a kindling, growing fire, falling on dewy petals.

The phone in his left hand started to buzz again. His accomplice in the dining room, called for his partner and on receiving no response, crept slowly through the bedroom and towards the adjoining bathroom.

The two men, clad in black, in sheer contrast to the whiteness of the room, were of a tall and lean stature. Full-sleeved *pathani* suits, gloved hands, black sneakers and chequered headbands draped them like bitumen, with bloodshot eyes flaming through. The man who had just approached the closet was taller and carried a rucksack on his back. As he raised his AK-47 and aimed it at her, the man with the phone hoisted his left hand, signaling him to stop and then advanced it towards her.

Moments, under such pressure, fuse together like ice-cubes that melt into each other and time becomes one misshapen lamina of events. She could feel a similar pressure building up between her ears. Her green pupils dilated in trepidation. It was the longest moment of her life. Without a warning; in a blink, there was a shot and Hansa lay in a heap on the floor, whiter than ever, stiller than ever!

Seven

Time seemed to stretch like a balloon, ready to burst with tensile strain. Hansa gasped and her long dark lashes fluttered through the mist that was making room around her head. The heat and fright had made her to sweat profusely and had caused the kohl in her eyes to smear her face. The air-conditioning seemed to have been turned off.

As she came to and opened her eyes, her gaze met the spot on the ceiling from where the bullet had ricocheted the second time after hammering the wall behind her. She tried hard to recall the turn of events and remembered seeing the taller guy taking aim to shoot. The click of the selector-lever was the last sound she had heard, as the other man's hand came up, clubbing the AK-47. The shot and her drop to the floor had been simultaneous.

She wondered if the bullet had been misfired on purpose or pretext. And did she faint with impact, nervous anxiety or something else?

Too many unanswered questions had started to rifle her now. She gathered her robe and composure and made an attempt to get up. Her right shoulder had taken the pressure of the fall and throbbed on movement. She still felt a bit giddy. As the haze in her mind cleared and she recalled the events, two impelling voices fell upon her ears.

"That's my order and you've to accept it!"

"You are a *kafir* and I'm not ready to obey one. We're out to kill and that's the only order I follow. Anybody who doesn't follow it is not a brother."

"You are not in your senses. We have only just begun and you are already cracking up. I think your brain is asking for its feed."

"Shut up! You can't fool me by this big-brother talk. I am in my right mind and my senses are well-fed. It's you who's turning into a crack-pot at the first sight of a fair-skinned woman!" The man was almost yelling now.

"How dare you raise your voice to me? You're calling me a kafir? You owe your life to me, pig-head!"

"I owe my life to my *kismet* and *Inshah-Allah*; I shall live to put every infidel to a just end."

A scuffle followed. Hansa could hear objects crashing to the floor. In a matter of seconds, there were three successive bangs, followed by a thud. Hansa stiffened and shut her eyes tight. She wished it was all one long nightmare which would end when she opened them.

A disturbing silence followed the crash, punctuated by sounds of explosions going off somewhere outside. By now, she had taken cognizance of the situation but was still unable to think clearly. She picked herself up and moved cautiously to the bathroom door. There was neither sound nor movement in the room.

She paused to think and then took a few steps forward. What she saw made her want to throw up. The guy, who, a while ago, had menacingly aimed a rifle at her now lay on the floor with a bullet through his throat. Blood pooled up beneath his neck and coloured the sun-bleached floor.

Something welled up inside her. She ran back inside the bathroom and threw up into the commode. As she reached out for the faucets, a few drops of water trickled out before the tap ran dry. Water supply had been cut off. The dolphins on the tiled floor now appeared dark and listless.

A phone hummed somewhere. She recalled that it was the reminder she had put on her phone to coordinate her travel plans with her secretary. The phone was in the tub, which was now empty. The water had been drained away. She grabbed it with trembling fingers and hastily speed-dialled the number three. The keypad was locked. Before she could unlock it; a shadow loomed up from behind her. Startled, Hansa turned around. Green pupils engaged with black and in moments piqued with dismay, the phone changed hands. "Lie low if you want to live", he rasped. She was not expected to answer. Masking tape clasped her mouth shut. He bound her hands behind her and as he bent to tie her feet, the fold of the bathrobe exposed her thigh. His hand moved and lingered precariously over her leg. She felt a shiver and withdrew. She could feel the heat of his breath, even through the layers of cloth around his face. It hovered over her thigh indecisively, but his eyes had found a stationary point in hers. Then as if driven by another purpose; it pulled the bathrobe over to cover her leg. She felt the spark of static electricity, as his rough palm brushed against her smooth knee.

"Stay here. Don't even think of getting out", he said as he finished tying up her feet. He picked up the haversack and the semi-automatic that the other guy was carrying and breezed out of the room.

Left to her fate and discordant thoughts, Hansa felt helpless. She couldn't understand how and why she was still alive and what had caused the altercation that led to one turning against the other. There wasn't much she could do except think, or pray. She crouched by the dolphins. It did not seem appropriate to hop her way out of the room to meet death in the face. Strangely enough, she wanted to believe and abide by the words of the man she had faced only for a few minutes.

Besides, she needed to calm her shaky nerves before she decided what to do next.

The noise outside had now become clearer and louder. She could hear a lot of gunfire and something going off with a blast at short intervals. Grenades, perhaps! The air too had a charred edge to it. She tried hard to hear human sound above the din but was unable to. There was a remote chance that the intercom in the room would be working. She wondered where Rajeev was and if help was on its way.

Rajeev had been her husband for three years now and his entry into her life had been quite akin to a romantic motion picture. He was nothing like the muscle-bearing, well-chiseled superstars of Bollywood. Instead, his only claim to fame were his intense black eyes, ready wit and an iconic father, who had built an empire within the industry, of which he was the undisputed heir.

Rajeev, the son of Srijann Walia, had met her on the sets of a film, in which she was to play the female lead and Rajeev had been signed on to play the part of her brother-in-law. Interestingly Sri-jee (as Mr. Srijann Walia was popularly known in the industry) was to play the role of her husband, the antagonist in the story. The film was based on the subject of incest and family turmoil. Hansa and Rajeev were to shoot a song-sequence in the paradisiacal landscape of Switzerland.

*****

Their rendezvous with romance had been like a well-drafted script, waiting to be read. Hansa had landed in Zurich a day prior to the shoot in order to accommodate jet-lag and reset her sleep pattern. She had been booked in at a chalet by the lake Thun near Interlaken. At that time of the year, boats serenaded the water, that shimmered with the cool mist of May frolicking over it, while crested ice-caps made for a picture-perfect background. It did not require much to fall prey to Cupid's game in an arresting ambience like that. However, Hansa had always been known for her stiff upper-lip and discreet attitude while at work. Crouching helplessly on the bathroom floor, she wished the bitterness of the past three years could be done and that Rajeev could come to her rescue once again, just the way he had promenaded into his life on that beautiful day at Lake Thun.

She had woken up that morning and stepped onto the balcony of her room that overlooked the lake. The wind had caressed her face softly as she felt a surge of amorous feelings inside her. She had smiled and her eyes twinkled as her gossamer gown flapped.

Something special was afloat in the air that day, like dreams made of candy-floss. She drew her arms around her waist and took a decision. Yellow, white and pink it would be. Yes, wild flowers in her hair in yellow, white and pink. Her mood for the day was set.

The shoot was to take place near a log hut by the lake. She had reached the set-location in an off-shoulder yellow dress with brown boots. With her curls perched high up on her head and wildflowers kissing the nape of her neck; she had heads turning, the minute she had stepped out of her room. The location was at a four-minute walk from the chalet.

She had asked the driver to bring the car around to the set, while preferring to foot it till there, with her secretary in tow.

"Madam, your costumes, for tomorrow are awaiting your approval. The designer has tried to make the changes you had asked for. When would you like to look at them?"

"Tell them they have been approved!"

"But, wouldn't you like to see them first. It'll save a lot of trouble later."

"If I've seen one, I've seen them all. Besides, I don't even require so many of them. You could actually keep just three and send away the rest, if he is in a hurry." "Madam, I think you are being a little hasty. The designer has spent a lot of time organising the fabric and accessories that you had asked for!"

"I told you, keep them or send them. It doesn't matter, really! Everything's Ok."

"But, Ma'am..." "Chill Ginny!"

He had not expected this. Apart from the nonchalant approval, it was the rare smile on her lips and her express wish to walk that were unusual. "Well, whatever! She's only twentyish," thought Ginny. The designer would certainly be happy, and make him happy in return. Ginny continued his prattle about launch parties and debutante directors as Hansa looked as far out as she could see.

Ganpat, alias Ginny, had been Hansa's secretary from the time she had ventured into the land of make-believe. He had not only been her professional confidante and Man-Friday but had also played an important part in business-networking which had landed her some meaty roles in award-winning productions. He was about ten years older than her in age and experience. A reliable associate most of the time; his only bane was his irrepressible desire to babble or perhaps sometimes, to make a few extra bucks on the side. The production crew was much younger, energetic and looked ebullient at the thought of being in the most romantic destination in the world. She seriously doubted if any of them, except the director, had work on their mind.

It was a cool, yet sunny day; the kind that does make you want to throw a wrap around your shoulders and lick on ice-cream with crunchy ice-flakes.

"Madam, shot is ready. Rajeev jee is on his way here from the airport. We will roll as soon as he reaches," one of the assistants said imploringly.

"He should've reached here yesterday. You know I like to do things on time and I certainly don't think much of people who waste my time. Where is he right now?"

"Ma'am, he is just ten minutes away from Thun. His flight was delayed."

"Ten minutes? Ya, I sure know what that means. If he doesn't get here in the next one hour, you can consider it a pack-up for the day, from my end. I'm not going to sit around waiting for a joker." She had met Rajeev briefly at a party during the early years of her career but had no professional interaction with him.

Incidentally, they had not been able to meet to discuss their roles for this film due to Hansa's busy schedule and Rajeev's frequent overseas trips. Whether these trips were for the purpose of business or pleasure, was a hot subject of gossip in socialite get-togethers. Besides, he was also remembered avidly in the circuit for his casual manner and lack of professional maturity.

On any other day, Hansa would have just walked away in a huff or perhaps settled down with a book. But that day the air had smelt different and her heart felt warmer than usual. The lake was spread out in front of her and a boat bobbed impatiently for its next love story. Hansa strolled down the pier and felt a sudden urge to take off on her own. She stepped on to the boat and was awed by the unhindered expanse of water and land that stood before her, holding hands. The foothills where the lake met the mountain, blushed with foliage in myriad colours. She could see the spires of a few Romanesque castles on the Northern stretch of the lake.

The next moment was one she was going to remember forever. A naughty gust of misty breeze, rushed in unannounced and flirted with her skirt. She swirled around, trying to keep the frock from its wild fling when the boat bobbed indecisively and she lost her balance.

As she tottered sideways, unexpected support found its way around her tiny waist. It was Rajeev, gazing out at the lake as he held her delicately. It was a few seconds later that he looked at her while she managed to regain balance.

"Hi! Rajeev, your knight in shining amour," he chuckled at his wisecrack as he introduced himself.

"I'm sure you are! Only a Walia can mix chutzpah with candour."

"I'll take that as a compliment. And I guess, that should make up for the time you had to spend waiting," he smiled coyly.

"A wrong needs many rights in order to justify itself," she quipped. "But thanks, nevertheless."

"So, considering this was my first, how many rights do I have left?" his eyes sparkling with intended mischief.

"Well, rights are not inheritance, they need to be earned. You could start by being punctual for once." She had snapped out of her early-morning mood but one charming moment had chosen to stay with her for the rest of her life. She could still feel the warmth of a strong arm around her dainty waist. A pair of swans waddled by oblivious to the world around them. The assistant came scrambling to the boat and told them that they were ready to shoot.

*****

She sighed. A grenade went off somewhere nearby and the lights in the room flickered. Her consciousness stumbled back into the present. It was a stark contrast to where she was a few seconds ago. It was interesting how thoughts could travel at the light of speed and yet have the potential to be sinfully dark. She couldn't see the action but the acrid smell in the air informed her of the increasing gravity of the situation. She felt silly at wanting to rest her faith in the words of a terrorist. She had to do something quickly. Now that the initial surge of fear had grounded itself, she could attempt to think and act sensibly. If the scene of her death had been scripted and bound, she would rather carry it out with the panache she was known for and not let it overpower her ineffectively.

She struggled with the masking tape on her wrists. The grip was too young to fray. She wiggled and moved in order to sit back over her hands and bring them up in front of her. Now, all she needed was to stand up on her feet. After a brief struggle and a few failed attempts later, she was able to bounce back up and find the ground under her feet.

She looked about and saw the first sign of hope. The candles had nearly burnt themselves out. She hopped around to the side of the tub and held her bound wrists over the diminishing flame, hoping desperately for it to work.

The first two candles fell as she tried to tip them a bit to reach to the flame. The flames struggled to live but died inconsequentially. The last candle, however, offered the assistance that she needed. The tape started to curl up into beads, singeing her skin. Deep furrows etched her forehead as she endured the slow, burning sensation.

As her hands came loose, she sat down and held the candles over her bound ankles. The second attempt was easier and quicker. She then scuttled into the room to clothe herself before she made desperate attempts to release the tape on her mouth. The skin on her wrists and ankles was now the colour of ripe raspberries. Freedom almost always leaves behind indelible marks of struggle.

She grabbed the first set of clothes that caught her eye and slipped into them. It was a pair of blue jeans and a white kimono blouse in cotton silk, which she had intended to wear the next day. She usually wore it with a red rose in her hair to complement the red trimming on the blouse. The red now seemed garish and ugly. Grabbing her tote-bag, she emptied the contents on the bed and searched for the nail-file which always accompanied her essentials in it. Her fingers touched something else instead. It was her business phone. She opened the message box and entered — "SOS, man in room *tuk fone*".

She had barely sent the message that she heard high-pitched voices in the corridor outside. Slipping the phone in her pocket, her shaky hands fumbled for the file and found it. Running back to the bathroom, she tripped over the rug and fell face down across the body of the dead assailant, retting in his own blood. Even without his gun, he looked menacing enough.

Hansa cringed in disgust. Then realising that time was not a luxury she could afford, scuttled over the hurdle, with a hand on her stomach, and made a dash for the bathroom.

There, with her heart drumming irrepressibly, she started to work on the tape with shaky hands and a filer.

*****

Outside, it was a scene from hell. The sixth floor was rapidly turning into the remains of a war-struck monument. Huge balls of fire rose intermittently from the lower floors, with the corridors belching smoke along its entire length. The famous central atrium that provided a palace like décor to the Heritage Wing now looked like a dilapidated relic from an ugly past. The music had turned into a rhapsody of devilish timbre.

On the fifth floor, two gun-wielding silhouettes emerged through the smoke screen and proceeded cautiously towards the staircase. The corridor on the ground floor, with its lustrous white marble chequered with black, was quiet and foreboding.

The corridors of the Palace Wing overlooked the central cavaedium from all the balusters railing them and; by the virtue of their architectural vastness; provided a safe vantage point for the apprehenders to keep all movement above and below within eye-shot. Footsteps were heard racing frantically across the aisle below.

Without deliberation, a hand-grenade went hurtling down the atrium and met the scramblers with an explosion. Meanwhile, the camouflaged man had finished his job on the sixth floor. He could see his accomplices on the floor below him. They gave each other the thumbs-up. His phone rang. He uncovered his veil briefly and muttered into it:

"*Ch'cha*, all rats rounded up. The Maharaja is bleeding."

"Good, don't spare a soul. Tell *Abu* and Ibrahim not to leave their post till I tell them to. Anyone still wriggling for their last breath; set them on fire!"

"Ch'cha, Azaan is gone. He was trying to save a rat. I shot him."

"May *paak* Mohammed-ur-Rasool forgive him. Every *Kafir* deserves his due. You have about ten minutes before the snakes come in. They are sliding in around the corner. Likely as well, to have eagles soon. Greet them with an inferno they won't be able to get out of … dead or alive. *Allah-hafiz*!"

The veiled man slipped the phone back in his pocket and moved noiselessly back to the suite where he had shot his aide. The men on the floor below were signalled to remain watchful and alert and keep their positions. He entered the room with his eyes scouring every inch of the place. The dead body presented itself, just the way he had left it. Shards of broken glass were strewn about and the bed-linen remained unruffled.

On the bed, his eyes caught something which was not there when he had left the room. He sprung into position, his back against the panelled wall and his gun, ready to shoot. There was no other visible or audible sign of movement in the room. A few seconds passed before he decided to go to the bathroom and complete his unfinished job. Treading like a jaguar, he moved towards the door, paused briefly outside it and shot off at the ceiling for effect. He had expected a reaction. Nothing moved. He inched his way in and stormed into the closet. There was no one. The place was empty. His game was gone.

*****

Hansa sat huddled beside the wooden chest, too scared to breathe. She had somehow made it through the clouds of smoke, unnoticed and alive. She had noticed two figures on the fifth floor, signalling someone on the sixth. She had kept moving, almost wriggling in a trance-like state, not pausing to think. What she had seen would probably haunt her for the rest of her life.

The flawless marble floors now looked like a dishevelled mortuary. Charred body parts and burning flesh had stupefied her senses and she tried hard to see through the haze as rheum and smoke seared her vision. Crouching low, she had now reached the spot where the landing met the aisle running in from the corridors. Fear had kept prodding her on.

There were likely to be more assailants on these corridors as well and she couldn't risk being seen. She had to make a dash across a stretch of about fifty metres spread out in a square to reach the next flight of steps, leading downstairs. Down on all fours, she evaluated her timing which was beginning to weigh down heavily on her. She had always taken calculated risks in life but this situation did not fit into any preconceived theory.

Before she could make a move, a hand had covered her mouth and a large piece of muslin shrouded her, blackening everything. She felt herself being dragged across the space. It seemed to be a lunge down the steps; as her feet rattled off the flight. She thought it wise not to put up a struggle. A few minutes passed by before she was thrown in somewhere and the cover pulled off. Before she could give him a despicable look, he spoke in his gravelly voice:

"Listen woman! The only place where you can stay alive is next to me. You want to run out to be blown up into a hundred pieces; you may as well but let me tell you, had I wanted you dead, you would be so by now. So use your brain and stay where I put you." He spat to his side to vent the residual anger. Once done, he came up uncomfortably close to her, and for a moment Hansa thought, he might grope her.

As his eyes bore into her body once more, she looked askance, trying not to unveil her fear.

"Destiny brings us together again, and *Inshah Allah*, a good life awaits us," he whispered hoarsely into her ear, turned about and disappeared into the thick darkness before her gaze could follow him. His words confused her more than they scared her.

Who was this man who had stepped out with the mission to kill hundreds of innocent people and destroy a monument with years of irrevocable history etched on its walls? And yet, he was talking about saving the life of a woman who was a complete stranger to him.

What did he mean by 'again'? She may have been a public figure and won the adulation of many men but to her, a terrorist would be far beyond the realms of love and adoration.

"Wear this," he said, throwing a set of black *pathani-suit* at her. The feel of the cloth was soft; like *mulmul*; quite contrary to her expectation. She picked up the clothing with nimble fingers and began to slip on the shirt. It reeked of male sweat. It was not too large, but ill-fitting for her lithe body. The collar was damp but it felt thicker than when it feels when it is drenched in sweat. She shuddered at the thought that flashed through her head. She was probably wearing a dead man's clothes that had been shot in the throat. She swallowed the lump in her throat and looked nervously at the man who was peering outside.

She couldn't quite identify the room either. The place was a few minutes' drag away from the staircase and was charred beyond recognition. It was bigger in size than her suite. Her peripheral vision caught sight of a foot behind a blackened pillar. The tall man was facing her now.

She felt cold, sweaty fingers tighten around her throat and coal-black eyes drilling into hers. Before she could put up any resistance, a volley of shots rang through the lobby outside. It seemed like a fresh invasion. He released his grip and rushed outside, turned back to say, "This is your last chance", before he stormed out of the room again.

*****

The face that belonged to the foot behind the pillar was pale and sweaty, and made quite a brave attempt at stifling her sobs. She approached the girl with a mixed sense of relief and anxiety. As she put her hand around her shoulder, the girl with honey blonde hair broke down and cried convulsively.

"Ssshhh," said Hansa, trying to placate her. "You're lucky, you're alive. Calm down. This will soon be over."

That seemed to reassure her a bit and her sobs trailed off into soft sniffs.

"Do you have anybody you want to talk to? I have a phone with me."

The girl took the phone that Hansa offered and timorously, dialled a number. It was unreachable. Fresh tears welled up in the girl's eyes.

"I can't reach him. I don't know if he's still alive. We were downstairs at the bar, when I decided to come up to the room and get my swim-suit. I don't know what might have happened to him down there."

"What's your name?"

"Simone"

"I'm Hansa. Don't worry. Let's just hope and pray for this to get over. I don't think it's safe for us to step out right now. I have reason to believe that the guy who brought me in, doesn't intend killing me. I guess you'll be safe if you stay with me. We'll have to put up a brave front."

Simone nodded in agreement. Hansa looked around and spotted a tiny, carved window-like panel, with filigreed wrought-iron work, at the far end of the room. Light filtered through in a tribal gush; inconspicuous, yet beneficial. The girls rushed to it and were able to get a peep-hole view of the world outside. A battery of police vehicles had cordoned off the area on the road below.

"Simone, do you know where we are right now?"

"Third floor. But I don't know which room. I got out of my room and was walking towards the lift when I heard the gunfire. I ran in the opposite direction, towards the staircase but there were these men running up the steps driving holes in everything that moved.

I saw people running about wildly and just dropping down dead in a matter of seconds."

Hansa took out her phone and messaged—Stuck on third floor, room unknown, firing on outside. She was now poised and in control.

"I think help is here. It won't be long before we are out safely."

They sat down feeling a little reassured. "Where are you from, Simone?"

"Switzerland. I had come here with my boyfriend Ulrich.

We'd just finished our Culinary Arts course and decided to holiday in India and learn about the local cuisine."

"Do you want to try calling him again?"

Simone tried once more but the phone was still out of coverage.

"Can send him a message?" "Sure, go ahead."

Simone texted Ricci and made a quick phone call home, apprising her family about the situation.

She sat down next to Hansa, looking at her with restless eagerness. Hansa wondered if small talk would help ease her mind a bit.

"Where are you from? How are you so calm?"

"I'm of mixed descent but very much an Indian now. And I'm not calm. Just keeping the faith," Hansa smiled.

"It's my fault to have brought Ricci here," Simone's voice became heavy again.

"Hey, guilt isn't going to help at all. I believe a rescue-team is already in operation. Just..."

There was a heavy thud outside. They huddled closer together. A few minutes of apprehension, circled them heavily and then fell quiet.

"So, what are your plans once you're out of here," Hansa tried to keep the spirit alive by infusing hope.

"We had plans to visit the Taj Mahal in Agra. Not anymore."

"Hmmm. You come from such a beautiful country. You know it's a favourite destination for set locales."

"O yes! I mean it is very beautiful." Simone paused. "Have you been there ever?"

"Yes. Five years ago. I was there for a shoot. For a film," she added hastily.

"Are you an actor? A movie-star?" Simone exclaimed with a hint of a twinkle dotting her blue eyes. "Wow, you must be popular then!"

Hansa was amused at the forthright question. The sound of police sirens drifted into the room and refuelled their hope. They looked towards the window.

Hansa's phone rang. It was Rajeev.

"Where's your phone? I've been desperately trying to reach you. Where are you?"

"I'm fine. Don't worry. I texted Pa."

"What d'you mean, you texted Pa? I've been killing myself trying to get in touch with you. Where are you right now?"

"Somewhere on the third floor."

She realised the call had dropped. She sighed. She knew that Rajeev was worried about her but she was unable to see him taking charge of things and driving them towards a solution. At most he would make random calls, yell at authority and be a perfect picture of a panic-stricken husband; unlike her father-in-law Srijann Walia, who did things differently and correctly.

She could almost foresee his plan of action and that's the reason she had chosen to keep her father-in-law informed about her whereabouts instead of her husband. Simply letting him know made Hansa feel more at ease and confident of her safety. She saw more of a man in her father-in-law than she did in her husband. He reminded her of president Jinnah as described by Ruttie Begum. Strangely at that moment, she was reminded of Ruttie's famous last words to her husband:

"When one has been as near to the reality of Life (which after all is Death) as I have been dearest, one only remembers the beautiful and tender moments and all the rest becomes a half veiled mist of unrealities . . . ."

*****

Hansa checked the time on her phone. It was half past eleven but it already seemed like they had been in that state for several hours. The phone-battery was on its last legs now. She wanted to save it for an emergency. If there could be one greater than this. Sitting next to her, Simone looked sleepy. She got up to peep through the chad-like holes in the wall. There were enough security personnel but activity was dormant. She could not see a sense of urgency. Taking a deep breath, she decided to call her father-in-law. She looked at her phone, reconsidering her decision. Before she could make room for second thoughts, her phone rang, flashing her father-in-law's name. In a split second, she took the phone to her ear:

"Hello, Pa!" and she broke down. Restraint came gushing down her cheeks.

"Sweetheart, don't you shed a tear. Nobody can so much as touch you with a bargepole. No harm will come to you, trust me. I'll get you out of this mess soon."

"I know," she sobbed, "but there are dead bodies and limbs strewn everywhere outside. It's creepy and I…"

"Relax. It's sad but it is happening and you've got to stay alert. Just lie low and don't make any conspicuous movement."

"Pa, my phone's running out of battery. I may not be able to…" and the light on the visual display went off.

Hansa had started to feel queasy again.

*****

From the moment he had caught the breaking news on his I-phone, Rajeev had been restless and agitated. He was too young to use experience as his advisor and analysis as his guide. So far, he had thrown his weight around at every place of authority that mattered. However, nothing much seemed to be coming out of it. The reassuring replies that he received did little to relieve him from the tremendous stress he was going through. His father was away to Delhi and without him, he felt like a headless chicken. Even though, he often felt cheated of a worthy place in the industry because of his father's monumental status; his Dad was still the bulwark of the Walia family's social existence. At the moment, Rajeev was unaware of his Dad's tacit presence in the spate of phone calis and compelling directives that were being exchanged between the political bigwigs of Delhi and Bombay.

It had been nearly an hour now that he had spoken with Hansa and all his phone calls thereafter had gone unanswered. He had tried her business phone as well but it was unreachable. Rajeev was a worried man, and for the first time in his life, he had felt the weight of responsibility on his shoulders. As his car wormed its way through the Mumbai traffic, it dawned on him that he had never noticed the harried face of the man on the bicycle or the distraught lady sitting by the road selling either droopy flower bands or stinky fish. For them, pain and discomfort made winsome appetizers. He was almost always busy with his phone or laptop, either tweeting or playing games while on the road.

For him, Mumbai, the Maximum City, resided in plush bungalows, travelled in expensive cars and walked about in signature clothing. What he noticed today was always within eyeshot but had never seeped into his vision.

A tall strapping lad of twenty-four, Rajeev had fallen in love with Hansa the day he had seen her on the cover of a glossy. Her light-coloured dewy eyes enchanted him and he had coveted her ever since, without distraction. His plan of action included staying away from loose flirtatious gimmicks and aspiring to sign a film with her. A girl with extraordinary charm would need an extraordinary wooing strategy. The first interaction by the lake Thun had given him a winning edge. "Be punctual," she had said but he had been able to decode the message encrypted in her body language. A girl sways differently when she is ready to give her heart away. The turn of the neck, the swing of the hand to straighten tangled curls or curl up straight locks, and even a simple supine movement has a rhythm to it.

He fervently hoped to make it in time today. Cross-browed, Rajeev looked out of his window. It had taken him nearly an hour to get out of the crowded *Juhu* streets. "Faster, *Balaji*," he urged the driver to press down the accelerator.

They were now crossing over from Bandra, the doorway for the suburbs to town, to *Mahim*. His bodyguards followed in the car behind them. The dark waters of the Arabian Sea in the distance were slowly gaining momentum, with the tide creeping into the shores.

"Water and fire," he thought, "the direst necessities of civilisation." His thoughts were refrained by an erratic halt. He cussed under his breath and barked orders into his phone.

The guards got down and strode up to check how the land lay. He rolled down his window momentarily. The eunuchs showed up with the breeze. Unannounced. Forced to roll it back up, he was even more miffed with the fact that they had identified him as Hansa's husband.

"It's a jam, sir. Accident ahead. Looks like a fatal one." "What's the scene of it clearing up?"

"Drunken driving, Sir. It's become an everyday thing now. There's a smashed SUV, a car that has turned turtle and a crushed body. May be two… difficult to see."

"Are the police there yet?"

"Yes, Sir. They are trying to manage the site and the traffic but it is difficult with two vehicles blocking the way."

"Come with me."

Rajeev got off his car and walked ahead of the parked vehicles, escorted by the three bouncers. There was a police Control-Room van, and a Gypsy that had come in from the wrong end to get to the scene of the accident. The down traffic was unperturbed and unconcerned with the chaos in the opposite lane. Uniformed men moved about their business as usual.

Rajeev walked up to the officer-in-charge and took him to a corner to have a private chat. The bouncers, standing at a short distance, saw the officer shaking his head vehemently while refusing to accept anything except the promise of an autographed movie-ticket. Smiles were exchanged. Soon, Rajeev and his security personnel were speeding towards their destination in the police gypsy with a star-struck cop.

The driver took an unexpected right turn to avoid the mid-town traffic. Not that Rajeev noticed. He was preoccupied with his phone, making random calls and yelling at authority, just as Hansa had expected him to. The Gypsy was speeding down the road leading to Chowpatty and towards Marine Drive.

As it approached a traffic signal near a famous restaurant, Rajeev witnessed a few gunshots, followed by a mass of people descending on a car that had hit the divider and stalled. It all happened in a flash and for a moment Rajeev considered stopping to enquire.

On a second thought, he asked the driver to make a quick exit before the crowd became a mob and blocked the traffic. The traffic was unusually disorganised. The jeep made its way through the busy road and Rajeev noticed another road block near the Oberoi Trident.

The place was a spectacle. The Marine Drive which usually looked resplendent with light, colour and carnal effects during late evening now looked botchy and threatening. The boulevard was devoid of pedestrians but the Queen's Necklace twinkled as a matter of routine.

“Damn! What the fuck is happening? Those rotten bastards are everywhere!" Rajeev was unable to hold back his thoughts anymore.

“Don't worry, Sir! Hansa madam will be totally fine! Ganpati Bappa will protect her," the cop had spoken for the first time.

The creases on Rajeev's forehead maintained their stance.

He had made futile attempts to reach Ginny as well.

“Ganpati Bappa shouldn't have let this happen in the first place. Why the hell can't you get to the goddamned place quickly?” he shot back at the cop as well as the jeep's driver.

God is everywhere, he had heard. For Rajeev the concept of God was just a notion to teach the human race to live in fear and also to have an unexplained dependence, to make irrational demands of someone and to be able to land the blame squarely on non-descript shoulders when things went wrong. Perhaps that's the reason employers subconsciously prefer to hire people with God-like names, as their drivers, maids or secretaries, he mused.

He called Hansa again and this time her phone rang. He pressed the phone to his ear.

“Where's your phone? I've been desperately trying to reach you. Where are you?”

“I'm fine. Don't worry. I texted Pa.”

“What d'you mean, you texted Pa? I've been killing myself trying to get in touch with you. Where are you right now?”

“Somewhere…” The call dropped.

*****

The Gateway of India had received many unexpected visitors that night. The place, which milled over with hawkers by the day and shifty hustlers by night, was now teeming with policemen, fire-fighters, journalists and photographers.

Lying on the ground, these men, and women too, witnessed the beautiful dome of the Taj going up in flames. The place had been cordoned off and the area, except the hotel, was well-illuminated with flood lights. Several windows of the suites in the heritage wing exhaled smoke.

It was a dour evening, smelling of death and destruction.

A grenade came flying out of a fifth floor and landed on the parapet. The cops ducked for cover and photographers, for a more strategic point to catch the action from. The Black Cats were yet to arrive.

Hansa saw the grenade going off and people scuttling around, directionless. The smoke settled down lazily. Through the haze, something looked familiar. Or someone. She couldn't make a mistake in identifying the shirt with a glorified dragon on its back. And of course, the lop-sided gait, accentuated by a sprained ankle. But clothes are usually more noticeable than people.

She wanted to shout out to him before he turned around and went the other way. It was imperative to catch his attention. However, she had neither the option, nor an advantageous position. "No conspicuous movement," Pa had said.

She looked around the room in desperation. Everything around was burnt. It was difficult to tell wood from iron, especially in the darkness.

Cinders glowed in a few corners.

"What are you looking for?" asked Simone, getting up to help.

"Like a stick or something," she replied.

After a bit of stumbling around, Simone picked up an iron rod. It would do just fine.

"Keep a watch on the door for me," she instructed Simone.

Simone gave her a wide-eyed nod and crept towards the door, apprehensively.

Hansa hurried back to the wall and started to disrobe. She removed the black kameez, followed by her kimono top. She always had the best of Victoria's Secret, next to her ivory skin; one of the many clandestine tidbits that she held close to her heart. Her hands shook as she smeared a finger with the soot around her and scrawled at the back of the blouse—"Hansa floor three".

"Someone's coming, it seems. I hear voices," Simone whispered loudly. Hansa looked out anxiously and quickened her pace as she tied the arms of the blouse to the rod. She was yet to clothe herself.

Hurriedly, she pushed the queer flag far out of the mole-size hole and moved it frantically to draw attention. She was unable to see him as the SOS flag blocked her view.

"Almost here, quick!" Simone ran back to the dark corner she had occupied earlier.

Hansa shoved the flag out of the opening and turned around.

She had barely grabbed the kameez, when the room received two new visitors, dangerously armed and dressed in black!

Eight

27th November 2008, Apollo Bunder, Mumbai, sometime after 12:00 a.m.

She shuddered and shook in cognizance of her state. The Grand Dame's modesty had been displaced. Surrounded by fire and water, Hansa shuddered too. There was a vortex of disaster spinning around her and she felt as if she was sitting in the eye of it, waiting for it to cave in on her. The smell of cordite was taking over her senses, clouding her awareness. The men proceeded towards her with their gaze fixed on the *kameez* that she had clasped in her hands. She returned their gaze with the green in her eyes reflecting the hue of their attire.

Both of them were of medium stature. One of them was perhaps a little shorter than her. They advanced with their intent written sloppily in their lusty eyes. The shorter one proceeded towards her as his accomplice stopped short a few steps away, without being told to. Hierarchical advantages and disadvantages are often spelt rather discreetly. This man with a non-descript face and a personality to match was now given charge of the backdrop. He toted two guns, one on his shoulder and the other in his hand.

Hansa pressed herself against the wall, hoping to disappear into it. Her knees felt weak and her stomach churned. The man was almost faceless. He was at such proximity where it is difficult to ascribe any form to features. Breathing down hard and heavy on Hansa's face, he slammed his palms on the wall, fencing her in.

"Feeling hot, *huh*? Can I help you cool off?"

Even though his accosting had not come as a surprise, yet, Hansa had anticipated a different set of questions. However, he did not seem to be concerned about the 'why' and 'how' of her semi-clad state. He was too smitten by the now. Clearly, men of his kind are inured only to plunder and not to perceive.

He slobbered over her for a few seconds while she looked away in another direction. He held her chin and moved it roughly to face him. Those few seconds provided the right filler between stimulus and response.

As the distance between their faces diminished, Hansa felt it coming and made no effort to hold back. Her stomach churned yet again, and a stream of puke, straight into the molester's face, set him completely off-balance. He puckered in repugnance. At the same instance, his accomplice fell down screaming in pain, with his hands cupping his eyes.

A second of distraction was all that Simone had needed. Hansa darted towards Simone, who had been quick-footed and taken good advantage of her cover in the darkness. She had scooped up the burning cinders of a piece of wood in the corner. The wood was red hot. Without wincing, she flung herself at the voyeur, thrusting the wood into his face and pressing the embers into his eyes. Even though her hands shook, her aim had been immaculate. The man had been so engrossed in the anticipation of his partner's moves that he had tuned out his senses to the movement behind him. The pursuit of untimely pleasures has often spelled a man's disaster in more ways than one.

The man with the reeking face lunged towards his aide. Hansa was agile enough to jump upon the marauder, while Simone picked up the gun that had fallen to the floor.

"You filthy bitch," he growled, "get the gun, you idiot!"

Hansa's light frame was no match to a body that had roughed it out in extreme and inhospitable conditions. As he tried to wipe his eyes and see clearly, he shook her off and onto the floor. He had her pinned to the ground in no time as she tried to feint his moves with all the strength that she could muster. Suddenly, his body fell limp on her.

Blood trickled on to her semi-clad body but she did not give time to stupor to get the better of her and rolled him off. Simone hauled her up. It had taken two blows; and one lay unconscious while the other bled fatally from the back of his head. Breathless and shaken, Hansa swallowed the lump in her throat as she tried to contain her breath. Simone held up the black *kameez* to her.

Hansa clothed herself as the girls looked at each other, unable to react. She held Simone's palms in hers. The reds matched. Fear is acidic in nature, invariably neutralising all barriers—physical, emotional as well as cultural. It now felt perfectly alright to hug.

Then, as if on the same train of thought, they leapt towards the door. Good luck, like a shooting star, often doesn't hold out for too long. A tall, forbidding structure of a man stood towering over the two girls. Familiar vibes, only colder, greeted them. Simone receded. A portly hand pushed Hansa aside to reach out to her.

"Leave her alone. She's with me," Hansa mustered up enough courage to speak, stepping back in his line of vision again.

"All the more reason why she should be out of my way," he growled.

"Wait! What is it that you want? Money? Prisoners? Political asylum, a deal with the government? You name it and I'll be able to arrange it for you. Just stop all this beastly madness," her voice was beginning to falter.

The man paused thoughtfully, his eyes drilling into hers. "You're in no position to negotiate."

A swift thrust of his bayonet sent Simone keeling over with her mouth gaping and eyeballs rolling back.

Hansa screamed.

"You beast," she threw herself at him, "what do you want from these innocent souls, you wretched bastard!"

He flung around and held her close, close enough for her to feel the reckless drumming of his heart. Molten heat poured out of his eyes into hers. Dry, red lips brushed over her soft pout as his hand caressed her waist. She thought she heard him whisper something. A name, perhaps.

"You're such a cursed animal...", she whimpered through her tears.

He stiffened and his thick palm came crashing against her slight cheek. Stars flashed across her vision as darkness engulfed her once again and she fell into strong arms.

*****

It was dark inside Chambers, the premium club of the hotel, with the spotlights over two paintings providing barely enough candescence for anyone to move about, even with unsure steps. Movement wasn't the order of the hour anyway. A few people crouched and huddled on the floor. Even the broadest of shoulders were now droopy and servile and the stiff-spined gentlemen seemed to have misplaced their social thrust.

The men in *thoubs* and *shumaggs* sat on well-cushioned chairs in the corner, peering through the space around them with quartz like intensity. The hostages, for the first time in their lives, regretted their affluence and prayed silently to trade it for survival.

Hansa opened her eyes to find herself in a room full of men and women, old and young. Some looked aghast, others tired. There was a cushion under her head and a dapper middle-aged man had his fingers around her wrist. A lady, with a greyish-black coiffure that was highlighted by slivers of silver in her hair, stood with indefatigable pride. Draped in crepe-silk and pearls, she loomed over her with generous eyes. Someone was rubbing Hansa's feet that had gone cold. Amongst a few others, a man in his mid-twenties, sat erect, staring at her with empty eyes and a face devoid of hope. He wore a grey-blue blazer with a flagrant Gallic Rooster embroidered on its lapel.

"You Ok Ms. Noorie?" the Parsi lady whispered.

"Yes, I think so." She tried to sit up. The world was still reeling. A few of the Taj staff members waited upon them, still on duty.

"Chambers?" she blinked, trying to dismember the haze from her vision.

"Yes, the staff brought us here. We were told they'd never find us here."

"Then?"

"Oh, you see that fat, balding man over there? He's an M.P. from somewhere. Smart Alec went live on a TV show with his phone, telling the whole world where he was holed up with a big group of important people. Can't believe he's been actually elected!"

"But how did I get here?"

"That one brought you in," she looked at the veiled man, standing beside the pillar supporting the window, shielding himself from being seen by anyone outside.

"We almost thought you were…you know… then he asked us to..."

"And he didn't try to kill anyone?"

"There was mayhem in the staircase but he stopped after he got here. Don't know what's on his mind!"

"What time is it?" "Half past three."

*****

It was a good view from the glass windows and the terrace provided a strategic vantage-point. The Gateway of India stood there like a mater-familias, heavy-lidded and full-bodied, chronicling the events that were unfolding before her.

To Zarrar, it was the gateway to his freedom as well as a symbol of parting and grief; like the void in the crow's nest when the cuckoo's off-springs spread their wings and go looking for a greener perch on the mango tree, leaving behind alien feathers and broken twigs. He tried hard never to entertain thoughts from his past but they, like intrusive neighbours, often crept up unto him, unannounced.

"*Mashah Allah*!" one of them commented at the austere presence of the Gateway of India, trying to join Zarrar in his thoughts. Zarrar spun around. Like a raging bull, he grabbed him by the throat and slammed him against the pillar. *Shivaji Maharaj* peered with sanguine eyes from the painting, overhead.

"*Haraamzaade*! Another word of praise and *Allah-kasam*, you'll have your grave in its foundation. I want this place turned into living hell; such that even vultures would hesitate to come here!"

The hostages flinched. The other two boys perked up their vigil.

Blood oozed out of a slight cut on his lip as Imtiaz caressed his throat that was throbbing with the effect of the rugged grip. He could never endure the ire of their leader's eyes, especially since he had never seen his face. Nobody had.

A reticent breeze, with its nimble fingers, played with the flames growing up from the dome. The fire seemed to be licking its lips after a good night's meal and the tide came in twiddling its thumbs. Change was setting in.

Something crashed. All eyes steered towards the narrow corridor leading out of the club's premises. Or perhaps it came from one of the halls. Another one followed. This time it seemed to be coming from the kitchen end. Zarrar gestured to one of the armed boys to move towards the door.

Imtiaz provided cover. He felt an unusual emotion come over him. His life flashed before his eyes. Incomplete images of half-thatched walls of his mud house in a village near Islamabad skirted his vision. He had never seen anything as remotely ostentatious as this beautiful hotel. The effect of LSD was probably wearing off. He felt uneasy and panic gripped him. It occurred to him that he was not supposed to be there at that moment but should be breaking sweat with his father in a tiny field in his village. He froze in his tracks, stupefied by the thought. His ally advanced towards the door.

"*Aise baahar naa jaao, pasha*! Don't move out like that, brother," he blurted.

The other guy ignored his mumbling to open the door, and stepped out. No sooner had he done this, that spits of blue fire came spinning towards him and devoured him. He fell down, writhing and oozing. Zarrar roared like a wounded lion.

Furious at the loss of a member under his umbrage, he opened fire randomly. Bullets ripped off the ceiling and walls, and flew about like mad bats, instantly putting five lives to rest. The sprinklers near the door went off.

"Non, non, non…. Mon Dieu," someone cried. Those who couldn't find their speech recoiled into an even tighter huddle, comforting each other with the warmth of their breath. Panic has a strangely adhesive effect on people, making them belong to each other. The Frenchman tried to disown the puddle that had built up beneath him and was slowly disappearing into the thick carpet. The Arabs stayed in their chairs and muttered something to Zarrar. He turned away. His satellite phone beeped. There was a message from *Ch'cha*:

"*Magarmachh* now out of the deeps! Eagles flying overhead!"

"Damn!"

MARCOS, the Marine Commandos, had arrived.

There was a pile of phones in his bag, which belonged to the hostages in the room. He picked up one and walked towards the group. Eyes, filled with fear, looked up at him like little children. Flinging the phone at Hansa, he gnarled:

"Srijann Walia … call him!"

Hansa gaped at the mention of his father-in-law's name. "Now!" he yelled, "And tell that filthy pig that each step that these ass-holes take towards me is going to cost them a few lives. And you, my darling, will be the last one to go but not before I have played such games with you that your own family will refuse to look at you, if they're lucky enough to find you!"

Each word fell upon Hansa's ears like molten lead. In a state of torpor, she attempted to dial his father-in-law's number. Network failed. She tried again.

"There's no signal here. Can I stand by the window and call?"

Zarrar snatched the phone from her and redialled. The call went through.

He yanked her up on her feet.

"You are too young to be playing dangerous games. *Inshah-Allah*, we'll be done with you soon. And since you're so used to attention, let's have a little performance from you. It will surely entertain these chickens here!"

The other lad chuckled. Imtiaz remained heedless. Zarrar summoned his two aides and instructed them without saying a word. One of them walked up to Hansa and brought her to a corner in the room. She was then made to face the audience. Imtiaz brought out a dagger and held it at her throat.

"And just so that you don't harbour any misgivings about your position here, let me send a little gift to your father-in-law."

It was nearly *fajr* time now, and the Arabs knelt down to offer their first prayer of the day. Fearlessly.

*****

Srijann Walia's plane was taxiing to a stop at the Juhu airport when his sat-phone beeped. It was a recently acquired asset, despite the strict regulations around the use of sat-phones in India. He had received an MMS. There was also a missed call from that number which, somehow, he had failed to notice. Normally, he would have deleted communication from an unknown number since his sat-phone number was known only to his closest confidantes.

However, his instinct urged him to look at the contents. What he saw made his maws crunch and his jaws to tighten with indignation. The course of action was now clear. He made two phone calls in quick succession. The first call was to the Chief Minister's personal phone and the other to his brother-in-law, a Commodore at the Western Naval Command.

*****

The iridescent sun had woken up to a full-day's work and the clouds seemed institutional. Even though the previous night had inked a page of history in grime and gore, hope still stood tall and unfazed. The faces of terror looked sub-human, with a few sleepless nights behind them. The people around them were now, nothing more than images, simulated and purported for their pleasure.

The number of fallen images was rising steadily and that was all the motivation they needed. They could choose to shut down the game whenever they wanted by simply wasting away the lives. There would be newer lives waiting to be toyed with at the onset of a new game. However, there's only one thing that prevented them from doing so. Like all compulsive gamers, they, too, had a manic obsession with finishing at the top level before giving it all up.

Zarrar wasn't ready to talk yet. He was enjoying the process and did not want a negotiation to ruin the apogee of this act of deliverance. Two hours had gone by and the crocodiles had not been able to make an inch of a head-way towards them. The MMS had done its job. He had even stopped answering calls from his base in Peshawar for the time-being, while he enjoyed the sweetness of this much-awaited moment.

He could see himself walking in the hills of the Khyber, hand in hand, with Husna. He would take her to the Taj, and make love to her on a bed of wild roses.

He shuddered at the thought of touching her for the very first time.

Haggling would have to wait.

"Hey you, pink shirt, come here," he called out to one of the stiff-spined gentlemen.

"Get that black *dupatta*!" The other boy sauntered up to a young woman in red and black apparel. Her plain face was smeared with traces of makeup and wispy hair hung unchecked around her face. She was well-endowed for her age and generation.

The lady parted with her scarf rather hastily, even before she was asked for it. The boy held it and stared at her breasts. She looked away, pretending to be oblivious of his gaze. High on steroids and unable to resist the temptation, he swooped down and grabbed her right breast, pleasure evident in bulging eyes as the woman screamed and parried his move.

Her male companion shut his eyes in order not to let the anger and humiliation spill out. He walked back to Zarrar, laughing like a psychopath, handing over the scarf. Beads of sweat surfaced on the forehead of the man in the pink shirt. The black dupatta was wrapped around his head, covering his entire face, except the eyes.

"Please don't... spare me, I beg you," tears welled up as he whispered softly, avoiding eye-contact.

"*Inshah-Allah*, we are not going to hurt you!"

"Take him away," he ordered. There was a sibylline exchange of glances between the men; an exchange that glorified the inane terror that they were spawning. The pink-shirt, with his face covered with a black cloth, was taken away towards the door that led to the terrace above the main entrance. A grand sculpture of *Chhatrapati* Shivaji, astride his horse, on the left was the key witness.

The gallant leader's Shiva Sutra was now merely an ornament from the past. The group that had huddled up closer inside, could now see him through the glass windows, walking out in the open with a gun aimed vagrantly at the personnel standing below. Before, anyone could comprehend this line of action, a spinning pellet-like sniper shot whooshed across from somewhere on the left and went right through the man, from one side to the other. He dropped down dead.

"Hah ... stupid bastards ... boys, snakes prowling on the exit. This route is sealed. Send Umer a message about the new invaders. *Alhamdu lillah*", bellowed Zarrar.

"*La ilaha ilAllah*," muttered the Arabs. The Parsi lady closed her eyes and recited the Ashem Vohu in a muffled tone.

*****

Rajeev had reached the Colaba Causeway just in time before all approach roads to South Bombay were shut out to commuters. He had to get off in one of the by-lanes behind the five-star hotel as there had been reports of firing in Café Leopold, the most popular stop for foreign tourists in South Bombay.

It had taken him nearly three hours to cover a distance of about twelve miles from Bandra to Colaba. He had started at around 10:00 pm. It was now well past midnight and he was still half a mile away from his destination. The police vehicle had made thoroughfare easier, though.

He now chose to foot the short distance to the site with one of his bouncers in tow. Nearing the Taj, his heartbeat quickened as he saw officers of the local police, the QRT, Army personnel and the NSG involved in rescue operations.

Like a real hero, he had intended to rush inside and rescue Hansa but there are always organisational procedures to slow down prompt action. A judicious flaw in this case, since he wouldn't have been able to come out of it alive.

As he walked towards the waterfront, he noticed the back of a man with a dragon motif glaring menacingly in his direction. There was no mistaking the limp in his gait. It had been his gift to him for casting aspersions on his wife. The man had a white silk blouse in his hand. Ordinarily, he would have ignored the dragon-shirt and perhaps not noticed the silk blouse. But together, they worked like nail and hammer, slamming in certain inferences. He ran up to the man in conversation with an officer-on-duty, talking animatedly about the owner of that blouse. Rajeev caught him by the collar and turned him around.

"What's this blouse doing with you?"

"I've no time to waste on you, you bugger. Just F.O.!"

"I want to know where the hell did you find this? Where's Hansa?"

"Oh, so you're worried about her having left it behind on my bed. Tsk, tsk…you're such a loser!"

Rajeev's fist flew into the air to meet the insolent squarely.

"Sir, you will have to vacate the premises. Please cooperate. It's for your own security," an officer suggested firmly, stepping in between them. The last thing the police needed right now was a public brawl.

A journo ran up to Rajeev to catch a byte. He waved her off and resumed his interaction with the man with a limp.

"Can you tell me what's going on? Do you know where Hansa is?"

Rajeev lowered his hand as his wrath dimmed and tone became tepid. He could see a woman being led off a first floor window by a fire-fighter.

Somebody somewhere must have heaved a sigh of relief on seeing her but it wasn't his moment of solace.

*****

Ginny tried to lift himself off from the floor but couldn't. Around him lay immobile pieces of human trimmings. He couldn't feel his right arm, and pieces of flachette studded his body. The floor was layered with shrapnel and blood. He was unable to discern what was more overpowering, the physical agony or the stench.

The previous evening, he had wished to step out of the plush hotel and walk down to Bade Miyan's for a feast of delicious mutton rolls. Bade Miyan was a well-known road-side eatery located in the by-lanes behind the Taj, famous for its non-vegetarian snacks and meals, made popular by the night-birds of the city. It was on the insistence of another crew member that he had changed his mind and decided to dine at The Zodiac Grill, which was now the abandoned site of an inglorious battlefront. He had seen the faces of the attackers. They looked like twins, with bulging eyes, flushed faces and flaring nostrils. They had streamed in spitting fire from their guns. They left as deftly as they had come in, hurling live grenades and disappearing behind the smoke-screen.

There was sound outside. He wasn't sure if it was wise to shout out. Neither did he have the strength. But there was something comforting about those sounds; something human. Footsteps got nearer and a figure appeared in what remained of the door. Ginny mustered all his strength to raise his left arm. He wasn't sure if he was able to.

Fortunately, in a situation like this, the slightest movement is inescapable. As pairs of hands reached out to him, his languid hope received a new lease of life.

*****

Even though, the man on the stretcher was beyond recognition; Rajeev ran towards him. He knew instinctively it was Ginny. Or perhaps it was the flash of the Ganpati bracelet on his left wrist. The right one was missing.

"Ginny…Ginny…where's Hansa? Is she okay? Was she with you? Ginny, open your eyes," Rajeev implored.

Ganpat could hear him but had no inclination to speak. Intent hearing and meagre speech had always helped him tide over demanding times, somewhat miraculously. Just like the Gods. The medic near the ambulance walked up to Rajeev. "Sir, I don't think he's in a position to talk. He's seriously injured and possibly under post-traumatic stress. Please, if you don't mind…"

Rajeev stepped away feeling helpless and his anxiety kept growing. His mother had been calling him incessantly but he had nothing to tell her yet. Dragon-shirt was nowhere in sight. He had assured him that Hansa was alive. This was the first and last time that he had wanted to believe that man.

If Hansa had flagged her SOS from the third floor, why didn't the rescue team find her? His thoughts were interrupted by the sound of gunfire going off inside. He stood akimbo, staring at the imposing structure in front of him and thinking of the many beautiful nights he had spent there, in even prettier company.

Right now, all that emerged from the beautiful facade were people, torn apart in limb and spirit and unable to coordinate the two.

The scraggly old man sleeping on the esplanade had been shooed away. He had jaywalked towards the lane bordering the Taj at right angles and now sat staring blankly at the goings on behind the large iron-gate which was a pool-side entrance to the hotel. The lane was empty.

He wondered if government vehicles would arrive with cartons of food and water, like they did during the time of floods. His eyes wandered in hungry hope and landed on a small, green pouch lying in a nook. Nobody seemed to have noticed it. Curiosity led him by the hand just when the large gate opened and a group containing hotel staff and guests scurried out on tip-toes.

*****

"Sir, the NSG-team has signalled clearance of the third floor. All hostages, who were alive or semi-conscious, have been rescued from that area. Hansa madam is not among them."

"Damn! You took an entire fucking night to tell me this? What about the upper floors?"

"Sir, we're trying our level best. You cannot imagine the scene inside. I cannot tell you anything more than this right now. Now, please if you'll let me do my job." The cop walked away.

Another thunderous explosion shook the ground and everything that stood on it. It had occurred in one of the alleys beside the Taj, near the pool-side entrance followed by minutes of non-stop firing in the palace-wing of the hotel. Groups of people, large and small, continued to be whisked out of the main entrance of the hotel at short intervals.

*****

"*Pasha, phone nahin lag rahaa* (the call is not going through)," Imtiaaz informed Zarrar.

He snatched the phone from him and tried calling his other teams. Even though their handlers had trained them to take death in the face after having completed the mission; he had no intention to die incognito. He had wanted to create terror of iconic proportions, and live to see the aftermath. Hansa sat in the farthest corner of the room, away from everybody else. She had managed to elicit much sympathy from the group but not courage.

"Okay, both of you grab one of these rats and use them as a shield. If one dies, pick another and keep shooting till the last one alive here. Don't touch those men, they're brothers," he instructed looking at the men sitting in the chairs. His vision then flew towards Hansa. She could not interpret the look in his eyes.

The hostages winced on hearing the instructions. The boys chose their squirming human shields. Zarrar walked up to Hansa and lifted her chin with his index finger. "You've got only one and a half hours on you. No point trying to make a silly move and cut that short!"

He then marched towards the boys and had a quiet debriefing.

"*Wa la tahsabanna alladhina qutillu fi Sabilillahi 'amwatan* (Do not think of those who are killed in the way of Allah as being dead)", he quoted from the holy *Quran* and they all stormed into one of the adjacent halls. The silent air soon echoed with the rattling of guns and explosions, right outside the Chambers.

*****

It had seemed like an eternity before someone broke the silence.

"I think we should step out on the verandah," someone remarked.

"Sir, it may not be a wise thing to do! You saw what happened to that man. And besides the snipers, we don't know if there are other terrorists in any of the adjoining buildings, waiting for ready targets. Anybody who steps out without cover might get caught in a cross-fire. They will not wait for you to produce your I-card. Moreover, those guys have locked up the adjoining door. There's no access to the terrace from here," one of the staffers spoke.

"Perhaps, we could separate the women and the old people and try to evacuate them first. Isn't there any fire exit or anything here?"

"Sir, we had tried an evacuation last night but they zeroed in on us from the other end. There are still many people lying dead on the staircase leading to the ground floor," the staffer reported.

"What about her?" someone pointed towards Hansa.

"We are all in this together. There has to be a way to help her get out of it," the Arab spoke for the first time. Envious eyes now looked at him a little less suspiciously.

"But that madman must've fool-proofed it. He wouldn't leave her with us if it was that easy to get it off her. Besides, I think he said something about a timer. So, probably it's already ticking. She makes the slightest movement, and a remote sensor detonates it. How the hell can she get out of it?" reasoned another.

"We have to try something. We can't keep sitting here waiting to die ... we have less than ninety minutes."

The molested lady's companions had found their machismo.

Their discussion was interrupted by the humming of a chopper, followed by the pattering of footsteps on the terrace. Before people could duck for cover, a mini explosion smashed the glass on the windows. Through the smoke, they saw six men in black overalls and balaclavas, wielding assault rifles, rushing into the room. They were in uniform with grenades and crossbows strapped across their chests.

Despite the tools of disaster on their person, their demeanour was quite reassuring to the petrified group. Guns pointed at the hostages, two of them asked everyone to raise their hands and face the wall in a single file, while the other three took various positions in the room in anticipation of someone coming in.

The last one, in his black aviators, lunged towards Hansa as he removed his glares and tossed them aside. Once again, piercing eyes from a concealed face darted across her face. She shut her eyes and waited for her fate to take its course.

She was too exhausted and traumatised to react. Once again, unfamiliar hands hovered over her body as she felt him lifting her *kameez*. Tears rolled down her cheeks this time.

*****

Outside, waiting in one of the police vehicles, Rajeev felt his blood pressure easing as he caught the action on the terrace from a safe distance. He had spoken with his father a while ago and felt relieved for the first time in the past ten hours. Yet, he couldn't be at ease completely till he saw his wife.

*****

“Sorry ma'am, I have to do this,” he said in his deep-throated voice. Working meticulously with his implements on the mesh of wires that made the bomb tick away like a little heartbeat, not once did he look at her. Time bombs are tricky business. There were four inter-twined wires on this one, all in different colours. The primer wire, reactor wire and the ignition timer wire had to be cut in the correct order in order to defuse the bomb. The fourth one was for the coordinates, which, if cut first, would mean a loss of coordinate signal, leading to an instant explosion. Getting the order of the other three wrong would speed up the process of detonation, exponentially.

Hansa couldn't believe that she was in safe hands. The rest of the group was asked to move towards the rear stairwell.

“What if the same thing as last night, happens again,” the Parsi lady asked.

“Ma'am, the bullets will have to get past me to reach you,” replied one of the brave-hearts leading them towards safety.

“I sure hope your bullet-proof vest is in good condition,” she tried to be humorous as she ambled along. Nobody responded.

*****

Finally, Rajeev's wait was over. A group of hostages descended upon the scene from the main entrance of the hotel. He rushed towards them, eager to hug Hansa. First the women, followed by the old people and subsequently the men came out with feeble smiles on their faces. Hansa was not amidst them. Rajeev's heart sank. He was about to quick-step towards the group and the commandos to enquire when a fresh round of firing started from within, targeting the buses that were loading the guests in. Rajeev stepped back into the car again with his hands running through his hair in frustration.

The firing was soon brought under control by the NSG team and the buses left for the police station in the vicinity for the verification of the hostages. The buzz was that three terrorists had been terminated. A few were still suspected to be hiding inside. The number was yet to be determined. They had been forced to lie low for the time-being. Rajeev brought out his phone once again to call his father.

Nine

Back inside the Chambers, Hansa had lost the energy and will to try and save herself. If not the bomb or the bullets, the fatigue and strain would certainly kill her. The MARCO was still fixated on the bomb while three of his mates engaged the terrorists from various positions. Hansa looked at him wondering what led certain men to choose a profession that involved endangering their own life for others. There was no dearth of lucrative career options. Yet, there were young men like him, living their life on razor's edge. They were the unsung heroes. And yet, the awards and accolades went to the virtual heroes who lived these lives on screen, and made it entertaining for people to watch.

Her pondering was intercepted by a sigh of relief. It was almost inaudible but his proximity to her made it otherwise.

"Let's go Ma'am," he said jumping to his feet. "My guess was right. This bomb was never meant to explode, at least not by these sensors!"

She was at a loss for words and tried to match his agility but her feet refused to move. He was a man with long foresight and short reaction time. Every second was worth a life.

"May I help?" and before she could answer him, he helped her to her feet, with her arm around his shoulders and his, around her waist. The bomb now lay beside them, innocuous and lifeless. He led her towards the stairwell exit through which the rest of the group had managed to escape. They were not that lucky. Bullets zinged through the gallery and the sound echoed.

"Ma'am, I'll have to leave you here and find a safe way out. Please don't worry, I'll be back. There's a restroom over there. I'd suggest you stay inside. You'll be out of harm's way. Step out only when you hear me say 'Marco Alpha Tango'. Right, Ma'am?"

"The bomb! Why wasn't it meant to explode? How are you so sure?"

"Well! No terrorist, with the intent to incinerate, would leave it ticking for one and a half hours; especially when he knows that time is not exactly in his favour. Surrounded by huntsmen, if he died before you, his purpose would not meet a justifiable end. And for all the observation is worth, the fourth wire was connected independently to a timer, outside the circuit of the other three! It was a dummy, quite cleverly used."

Hansa was now so overwhelmed that she could neither reason nor respond. She walked quietly with him towards the washrooms and stayed where she had been asked to.

"Then why did you labour over it as if your life rested on it?"

"Ma'am, when it comes to saving a life, there's nothing called 99.9 per cent precision. I've got to run now. Be brave and stay safe. Remember, I'm not leaving this place without you."

He was gone like the wind. Outside, the sky seemed to be clearing up.

There was no water in the taps. She tore some toilet paper and wiped her face. Squatting over the toilet seat was avoidable. Besides, her legs ached. So, she stood against the wall and breathed deeply, allowing blood to circulate through her body.

Thankfully, the doors were of floor-to-ceiling height, unlike most restrooms in hotels and malls.

She closed her eyes and tried to dissociate herself from all thought.

An agitated mind doesn't allow vacuum to exist. Her thoughts travelled instantly to Rajeev, and fleetingly to the man in the dragon-shirt. She wondered what he would do if she died today. Would he mourn her loss forever, or come to terms with it and move on in life? Or would he be too heartbroken to continue and like the mythological cob, breathe his last by the side of his lifeless pen. There would be no dearth of girls wanting to hook up with him after she was gone. After all, he was Srijann Walia's only son.

The face of her mother surfaced in her thoughts after a long time. She wondered if her mother was watching this carnage. Did she know that her daughter was waiting by the edge of life, not knowing whether she would emerge alive or dead? Her mother had been the single most important and the sanest influence in her life. But like all mortals, she too had her shortcomings.

To Hansa, she was the paradigm of blind faith and immature love. Her father, *Zain*, had been the most charming *wooer* those times could have produced. No sooner had Noorie, her mother, fallen for his coquettish ambush and committed her life to dreams of royal bearing; Zain realised he was not ready for responsibility of any kind, either marital or paternal. He left her without remorse and was never heard of again.

The story of her life had taught Hansa not to trust men blindly and always suspected their intention, no matter how convincing they sounded. Reading about Ruttie Jinnah had a near-cathartic effect on her as she established parallels and a semblance between the two women. Hansa remembered how her mother used to tell her a story from Indian mythology. It was about the *garuda*, the falcon, and *naga*, the serpent. Naga had held *garuda's* mother captive and would release her only if *garuda* brought the elixir of life to him.

Garuda wanted to save her mother at any cost and did the needful. However, on the insistence of Indra, the lord of heaven, garuda placed the vial containing the magical liquid on the grass, instead of tipping it on to it. Oblivious of this misappropriation, weak-sighted Naga came and licked the grass blades, causing his tongue to fork. Riled and vengeful, Naga vowed to avenge the deceit by claiming power over Garuda's life.

Hansa, the swan, her mother had said, symbolises the union of the diametrically opposite traits of Garuda and Naga. Yet; this conjugation is an embodiment of the highest wisdom and spirituality, the swan. As a child she had heard the story with great interest and bemusement but as she grew up, the disguised intent behind the telling of the tale, gradually unravelled before her.

This distrust of men that had taken root during her childhood, found moist ground to grow on when *Kuber* went over the moon trying to impress her.

She was certain that it was nothing more than a rich kid's fancy for a new gadget in the store. He would get over it the minute something newer and fancier caught his eye.

She was charmed, beyond doubt, on the day that he had publicly proclaimed his love for her. She had many suitors but nobody had invested time, money and thought so cohesively and thoughtfully in wooing her. Yet, she wasn't sure if she should express her gratitude or tell him that he wasn't the one for her. She found herself besotted but not in love. The emotional baggage of her mother's travails was too much to handle.

Besides, to her, love was something that left no room for critical evaluation. It was not a business deal. She had asked for time to think. He wasn't prepared for anything other than a spontaneous approval.

However, he swallowed his pride and decided to let her manage her thoughts more wisely. There was a lot at stake and she was certainly no fool.

Their film was released in due course but did not rake in business as was expected.

She, nevertheless, won an award for making an impressive debut. As time passed, Kuber became pushy and sometimes, even intimidating. Tired of playing dodge-ball with his flirtations; eventually, Hansa gave in to his overtures, carefully passing up any opportunity to let him cross the proverbial line. As time passed, she started to find her feet in the industry. Heavy-footed months passed by and started to metamorphose into a year. After the first year went by insignificantly, Kuber started to show signs of an obsessive lover. He was now desperate to have her.

She had signed another film and was looking forward to working in it. It held the promise of a significant milestone in her career. The trip to Switzerland had been the most unforgettable three weeks of her life for all the right reasons. Rajeev had been an incorrigible romantic throughout the time they had spent on and off the sets. When flowers and chocolates had done their bit, he humoured her, all of which was good enough to put a glint in Hansa's eyes. Sometimes, he made her laugh. On other occasions, he just made her want to laugh.

It was a pleasant Sunday morning, and the production-unit had been given half a day off to rest and gain momentum for the tough schedule ahead. Shooting was to resume post-lunch in the dimming southern lights.

"Let's go fly!" Rajeev had suggested. "What d'you mean?"

"Du-uh! Paragliding babe! The best way to travel in Confederation Helvetica. C'mon, grab your puffs and muffs and let's go!"

Before she could show any reluctance, she was on her way to get enamoured by the verdant hills and tantalising breeze. She was also totally taken in by his gift of the gab. He could continue to have a conversation with himself while the world around him fell down guffawing.

They didn't have to wait too long to get harnessed. She hadn't thought that they would be harnessed together and were going to be in tandem flights with the guide. Not that she objected. It was a strangely ticklish feeling. As they took off from an arboreal cliff, she felt like an albatross, manipulating the winds. It was another world up there.

"Let's play a game," he said after a few minutes of enraptured silence. The gap between their harnesses was just about enough to accelerate the rush of adrenaline.

"Now what do you have up your sleeve?" she giggled.

"It's called monologue. We try and make conversation but are allowed to speak only one word at a time. Whoever uses more than one, loses. The only condition is that the next word cannot be totally disjointed from the previous. And no more than three seconds to a response. Not too easy for you, eh?" he egged her on.

"So, you are telling me that I'm the one with verbal … whatever … Okay, here we go …"

"Wait a sec'. We need a subject to begin with," he suggested.

"Okay…mountains. Start!" Visual and vocal skirmishes hardly ever happened together in a romantic setting. She was getting excited and felt colour rushing to her cheeks.

"High," he responded effortlessly.

"Slopes," she chuckled.

"Valley", he was quick.

"Lake", she was too.

"Banks"

"Trees,"

"Birds"

"Nesting"

"Together"

She felt his breath on her neck as well his gaze as he spoke. She fumbled for a response, now a little nervous to play along.

"Hope," she would've stuttered, had the word been any longer.

"lessly"

"what?"

"in"

"hey!"

"love with you!"

"three words … you lose," she craned her neck to look at him, hoping that he wasn't able to hear her heart beating wildly.

"Yeah, I lost it," and he planted the softest kiss on her dewy lips; and lingered. The breeze took them a wee bit higher. It was 12ºC. And pleasantly warm.

*****

Gunshots, once again, drove holes through her thoughts. She found it a bit odd herself that in a crisis like this; she was delving in the past. Maybe, that's what people mean when they say that your life's most indelible moments flash past your eyes just when you can see the finish-line, or are made aware of the proximity.

So many lovers proclaiming undying love for her and yet, today, when her own life was in danger, she was looking up to a stranger hoping that he would be able to save her. She thought she heard him call out. Or was it somebody else? She must be getting delirious. She strained her eyes to see clearly but couldn't. She needed some water, desperately.

Water … water and fire … she had told Rajeev once how water and fire were vital to survival and yet, can be the most devastating forces, both, in their presence as well as absence. They had been instrumental in all the key events in her life. Like the time when Rajeev had popped the question.

*****

It was a late night flight to Mauritius. He had wanted to get there three days prior to the shoot. Rajeev had made all the necessary arrangements. Hansa reached precisely three hours before the boarding time, bag and baggage in order. Rajeev was late as usual. Despite her mind's non-stop chatter on his irresponsible ways, she waited imperviously. They had just about an hour left to board, when Rajeev's car rolled into sight. He jumped out with his duffle bag and instructed the driver to leave. His luggage was to arrive with the production crew.

"Sorry, *jaan*, the traffic was unforgiving."

Hansa tried to force a smile. There was no time to squabble. She turned and headed towards the departure terminal.

"Tickets?" she asked him. There was no response. She turned around to repeat her question but *Raj* was missing.

She riffled through the faces and finally spotted him near the drop-off point, talking on the phone.

"What's wrong, Raj? Do you have any intention of boarding this flight?" Her tone was now getting sharper.

Before he could answer, his driver came jogging up to him with a folder in his hand.

"Tickets! Left them on the car-seat!" Raj smiled sheepishly as Hansa looked at him in disbelief. Thereafter, it had been a long run through immigration and security check before they finally boarded the plane.

*****

Mauritius was everything that dream destinations are made of. A wet-July ordeal in Mumbai can transform into a heavenly experience on the little island, despite the humidity levels. They were booked in a luxury resort on the south coast. The six hours of travel time were spent chatting, snuggling, kissing and giggling while the other passengers slept and the in-flight crew tried to keep their eyes off them.

They had landed in Mauritius in the wee hours of the morning, and their resort was over an hour's drive away. As their hired cab brought them on to the North-South freeway, the Sun was just beginning to peep from behind the sugarcane plantations. The ball of fire was captivating in its innoxious avatar.

The resort was like any Six-Startar luxury hotel with the frills expected of an indulgent stay. Hansa and Rajeev walked up to the reception desk to collect the keys to their rooms. She had expected a single key.

However, Raj picked up two and elbowed her towards their rooms that lay adjacent to each other, over-looking the Indian Ocean.

"I know what you're thinking and yes, I've got to be crazy to be doing this!"

"Ah, you're such a saint," she smiled.

"That doesn't make me any less of a man!" he smiled back as Hansa blushed.

She was to meet him by the pool deck after two hours. She was punctual and by now, getting used to waiting for him. It wasn't a long wait this time. He was hungry. As they turned to leave for the restaurant, Hansa thought she saw a familiar face, lying under a deck umbrella. She wasn't sure where she'd seen him. It almost felt as if he had been staring at her for some time from under his wide-brimmed hat. She shared her concern with Rajeev.

"Oh baby, people love Indian cinema around here you know. He must have recognised you from your last film."

She cast her worries to the ocean breeze and drifted away with Raj.

*****

The ocean was like Prussian blue glass. They stood on the diving deck, gearing up for their under-sea walk. The last thing to go on to their diving costumes was the oxygenated helmet.

Hansa had always loved the sea and its many mysteries. Water was second nature to her. Walking on the ocean floor at a depth of about fifteen feet while holding Rajeev's hand was an experience she would cherish for the rest of her life. They stepped down the ladder, cutting through the water-surface and leading to the ocean bed. Hansa stepped down, guided by the instructor and as her feet touched the sand, a tingle ran up her lithe body. Raj held her hand and together they bobbed through the schools of tiny fish that came to feed off the bread in their hands. Striped yellow fish, corals, sponges and baby turtles frolicked about fancy-free in their peaceful world.

Then it happened, quite literally out of the blue. Rajeev went down on his knee. The instructor handed him a tiny red box. She held her breath. He brought out an oyster that opened to reveal a flawless pearl, encrusted in glistening diamonds, beaming at her for approval. Hansa had to hold back her excitement as the diving gear was too bulky for her to get ecstatic. Her body language was enough to prompt Raj to his next act. From the box, out came a scroll that read:

"Marry me my mermaid. I've been fishing…er…wishing for you!"

It was something Hansa had not anticipated, even though she did have a feeling that Rajeev had a surprise up his sleeve. She was overjoyed and of course, the witty proposal was a clincher. She wanted to seal her approval with a kiss but the life-saving oxygen helmet, that now appeared

Draconian, wouldn't allow any smothering. Hansa's laughter caused the bulbous apparatus to jerk and shift out of position. Blobs of sea-water rushed in to replace the oxygen. Hansa coughed it in. Panic struck and the instructor yanked the support cord to have her lifted to the surface immediately. She choked, spluttered and passed out. Rajeev couldn't believe his luck.

*****

When she opened her eyes, she was in her room at the hotel, in her bathrobe. The memory of the mishap ballooned itself but was immediately distended by the preceding incident. A smile played upon her lips. Raj stepped in with room-service. The attendant left after pocketing a generous service tab. Hansa hauled her groggy self up and noticed the ring flashing on her left hand.

"Well now, my pretty, just in case you have overcome the desire to empty the ocean of its contents; may I have an official approval with the signature it deserves? And not to forget the rights to record and publish it digitally."

Hansa wrapped her arms around him and expressed herself with a long, amorous kiss. It was a yes. Rajeev wasted no time in sending a message to his mother.

*****

Her mind zoomed back into the present. Outside the toilet, Hansa could hear a lot of commotion. Someone was shouting instructions while someone else was mouthing expletives. She stiffened in anticipation of the door flinging open in her face. What lay beyond, she couldn't imagine. Her nightmare was not to end here. A cold voice called out something she had been waiting to hear.

"MARCO Alpha Tango," someone called out. Then there was a volley of bullets, followed by a funereal silence. Hope, now on its last legs, passed away quietly. She slid to the floor in despair.

Ten

It was the silence now that was unbearable. She wanted to hear something, someone … anything. Then as if someone tuned in to the energy that she was transmitting; there was a knock on the door. She waited for the knocker to speak. There was another rap on the door with increased intensity, followed by another. She looked around, not knowing what exactly she was looking for. It was pointless.

For a moment she even wished she had been one of the many people who had died. Trying to regain her composure, she chided herself for being so selfish. The reason to live was much stronger than the pretext to die.

She heard shuffling feet outside the washroom-door. Whoever had come in was looking for someone or something in particular.

"Oh please, open the door," someone sobbed.

Hansa was a bit apprehensive to open the door to an unfamiliar voice. However, the plea coaxed her heart to take over the brain's dismissal. Holding her breath, she opened the door a wee bit and saw a little girl looking up at her with tearful eyes. She was no more than seven or eight years old.

"They shot my mummy on the stairs and I ran back up," she told her while trying to stifle her sobs.

Hansa pulled her in and shut the door. Wiping her tears, she thought of what she could say to comfort the child. There was nothing.

"How did you know I was in here?" "Your door was locked."

"Did they see you running back up?" "I don't know … couldn't see them." Hansa took in a few deep breaths.

"Ok. Sit here. Was there anybody else with you?"

The girl shook her head. "My Papa had gone to another room and left me with my *Mommy*. He said that since he was British, they might kill him first."

"Was…Is your mummy British too?" "No, she's Indian."

"Where do you live?" "In the U.K."

"Here on a holiday, is it?"

The girl nodded, wiping her eyes with the back of her hand. Hansa had managed to distract the little girl enough to take her mind off from what she had just seen.

"Do you have any relatives here in Bombay?" "No… in Delhi."

"You know, the Indian soldiers are here to fight these nasty men. They'll soon be caught and punished. Till then, we have to be brave and stay safe."

The distraction proved to be short-lived.

"What will happen to my Mommy there?" the girl was about to cry again.

"Oh sweetheart, let's just pray that those soldiers find your Mommy and take her to the ambulance outside." Hansa was now running out of positive things to say. Her own belief was shaken after Simone's ruthless elimination. She garnered the vestiges of hope that were left with her, in order to comfort the child.

*****

The presence of the little girl inside the cubicle was very comforting. Even though both of them sat quietly on the bathroom floor with their legs entangled, each one gave the other a sense of being alive. One can spend an entire lifetime trying to live perfectly and yet not realise the importance of having live people in it; who inhale, feel, absorb and exhale just like us and yet are so different in thoughts, perceptions and responses. Hansa observed the little girl and wondered what could be a child's thoughts in a situation like this. Was she thinking of a safe exit or was she praying for her parents to be alive and well?

"I'm so thirsty," whispered the girl. Hansa couldn't help. "Hey, what's your name," she asked the girl.

"Rabaab," was the faint reply.

"Rabaab, there's no water here. But it won't be long before we'll have chilled water and juice with us. But we'll have to hold on till we get out of here."

The child seemed to be swooning.

"Ok Rabaab. You can rest your head in my lap. But remember, we're getting out of here soon. By the way, do you know the meaning of your name?"

The little girl tried to nestle herself comfortably in Hansa's lap. She did not have an answer.

"It means the radiance or glory of God…Rabb plus Aab. So now you know why I'm so sure that we're getting out safely?" "Then why did my …"

"Shhhhh!"

She rested her head against the wall and her hand on her stomach, and let her consciousness dwindle into oblivion.

*****

The MARCOS team was positioned strategically through the labyrinthine plan of the hotel. Gaining entry to the besieged hotel was not such an arduous task. The difficult part was locating the parasites and neutralising them, especially when their number and ammunition-strength were unknown. Bullets hailed through the lobbies as the enemies exchanged fire. Twenty of them had descended upon the territory like a swarm of locusts. Entry had been through the fire exits and air-drops.

The soldier leading the group had deftly dodged all danger to evacuate the hostage group from the Chambers. It was a group of guests in the Taj Towers, lead by two commandos, which had panicked and revealed their cover to the terrorists. However, the men-in-charge had managed to take a circuitous route and lead them to the fire exits.

MARCO Alpha Tango had managed to thwart all efforts of the terrorists to sabotage the evacuation-plans. He had managed to gun down three of them and injured one. He would have eliminated the fourth one too, had a lady, with her daughter, not appeared suddenly at a bend and in the visible range of the hidden terrorist. She was shot in the arm and collapsed with shock. The child had run up the steps. Now that the firing had stopped, it would be safe to go back up to look for the child and lead the lady to safety. He double-stepped it up the stairs. The child was nowhere to be seen.

Still looking, he reached the ladies' powder-room. Positioned a little away from the door, he called out softly "Alpha Tango". The place was quiet. He spoke again, a little louder this time. Silence answered back. Cautiously, he started to check the toilets. One of the doors opened a little but refused to move further. Something was stopping it on the inside. He pushed it a bit further and peered in.

There lay a little girl in a pool of blood. Hansa Noorie Walia was missing.

*****

It had been more than twenty four hours now since their ordeal had begun. Rajeev was exhausted and had decided to check-in at one of the hotels nearby. A comfortable place had been organised for him, which was a short walk from the Taj. Lying on the bed, all he could do was recall the first year of their marriage. The movie that they had shot for in Switzerland had been well-received and critically acclaimed. It had scrabbled upon the underbelly of social stigma. Even though he had failed to make a mark as an actor, Rajeev took solace in the fact that his father and newly-wedded wife had managed to make the critics sit up and take notice.

It was the morning after the grand awards ceremony that he had confided in his father.

"Pa, I'm thinking of starting a production-house and directing my own film!"

"Really, Raj? I'm happy to hear that; but don't you think you need to give your acting career a couple of years before you shoulder the responsibility of something so big?"

"You need to invest your time and energy in developing your potential, son. Stay focussed. Producing and directing a film comes after one has learnt the finer nuances of filmmaking and selling. It's not just about getting people to invest money. There's too much at stake there and one mustn't jump into unfamiliar territory without preparation," added *Gargi*.

"Aw c'mon, ma! Do you think all these pot-bellied producers hanging around here; know a shit about filmmaking? All one needs is wealthy clout and the ability to sell well!"

"Rajeev, it's good to be ambitious but one needs to take calculated risks in life. Short-cuts never lead anyone to the top. You decide what you want to do and we'll stand by you but if you ask us to hold your finger and help you escape from every wall that you face; well then son, it's about time you learnt to scale them by the sweat of your own brow!"

"Ma, can you stop getting philosophical each time I come up with a plan? Pa, look! Right now, I don't have any films on hand and the producers that I approach are keeping me on the hook, and you never seem to use your position to give my career a boost. Since you have no intention of pushing my acting career, then the least you could do is to help me set up a production house."

"Stop right there, Raj! You know when we are young; we have many dreams and are highly ambitious.

So we set our vision high up there, far away from the ground. Which is fantastic! But what we often fail to see is the inclined path that leads us to that summit.

The summit is scalable only for those who set their vision low and learn to find ways to overcome the obstacles, one at a time, with wisdom and courage. That's the only path. Like I always say, there aren't any short-cuts!"

"Gosh, Pa! Why is it so impossible to talk to you about anything? What are you trying to tell me? That I should keep waiting for some producer to sign me up for a piddly-shit role of a side-sweep? Or should I look at jump-starting my career by becoming an extra hand on the sets like the great Kapoors? I'm trying to do something here, in which you and Hansa can prove to be such an asset. I don't see where the problem is."

"Raj, the problem is not in your idea. It is in the approach. You want my support; that is always there for you. But believe me, the pursuit of success without enhancing one's sphere of knowledge and experience is like following the rainbow for the pot of gold. You'll find neither. On the other hand, invest time and energy in expanding your horizon, then whatever you do will become the rainbow and you, shall be the pot of gold! Find your feet as an actor first!" Rajeev knew the discussion was over when his father resumed reading the script of his next film. His mother put her hand on his and looked at him in consolation.

He needed his mother's hand on his right now. Those hands had been instrumental in bringing many joys into his life, as well as adding a sparkle to them with her presence. As he looked outside the window, he could see the birds of prey that had been circling over the spires of the Taj during the earlier hours of the day, now gliding down swiftly for a quick meal before the day came to an end.

*****

Zarrar had not expected such a deluge of soldiers invading the premises. Or at least he had expected a heads-up from Zaki chacha well in time. Ch'cha had called to tell him about the fresh onslaught but it was too late. He had to devise his own plan and take complete charge of the situation. His men had received his instructions and were already setting fire to the rooms in which they had found people hiding in closets and corners. He was in one of the rooms in the Taj Tower and huddled in the room were eleven people; and one of them was Hansa. Bleeding from her ear-lobe, she stared blankly at the five faces of terror that stood arrogantly before the hostages. The only familiar face was that of Zarrar.

She had screamed and cried and pleaded to them to spare the little girl. They had shown no mercy. Hansa was losing control of her sobriety. She almost felt responsible for the loss of two gullible souls, who had hoped to find refuge in her company. She was beginning to believe that she had become the reason for their untimely deaths. The three men had carried her to Zarrar, who had been watching over a group of people.

"Ah! *Ahlan-wasahlan*, Husna, my love! Or is it Hansa? Husna, Hansa, Hansa, Husna…oh how does it matter? Both are Allah's chosen ones. For me. So you managed to outlive the bomb, hanh? So, Allah has expressed His will yet again, and sent you here for me. You are such an asset wherever you go! And you shall go far…as long as you remain with me…for me!"

Hansa had given him the most hateful glance. "What do you know what Allah likes or dislikes? You are slaves to the devil. And you'll meet an end worthy of…" Before she could finish venting her anger, a blow across her ear ended up resounding inside her head. There was a death-like stupor and she almost thought her ear had fallen off.

"I have given you permission only to live, not to speak, you side-switching whore! Save your breath, you don't have much left to waste away!"

She couldn't care what he called her or what plot of horror was to unfold next. Her agony, fatigue and desperation were beginning to take their toll and were slowly coalescing into death-defying anger as she heard him shout instructions over the phone.

"*Aag lagaa do chaaro taraf.* Set everything on fire. Gather whatever you can and douse it. Every room has a mini bar with some liquor in it. Use it to get the fire going and vacate the room as soon as you're done."

While he was still yelling into the phone, two of the other four men started to empty some bottles on to the beds and curtains. They were soon ablaze. It was an instinctive reaction for people to get up and run towards the door. The fat, balding man in the far end of the room seemed to be an important figure to some business. Nobody cared for those facts right now. The group had started to choke and gasp. They were all herded out at gunpoint, except the fat, balding man. He would slow them down. His mercy-pleas distorted Zarrar's face with pleasure. Except the wriggling man, who was now engulfed in flames, they were all led out of the room and into the corridor. The single file was pushed through the narrow corridor towards another room on an upper floor. The screams for help faded away in the background.

Outside, night had crept up on the sun stealthily. The last twenty-four hours had been life-changing in many ways for manv people.

*****

In a movie, Hansa could have expected to have the hero come and rescue her. But life does not measure up to 70 mm and in it, there exist no heroes; only fallen angels, with their hopes, desires, fears and failings. In this moment of truth, who would be her knight in shining armour? Rajeev, who had left no stone unturned to convince her that he couldn't live without her; or Kuber, who had left no promise unfulfilled, of making her see the dangers of unrequited love?

For some strange, unknown reason, her captor was the reason she had been alive so far. She struggled with the answers and needed someone to read them out aloud to her. Being shoved around in a single file with strange men and women who were uncertain of which breath would be their last, she had shed the garb of a diva and had become one with the commoners, as well as with herself.

Eleven

What you do is not so important; it's how you do it that makes the difference. She had heard this somewhere, back in saner times. Right now she couldn't recall. However, figments of lessons learnt and things heard, seem to pop up like teaser-trailers during trying times, prompting the bearer to endure and move on. Whoever had said it had lost their bearing in her memory but had stayed alive in the thought. Ghosts from the past need not always be frightening.

As they were being bundled into yet another room, Hansa knew that she had to break free from her physicality and let her mind take over. She had only as much time as the men had, to stay under cover and maintain their line of fire. And by the way, things were proceeding; it was evident that Zarrar was gradually losing control over the sequence of events. She had a plan.

It was a bit desperate, not foolproof, but under the given circumstances, stood a good chance of working favourably. She, however, needed someone with whom she could coordinate her plan of action; someone who would be fearless and yet, would shoulder the responsibility of keeping everyone alive. Not a reckless hero but someone who could communicate well and understand effortlessly, while maintaining a stoic calm. To her, the people in the group seemed ill-equipped, both mentally and physically, to carry out her design. There were ten of them now, including her and the four adversaries, as well as Zarrar. She could bet her chances upon the chap in the beige *sherwani*.

Tottering towards the middle of the narrow corridor, she called out "Doctor!" The man in the beige *sherwani* swung around as Hansa fell to the floor in a spasmodic fit. Attentions diverted and commotion ensued. The man bent upon her was trying to adjust her body posture in order to prevent the concussion from causing much damage. He peered at her for a few seconds and then let her be.

"Husnajee, Husnajee…" he called out the name rather discreetly.

Zarrar turned around and bellowed. "She's Hansa! And what's wrong?"

"That's what I said! She's having an epileptic fit, it seems," he answered unwaveringly. Zarrar muttered something under his breath and then yelled again, "How do you know?"

"I'm a doctor. I'm supposed to know."

The doctor opened his wrist-watch and adjusted it inside her frothing mouth, between her teeth.

Her guess was spot-on. She had noticed his hands when he had meticulously wiped her bleeding ear with a damp towel.

"Damn, I want her to stay good. I'm giving you five minutes. Get her up on her feet."

"I have nothing to treat her with. Besides, even if I managed to revive her, she wouldn't be able to walk for the next few hours at least."

"Stop bullshitting me. You know what; I think I should just blow your brains out right here."

"If that helps you save her, go ahead! We are as good as dead, anyway. You can choose to kill us now or later. It doesn't matter. But the fact remains that killing us will not do this lady any good, and I guess that's not what you want right now."

The others were being manned by the team of four. Hansa's fits continued in brief intervals, as drool trickled down the side of her mouth.

The group was split up into two. They were shoved into a room once again, while the other men, with the rest of the hostages, were asked to spread out and take position outside, along the length of the corridor.

Zarrar stayed back with them. This was something exactly opposite to what Hansa had wanted. The ratio was now five to two.

"Her seizure seems to be in control, but she will have to stay put. You don't know when they'll start again. She'll need some water," said the doctor.

Zarrar was now beginning to feel the pressure. It was important for people to be mobile for them to provide cover for his men. A dead man did not make a useful shield. It was now, an appropriate time to strike a bargain.

"Hansa, in lieu of a clear exit" was the message that he sent.

As he tucked the phone into the pocket of his black kameez, the veil fell away from his face, and through half-closed eyes, Hansa caught a glimpse of the mysterious undertaker. His conventionally handsome looks were marred by aggression and a deep-set scar in the form of an inverted crescent on his left cheek. His face looked vaguely familiar. Strangely, it reminded her of her father who she had seen only in a photograph. The veil went back up in its place as swiftly as it came down. The doctor came back with a towel dripping in water. Gunfire resounded in the corridor yet again.

"Allaaah!" Zarrar had recognised the sound of the guns they were carrying and this one was not from one of them. There was no returning gunfire. The hunters were now the hunted. Things didn't look too upbeat.

Hansa, on the floor, was thinking rapidly about her next move. The doctor was still sitting beside her, and with the edge of the wet towel, tucked between her teeth, she had managed to get her first act right. It's how you do it that matters; and she remembered the person who had said those words. Zarine Nawaz, the timeless, ageless diva of tinsel town and an unusual stake-holder in her life.

*****

Hansa continued her act as the indisposed. Zarrar kept pacing in and out of the room restlessly. He had agreed to the condition put against his demand and was now waiting for a response. Seconds moved at an elephantine pace.

"You were really convincing," the doctor whispered to her when Zarrar had stepped out.

"And you were pretty bright too, to have caught the cue instantly," replied Hansa.

"But how did you figure out I was a doctor?" "You have tell-tale hands."

He looked at his hands briefly. An expensive watch on his wrist showed the time. It was 9:20 pm.

"Brilliant! So, what's the next move?"

"I wanted him to stop moving upwards. Just contain his movement, you know. Escape would keep getting more difficult with each ascent. But I wanted the group to stay together.

I wonder what happened to the others!"

"And what made you think, he would spare the others?"

"Woman's instinct," she felt a bit silly saying that. "Well, if there is no other end than sure-fire death, then what's the harm in trying every possible way of delaying it?" She had now justified her previous statement.

The doctor smiled. "Woman's instinct? Good one there. Especially, since it was such an A-one plan. By the way I'm Tapas, a software engineer from Ahmedabad."

Hansa's eyes widened. But she managed to disguise her expression as soon as Zarrar stepped back in.

*****

At the Chambers …

There was no time to pause and think. He had to find her. Reasons were deterrents. Purpose was the driver. If she was alone, she couldn't have gone far. The fusillade and the fear would have prevented her. He looked around, straining his ears to hear the sound of muffled breath. He was vigilant of the 360 degree space around him, and his ears kept a tab on the movement on the floor as well as the ceiling. She was not in the Chambers, or the exit staircase. Walking down the steps or through the corridor outside the Chambers, would be like walking straight into the enemy's trap. He spoke into his microchip: "Eagle 5 come in; Tango flying NW; Cover." The only safe way out now, was from the terrace to the ground.

And within a matter of minutes, he had rappelled down the side of the main entrance, made a swift entry into the lobby and glided past The Zodiac Grill. The NSG were at work with a fire-fighting team on the ground floor, dousing the fire in certain areas inside the hotel.

His team, along with the Black Cats, had already evacuated groups of people holed up in areas trapped by fire.

Outside, he had seen another team of fire-fighters stationed on the northern side of the main entrance. Flames had started to engulf the first and second floors and were gradually moving upwards. He had seen a ball of fire hurl itself out of one of the balconies on the second floor. An ill-fated hostage! Indignation was a natural emotion. But he was trained to express it at the right time and in the right measure. A jaw for a tooth and two eyes for one was the unwritten rule of his training. His instruction to the backup team of three men was to land on the twenty-second floor and make swift progress downwards. The idea was to hole up the rats in the centre, with all entry and exit points, above and below, blocked.

He went past the lift lobby. Avoiding the lifts, he made a quick-shot towards the stairs, to meet his accomplice. There was no sign of movement through the first two floors now. The terrorists had moved on after pushing a burning man out the window. After having combed the first two floors thoroughly and positioning their selves on the landing of the third floor, the MARCOS decided that they needed to scour each floor right up to the twenty-second, in order to hunt down the vermin.

Hawk-eyed and shark-brained, the two men stepped on to the second floor corridor, wary even of the soft cushioning of the carpet under their feet. They advanced in tandem; one keeping the other's back covered. Most doors were closed. They knocked on some and broke open a few.

These were the rooms that were made inaccessible, either because of the dead occupants or because of the furniture stashed away in front of the door. The ones that were jammed in place with the help of the room's furniture had people hiding inside closets, under beds or waving frantically from the balconies. It took them laborious hours to comb through the third floor with moribund results. Four of the team members were now together, as they brought together a group of about twenty people, who had escaped death by the sheer power of their will. Later, some would call it destiny.

The rescued guests were led to the balcony of one of the rooms, where the fire-fighting team helped them step out of the nightmare.

For the MARCOS, the challenge was getting tougher with each fiight of stairs. Not only was the damage done by the fire making it difficult for them to find a clear way upwards; the smoke, the darkness and the smell of charred human flesh was compounding the degree of difficulty, exponentially. But neither sight nor the virtual movement of the sun could sway them from their purpose. They had set out to decimate and dying was not an option. Out of the four, one stayed on the third floor to man unforeseen activity, while the other three moved up, providing adequate cover and keeping safe distance. By the time they reached the seventh floor, fire was beginning to embale some of the rooms. From the smell and the state of the corridor, he inferred that things had been set alight just as they were stepping on to the floor.

"Activity on floor Seven," Alpha Tango mouthed into the communication device strapped to his wrist. Then, as if to verify his observation, a roar of gunfire from one of the rooms, met them at random. It lasted a few seconds and the sound reverberated through the length of the corridor, making it difficult to ascertain the source.

The fire-extinguishers on the wall could be handy but they did not want to run the risk of disclosing their position.

His team had learnt to trust his insightful analyses of situations and infer correctly in 99 per cent of the cases. All of them carried motion-detectors on them but nobody had received any signals. Nobody questioned him either and they spread out quietly like fungus. Two men would provide cover while one moved forward. The corridor was pitch-dark with smoke beginning to creep out of the doors. There were no pillars or buttresses to provide any stronghold. The only light that would come towards them would be in the form of gunfire from the enemy. Covering the length of the corridor to reach the infected room at the far end, would be like walking straight into the enemy's hands.

*****

Zarrar had received a response to the message that he had sent earlier. They had asked for everyone along with Hansa. Either it was the waning effect of the drugs or a nervous breakdown, but Zarrar had started to feel jittery like never before. Three of his pawns had already fallen to the opponent, while he himself had permanently terminated the services of another. Bouts of anger were now waxing and waning as their perpetuality stood broken.

Cracks were now starting to show up in his do-or-die resolve. Before he could decide his next move, there was a gunshot that rung through the corridor. He asked his accomplice to check for danger but he sensed no sign of movement outside. Zarrar wasn't convinced. As the younger gunman stood guard over the hostages and he took position near the door, another bolt of blue, shot across the length. On the terrace outside the room, a shadow moved stealthily towards the entrance to the room.

It was the second night now that Hansa had been trapped in the quagmire. An unassuming dart shot through the darkness and pierced the nape of the gunman's neck.

He fell like a stump in a storm. Incidentally, it had missed Zarrar's notice as the door shielded his vision. Someone moved around the dark room.

“Stay where you are! Don't move,” he hissed at the same moment when there was a roll of shots exchanged outside. Hansa knew that voice. Someone replaced the gunman who had fallen to the floor quite painlessly. The other three watched like mute spectators, waiting to be rescued, or killed. They were the ones who are never in charge of their life's events and like to call themselves ‘destiny’s children’.

It was getting difficult for Zarrar to handle the crossfire all by himself. To him, there seemed to be more than five people as the line of fire kept changing.

He had spent less than ten minutes parrying the attack when he decided to call his accomplice. He called out to the man guarding the hostages. When a couple of shouts did not bring forth a response, he turned back in. His eyes were now better accustomed to see in the dark. The room was empty except for the motionless body of his accomplice. He checked the terrace. There was no trace of his tickets to freedom. Aggression started to get diluted by fear as death and freedom were now precariously balanced. He didn't believe in mysteries. They had to be somewhere inside. He took out his torch and started to inspect the room. There was a disquieting silence outside.

*****

Outside, Alpha Tango had managed to secure a cord to the balcony of the room on the sixth floor. He had messaged the fire-fighting team to move out of sight. Their visibility to the assailants would spell instant doom for the hostages. The youngest in the group was the first one to be lowered. The others remained plastered to the wall. He reached the balcony and gave the cord a tug. Even though, the darkness made the escape-route quite inconspicuous, yet, time was at a premium. He kept his calm and without uttering a word, prompted everyone to a safe landing on the lower floor.

Hansa was the second last to go, while wondering why he didn't put an end to the lone man, who had been leading the terror-trail all along. As their rescuer started his descent, a voice hollered from inside and came chasing after a round of fire. Zarrar was enraged at having been outdone. While his gun spat fire, his mouth spat expletives.

A bullet caught the MARCO's shoulder just as he descended into the balcony. He swung in with the others and tugged the cord back into the entrapment on his wrist. They broke open the door of the room and rushed in.

"Cover floor six."

It was now unsafe to make a dash for the ground floor as the spited terrorist was sure to try and hunt them down. Since their exact number was still unknown to the rescue team, the hostage-group needed to lie low and play it safe. Offence was an option only with the MARCOS but not at the risk of putting innocent lives at risk. It made sense, therefore, to change rooms. The group was moved out again and made to crawl across to the adjacent balcony. They were much safer there, a room away from the approaching danger. Alpha Tango decided to go back in the adjoining room; where he was likely to come face to face with terror; and get offensive.

His shoulder bled profusely. For the first time, Hansa had met a man whose actions really did speak louder than his words.

*****

On the ninth floor, the two assailants were in a predatory mood. The rooms had already been visited by a few of their accomplices and hence, left no visible sign of life. Their objective was to set fire wherever they could. Soon it became difficult to proceed with five in tow. It did not take them long to decide that the heavier as well as the puny-sized were liabilities. While one would cause disadvantageous motion, the other would provide negligible cover in case of a contingency. It was easy to get rid of them. Now, armed with only two well-built human shields and a girl, they proceeded with their task. However, as they stepped out of a room, they had not expected to find their way blocked by furniture on one side and fire on the other.

*****

He was now ready to take his adversary head-on. He stepped out of the room, with his gun aimed at the steps. He waited for a few minutes. There was furore on one of the upper floors. He did not let that distract him. He waited for the bellowing man to run for his escaping prey. It shouldn't have taken him so long to get there.

"Looking for something, soldier?"

Alpha Tango turned around to find a gun pointed to Tapas's temple. The others looked at him with a pained expression.

"You harm him and that's the last movement your body shall make," the MARCO promised, creeping towards him.

"Really? But what if I don't intend to hurt him at all?" Zarrar's distemper was changing to a defiant laughter. And then he shot at the commando.

Blood spurted out the side of his right thigh. He continued to advance. The next bullet shot through his right hand and disarmed him. Alpha Tango was now as vulnerable as the hostages.

"Now, my hero, you may join your friends here. Oh, but I can't carry too many of you on me and you are quite an asset to have. Therefore, to balance things out, someone will have to go!" And he zinged the bullet that scraped past Tapas's head, taking away a tuft of hair, while grazing his skull. He fell down in pain.

It would have surely gone through it, had Zarrar not been writhing on the floor with his right leg caught in a metallic cord. It had taken Alpha Tango, a nanosecond to react. His veil fell off once again but the darkness kept the intrigue undisturbed. Zarrar wriggled like a cobra caught in a snake-trap. The black veil played on his forehead, streaking it with red.

Traces of blood added to the gothic appearance of his face. Before anyone could understand what had happened, there were two figures on the floor, engaged in mortal combat.

*****

The confrontation in the darkness lasted for more than five minutes. Zarrar was a surprisingly meticulous fighter, even without ammunition. He had received several decapitating blows from the combatant, one of which had given him a broken jaw. Blood dripped from his injuries too, as Hansa's rescuer lunged for her. Before he could get his hands around her, a shoe-knife in a big and rough hand hovered dangerously at her throat. But the game of turnstiles didn't last long, as there was a thunderous explosion on one of the upper floors. The ceiling caved in near the exit from the corridor and debris started to fall like the sands of an hour glass. Three bodies fell through the cavity in the ceiling. Two of the bodies were charred and the third, which was in combat gear, had parts of its limbs blown away.

Four of the hostages made a bee-line for the staircase, while the battling men continued their *ninja combat*, with Hansa trapped in a corner. The hostages weren't too lucky either, as their attempt at escaping was stopped short by two gun-wielding men, aiming straight at Alpha Tango. It was Zarrar's winning moment. And the last one!

For the MARCO looking at impending death in the face, it was all in a day's work.

*****

The men on the upper floor had managed to rope in two attackers. There was no escape-route. As they moved towards them from one end and the fire flared from the other, one of the men bit the inside of his cheek and fell to the floor. He knew that cyanide would provide a more painless death than eating a bullet. The other one decided to fight it out. As he was hurling a grenade towards the soldiers, a lecherous flare had crept up on him and started to devour him. Before the uniformed men could counter his move, the grenade went off between them and took three people down to the floor below them.

One of the soldiers had managed to shield himself by falling through the door on his left. He was lucky to not have the door blocked by the furniture in the room. His fall was intercepted by the cry of a little boy. His parents, who had managed to keep him quiet so far by talking to him incessantly in whispers, now panicked. He resumed his posture and walked towards the sound of crying. He took the boy in his arms and whispered something in his ears. The child stopped bawling and looked at him in disbelief. The man then gestured to the parents as he returned the child to them and the trio followed him.

“There is no superman!” the boy informed the commando.

“I'm taking you to meet him,” the soldier replied. Anyway, his loose talk had achieved the objective of calming down the child.

“Mummy, do you know this *bandaa* (man) is Superman's Daddy?”, the boy told his mother with a tear-stained face.

*****

"It's never final, till it's final!" said Alpha Tango, placing his knife at Zarrar's throat again. The two gunmen now lay on the floor; their body perforated with bullets. The commando, who had rescued the trio on the upper floor, had intervened as he had arrived at the scene. Darkness had become an aide and was beginning to work to their advantage now. The magarmacch had captured his piranha alive and his shoulder, thigh and hand throbbed with the intensity of his purpose.

Hansa's fear had now become passive. She was sure she was going to live. There was an impenetrable shield around this man 0 that surpassed the magnetism of a superhero. His valour made him a hero; and his ordinariness made him extraordinary.

*****

A group of twelve guests sat huddled on the rooftop of the Tower wing of Taj Mahal Palace Hotel. Behind them, the dome of the Taj, engulfed in flames, was raging red. Minutes were stretching into hours and the wait made them arduous by a long measure. The men watching over them were young lads, dressed casually in jeans and T-shirts. The only things that set them apart from the others were the backpacks they carried and the guns in their hands. Each time there would be a sniper fire; they would shoot one person and hold his body up in the air, in full view of sniper-vision.

Three people had fallen to this game so far and the last victim had been a six-year old boy. The firing had stopped now, and the mother sat sobbing, drifting in and out of consciousness. She had begged them to shoot her as well, jumped and clawed at them for release, of either kind; but had only managed to fuel their psychotic fires. The night of horrors had peaked and the moon had started its descent westwards.

The chopper had stopped drifting in and out of view. The terrorists had opened fire once and driven it away. Several floors below the rooftop, a soldier and a combatant fought tooth and nail; one to kill and the other to save. Something buzzed in Alpha Tango's ear. It was disheartening. He wished he had received the instruction a minute later. By then, he would have eliminated the mad hatter, whose breath now moved hazardously along the edge of a knife.

Twelve

Friday mornings in Tinsel Town, almost always arrive laden with nervous anxiety and fringed by apprehensions. This Friday had all of it and more. Not only were precious lives trying to dodge near certain death; it was to be the blackest Friday for Mumbai, as corpses mingled with debris and became unidentifiable.

Despite the news that most of the terrorists had been exterminated; many families of the hostages, hung on to prayer by a fraying thread and hovered around their TV sets. Anxious steps anchored each minute in desperate hope, as mobiles rung and thumbs typed in text messages impatiently. There were homes where mournful weeping had already found its way in. *Bhais* (goons), heroes, people; and politicians; all were glued to their TV screens alike, as channels vied with each other to capture the most disturbing bit of the news in the most scintillating manner. Strangely, some of the channels did choose to keep a sensitive tab on the way stories were delivered to the masses, and refrained from dramatising the turn of events to a cinematic scale. Business-drivers and number-crunchers, usually found in the plush board-rooms of channel-offices, were not available for comment. This was much larger than life.

Srijann Walia watched all of this on the three TV sets perched in front of him. From the classic elegance of the TV's frame, oozed tales of inhuman apathy, in forms less merciful than the terrorists' rampage. The suite had been set up and customised for him before he had stepped in. Rajeev was in the adjacent room and had been advised by his father to take a nap.

He had started to show signs of severe stress, when he broke down in front of his father and started to speak incoherently about giving Hansa a life that she deserved. He was willing to make any promise to keep her happy so long as she came out of the "hell-hole, alive and unharmed".

"Dad, I can't go on without her. Please get her out. Had this security-issue not been a bother, I would've gone in and rescued her myself!"

"Calm down, Raj. Your panic will not bring about any solution, and no sooner than it is meant to take. You need to take a shower and catch some sleep." Srijee consoled his son and in his trademark baritone told him, "The true test of a man's endurance comes in the direst of situations. Those who can control their actions and reactions are the ones who deserve to be called men. Go and take some time-out. You'll be able to think and behave more rationally."

Rajeev did not have the energy to refuse. He went back to his room to sleep over his troubles. Srijann Walia picked up the remote-control of the TV set and was about to switch channels when his phone rang. He answered.

"Hi! Don't worry. Things will soon be under control." "Where are you right now?"

"In the vicinity…you know where."

"I wish I could be there with you. I'm feeling so anxious." "Don't worry about me. I have ten people to look after me.

Pray for Hansa. I have given her my word. I have to live up to it."

"Is Rajeev with you?"

"He's taking a break right now; hasn't slept in two days."

"What about the hounds? Are they a bother?" "Sweetheart, do you think I even care about them right now? They need live stories. We need live people. Have you looked at what the channels are floating? Anybody who can benefit from the situation is busy grinding his axe. Those who are unable to or are answerable are either pretending to be out of the country or are holding their hands up. Bewilderment is the best way to escape responsibility."

"I've never seen you so flustered. Take it easy on yourself."

"How can I take it easy? Many lives have been lost merely because even in a crisis like this, people are awaiting approvals and direction. Accountability has taken priority over responsibility and therefore, action is disgustingly slow; and that's exactly what the hounds are sniffing for. I wish it were the slow-moving file-pushers trapped inside right now and not those inoperative people in there, at least not my Hansa. She doesn't deserve to be there."

"Relax jaan! Hansa is an extraordinary girl. She'll not only come out alive but perhaps help many others to safety. This is one of our many tests. We've always passed in flying colours, haven't we?"

Her straight and guileless outlook towards everything that life threw at her, made the direst of situations appear surmountable. He smiled. On the TV screen, he could see the entire nation coming together to express solidarity and cohesion. Why, he wondered, did it always have to take a bloody event and a few dead people for a nation to come together as one? Why didn't the fraternal instinct bind them together when episodes of communal violence are perpetrated by those in power?

The phone rang again. It was a well-known former scribe-turned-newsmonger from one of the leading TV channels that powered a leading daily too.

He was not interested in answering the call but did so, instinctively.

"Good afternoon Sir!"

"Yes Sheona! I'm sure you haven't called for comments on the current situation. You've got too much of a head-start to have a clichéd HAYF (How are you feeling) talk. What is it then?"

"Sir, I need to meet you ASAP. I got my hands on something that may be of special interest to you."

Srijann Walia looked at his watch. What could be more important than the Taj scenario right now?

"In forty-five minutes. By the clock!" And he disconnected the phone.

"Has Ginny been discharged, yet?" Srijann asked his secretary.

"No Sir! He is still in the hospital." "Does he have a phone on him?"

"Not yet, Sir."

"Get him here, now!"

Srijann Walia always took all his decisions with his head and heart in the right place. And it was unlike him not to have a back-up plan for any of his plans. The middle-aged spinster he was about to meet was overtly crafty and dangerously ambitious. However, she was an important link to the pulse of news-production and circulation in the country; the kind who make and break the news on prime time television. He needed some foresight into her plan of action. Within ten minutes, he received a message telling him that Ginny was on his way to attend to Mr. Walia's call.

In his suite, Srijann changed his phone settings to silent and pondered over the situation. He had managed to stall immediate action by the Navy after a heated debate with the senior officials in command. It took highly diplomatic skills to be able to deter the course of action with the nation's interest at stake. He could have circulated the MMS that he had received but it would only initiate a parallel charade on TV channels and the seriousness of the issue would be made trite by exposure, affecting Hansa's brand equity. He had managed to throw around a significant amount of weight. The MARCOS had been prevented from taking extreme measures. They only needed to keep the *mujahir* engaged and the hostages out of danger. Now this newsmonger had called him with some sensational secret up her sleeve. Srijann Walia was gearing up to speak with the C.M. of Maharashtra when Ginny walked in.

"Ganpat, what is Sheona up to these days?"

"Sir, nothing very important, as far as I can remember. She's been trying to fix some entries to the International Awards. I haven't seen her much lately. She's turning into a bit of a mad bitch, Sir!"

"Language, Ginny! When did you see her last?"

"On 26th Sir. I saw her chatting up Kuber Narang, here at Shamiana. He was giving her some envelope." "When is Kuber's next movie due for release?"

"Sir, it will take at least three months to get completed. Even the promos haven't come out, yet."

"I want to know about all the projects that he is involved in. Also, find out Sheona's current PR equation with him."

"Don't worry, Sir. I'll find out everything. My sources are very reliable. A little expensive but they can't refuse me. Besides, if I…"

"Shut up, Ginny!"

Ginny was a good pitcher. He could spin his expectations in the least intimidating manner. That was the reason why he had retained his job with Hansa for so many years now. Moreover, Srijann Walia could read people well. Even between the lines. Said and unsaid.

He removed a few thousand rupees from a bundle lying in a bag by the table, handed them out; which Ginny bent over and received with one hand and an expressionless face; and dismissed him with a polite thank-you. After Ganpat left, Srijann Walia gave a few instructions to his secretary. He recalled having seen Ginny at the hospital, when he had gone to look up Zarine. Ginny had not noticed Srijee in the distance while waiting in the waiting-lounge. The brown envelope sat threateningly in his lap. Mr. Walia had considered it best not to draw the man's attention to himself, as he quietly slid outside towards the parking lot.

He wondered if he should summon his son for the meeting. It did not require much thought to dismiss the idea. Rajeev had been under tremendous stress and needed to stay away from any kind of buzz. Srijann had advised him to sleep for some time in order to clear the fog seeping into his cognitive ability. Ever since Hansa's miscarriage, he had sensed a change in the dynamics of their relationships with each other.

Hansa did not look as cheerful in Rajeev's company as she did earlier. Rajeev had been getting edgier in his interaction with his parents and Hansa had been restrained and thoughtful, when in conversation with him. Even though, she was a brilliant actor; she was still not good enough for Srijee to be taken in by the respectful guise. He could tell when a performance is coming from the heart and when it is being forced through by the head.

It was not difficult to relate the change to the startling run-in at the hospital. Did she know? Had she guessed or been informed? He could trust Zarine but trust often became an object in a china-shop in an industry hounded by a bull-headed Press. Ayway, that was not what was top-of-mind right now. It was Hansa they were all worried about. It was unnecessary for Srijann Walia to be present near the site of the incident. He was there only for his son. It took a big deal to ruffle Srijann Walia's feathers; and this was bigger than that. In the middle of his idle thinking, his phone rang. It was Gargi. It did not need to be answered just yet.

*****

Gargi Walia had never felt so helpless ever before; and certainly not at times when her family needed her the most. She had arrived in Chennai on the evening of 24th November to be a part of the wedding celebrations of her best friend's daughter. Unexpected and incessant rains had lashed the city after her arrival. Most of the city was flooded and commuting had become impossible through the water-logged, crater-punched roads. Some of the customary celebrations had been postponed as it was impossible for the guests to arrive due to non-commutability.

On the night of 26th, when Gargi plopped into bed, tired and restless, she switched on the TV set to de-stress before tucking herself in for the night. To her horror, she found the news channels reporting terrorist attacks in Mumbai. Immediately she called up her son, her husband and her daughter-in-law, in that order. Rajeev was fine, Srijann was still in Delhi and Hansa was unreachable. Rajeev had apprised her of the situation while on his way to the hotel. She had insisted that Rajeev send his secretary and security personnel, instead of going there himself. However, her insistence had not been received very well by her son. She knew it would be futile to explain to him that her suggestion came more out of concern for him than a lack of love for his wife.

Rajeev was quick in judgement and impulsive in expression. Thereafter, she had not been able to sleep through the night and had called Rajeev every hour to get a live update of the situation. She knew her husband would leave no stone unturned to get their beloved daughter-in-law out of harm's way.

Meanwhile, she called up her office staff to book her ticket to Mumbai on the next available flight. The rains, however, had been rather opposed to the idea and continued to rattle the city. Flights were non-operational and rail service had been stalled. Gargi had no choice but to stay put and pray hard.

*****

It was now Friday morning and she had called Sri a number of times. His phone kept ringing without an answer. Gargi understood. The situation was not yet under his control, else he would not have kept her waiting. Like a true hero, he would surface from the deeps, only after he had ensured the best possible outcome. Even though, she was getting regular updates from Rajeev; she knew that only Sri could allow her to breathe free and easy.

*****

The clock kept its time and so did Sheona. After precisely forty-five minutes, he received a call on the room's intercom about her arrival, along with a colleague. She had a boisterous air about her that forced people to make way for her will. It was expected of her to create some brouhaha around her presence.

No matter how serious the situation, her moves would almost always be cinematic. He waited for her while trying to analyse the political statements being made and diplomatic condolences being floated. The door opened and Srijann turned around to meet the guest eye to eye. She stood in the doorway, pleased to have brought him such surprise.

As Srijann dismissed the bouncers at the door, she walked towards him confidently and wrapped her arms around him, planting a kiss on his cheek. At the same moment, the door swung open again and in stepped Sheona, flashing a smile at the most talked-about couple from yesteryears, breaking their arm-lock.

There wasn't much reaction-time for Mr. Walia, as he saw someone slip away into the corridor behind her, after having stolen and stamped the moment with a click. Zarine carried her unruffled demeanour like a permanent accessory on her forearm. Quietly, she drifted to the window that overlooked a busy road. It was just another Friday in tinsel town.

"What's going on, Sheona? I don't expect such uncivil behaviour from you."

"Srijee, pardon me but I'm just trying hard to retain a ruthlessly boring job. Occasionally, it turns out to be a bit interesting, though. Anyway, I walked in fully announced, didn't I? I came in to share something with you but it seems that you have some commitments to keep." She carried the smile of a young witch, who knows that her craft is all about articulating her spells; and timing was the key to perfection.

"What is it that you want to show me that couldn't wait till this crisis is over?" he asked, choosing to ignore her remark.

"Er, Sir, you might want to keep this, sort of, under-the-carpet." She glanced at Zarine, who could feel the girl's perceptive gaze boring through her.

"It's alright. Zarine is a confidante." Srijee didn't believe in pretence.

Sheona opened her bag and brought out an A-4 sized envelope and placed it in her hands. Srijann Walia opened it and looked at the photographs, turning one on the other quite casually.

"That's it?"

"You should look worried, Sir. These photos were due to appear as breaking news at prime time, and in tomorrow's newspaper on the same page as the half-page promo of 'Ruttiebai'. Thankfully, they reached my desk before hitting the newsroom. The Taj disaster saved Hansa's film, and perhaps her career."

"Where did you get these?" "Sir, is that important?" "Yes"

"Not difficult to guess!"

"Who else has access?" "Two editors. Alligators." "Price?"

"You know me, Sir. Money can't buy me…love!" she winked and looked at Zarine as she said; "I am working really hard for the position of

Head of Operations. All I need is a word from your end and that'll settle the gators and I'll be able to cross the river."

"Can't promise you that!"

"Oh Sir, you sound miffed but look at it this way. I could have used these photos to auger the prospects of certain key people in a competitive channel and they would've ensured that the position came to me anyway. I did this as our business relationship goes back a long way. I just kept you in my noble thoughts. Now one good turn deserves an equally good; if not better; return, doesn't it?"

"Meet my P.A. in office in an hour. He takes good care of wagging tongues. And by the way, just remember, it's easier to destroy a career than to build one. Gossip, loosely thrown, can cost you dearly sometimes."

"Sir, I work only for money ... not for pleasure; and gossip gets me neither!"

Sheona talked her way out of the room; just the way she had always walked out of tough negotiations.

And Srijann Walia never wasted any time in keeping his promises.

*****

Zarine wasn't prepared for a public disclosure yet. She spoke after Sheona left.

"Jaan, this shouldn't have happened. I'm sorry. Spontaneity, it seems, never meets a dead end but, when least desired, surely a deadly end."

Srijann couldn't help smiling at her childlike abandon even in undesirable situations.

"Don't worry. That girl can't afford to lose her job. She'll be a pest for sometime but knows how and how much to behave. Relax."

"Has Gargi managed to get out of Chennai? I believe, the climate there has been like the local newspaper. Totally uninspiring!"

And Srijann held her hand and looked at her like a devotee.

"Zara, do you think Hansa and Raj really love each other? You have such a perceptive view of relationships and their loops. Do you think that between them they share an ounce of what you and I have shared in the past two decades?"

"C'mon Jaan, you can't compare the kids to us. In fact, you can't compare anyone to us. Between Raj and Hansa, I think Hansa is a girl with a steady balance between her head and her heart. But when on an emotional joyride, she tends to lose that equanimity. Her relationship with Raj probably found a direction on one such joyride. Now they need to ride through a rough patch to test the strength of the hinges that hold them together."

"I don't think they can survive any potholes, let alone a rough patch. This is going to be tough to explain."

"Sri, "Zarine looked into his eyes," I know you've seen something disturbing in those photographs. But whatever it is, believe me, it will help sort out many kinks. Y'know, my 'trying-times theory' applies to all relationships. Didn't your relationship with Gargi stand the test of public disgrace when her father was roped into a sex-scandal? Considering you initiated the proceedings, it must've been very demanding on Gargi, no? Yet, you both still love each other. So, there you go!"

Breaking news on the TV screen caught Srijann's eye. It said "two terrorists killed, one MARCO injured in cross fire; group of hostages seen on the roof."

*****

When people are unable to respond with an answer, they react. The reaction is more of a reaffirmation to self about one's capability. It started with silent candle-lit marches with a commiserative feeling, which was quickly usurped by NGOs to gain visibility on national television. This, in turn, caught the roving politician's eyes and became reason enough to slander his friends-in-power.

Newsrooms were full of ambiguous statements on the number of terrorists killed. A news channel came up with the idea of broadcasting the conversation of a reporter with a terrorist in another hotel. The idea caught attention like a house on fire and the race for TRPs began. Soon, a few channels were broadcasting conversations and those who couldn't, broadcasted proof of the clips having been forged. The policemen who laid down their lives in the line of duty were given a state farewell, caught live by media-persons thronging their mournful homes. School managements perked up and saw this as a marketing tool. Children were made to sing patriotic songs in public places, the meaning of which was little understood by singers and listeners alike.

Afternoon had uneventfully slipped into the twilight gown. Rajeev had sobered down a bit after an eight-hour rest and a decent meal. He walked into his Dad's suite. There was no one in the room. The shower in the bathroom was on. His Dad was probably inside. He sat down to catch some news. As he surfed through the deluge of news, he found a lesser known channel flashing his father's name.

*****

Friday went by with snippets of hope doing the rounds, in the streets of Mumbai, over cutting-chai. The MARCOS team was reported to have eliminated all but two of the extremists. Rajeev and his father had discussed several issues through the night, some leading to extravagant arguments.

"Dad, what's going on? This ridiculous channel has the audacity to float such news about you and Zarine Aunty? I'm going to fuck the life out of their happiness and ...!"

"What are you going to do, son, and why?"

"What do you mean, why, Pa? Aren't you disturbed over this?"

"Right now, the only thing that is disturbing is that your wife is inside that place, fighting to survive! Do you love your wife enough, Raj?"

"Pa, I can't understand you! I'm bloody stressed over her, and this piece of news has completely yanked the rug from under my feet. How can you be so cool about this? Have you thought how Ma is going to feel?"

"Raj, when will you ever learn to put things in the correct order of priority? Your mother is my responsibility and I will ensure that her questions are answered to her satisfaction. Meanwhile, can you focus your energies on your responsibilities?"

"No-no-no…something's not right here. I think I'm quite far off from something that I should know. What's it, Dad? Do you mind telling me, what's going on?"

"You still haven't learnt to time your time well! You'd be ahead of everything if only you could do that." His father's response led Rajeev's mind away from Hansa temporarily. He wondered if his mother had been made aware of this situation and if yes, what would she be going through right now?

The floods in Chennai had abated and his mother was expected to arrive in Mumbai on Saturday morning. There were about ten to twelve people left to be rescued, half of which were stranded on the rooftop of Taj Towers. Five people and a few corpses filled up the TV screens of most news channels. It was nearly impossible for the choppers to place the evacuation team on the rooftop as there was indiscriminate firing from a covered area and the terrorist had an advantageous position.

Saturday morning arrived with renewed hope and vigour. Srijann Walia had received information about the operation nearing its end and the hotel premises having been nearly sanitised.

The hostages on the rooftop had been rescued and the terrorist who was holding them up had been terminated. Rajeev's confidence of seeing Hansa alive and well had grown manifold and even though he couldn't sleep through the night; he had fought his panic attacks.

Mornings almost always arrive packed with enough adventure for a day, just waiting to be unfurled. Rajeev ordered some coffee. It arrived ceremoniously on a trolley with cookies, fresh brew and newspapers as accompaniments. Rajeev picked up the newspaper before the cup with hot, steaming beverage. The coffee was not meant to reach him. The front page of the city edition was scalding.

What stared at him from the supplement on Bollywood news were pictures of his father and Zarine Nawaaz in an arm-lock, in the hotel room where Srijann Walia was currently staying. The story that accompanied the photographs had crossed limits of couth reporting and had touted the two actors as adulterers who had been caught red-handed for the first time in twenty years. For Rajeev, twenty-ninth of November had dawned no better than the twenty sixth.

Thirteen

Hansa had no idea, where she was or who she was with. The room was pitch-dark and someone had hissed at her to stay put where she was if she wanted to survive. She had only heard gunfire for the last twelve hours and was now rapidly losing her ability to perceive or infer. She thought she had heard people in her group talking intermittently but wasn't sure if it was them or her hysteria. She recalled being pulled and pushed into rooms, up and down staircases and at one time she was also holed up in a tall cubicle, where she could just barely stand straight.

Briefly, a few intense words, had kept her hope alive.

At times, the strength in a man's arms becomes known by the strength of his character and sometimes, merely by his conviction in his action. She had gauged the strength of his arms by his indefatigable spirit. Thereafter, she did not fight her fear and allowed it to come uninhibited and leave unattended.

Throughout the misadventure, her eyes had been half-shut. She only became aware that a new day had dawned when she was pushed onto a terrace and her eyes were unable to receive the warm morning rays kindly. She had lived fifty-six long hours of darkness.

Zarrar had lost sight of his objective now. What had begun as jihad, inspired by owls and badgers, had now become an insatiable thirst for blood. The more it was shed, the more the thirst grew. Animal rage had replaced the need for food, water and oxygen inside his body. In a state of delirium, he was driven by a pair of grey-green eyes and an animate, involuntary desire to kill.

They were now on the rooftop of Taj Towers. The drone of the choppers could be heard in the distance and Zarrar had taken strategic cover with Hansa, who had been made to drag herself along his side. Her mouth was clamped shut and wrists tied behind her back. He stood in a slightly covered niche, out of view of the chopper, facing the door to the stairwell and gun pointed at Hansa. He was not letting anyone take her away this time. She was too ethereal to be touched by gun-toting wild animals. He needed to protect her from all harm. The predators were creeping up on them and he was the saviour. His brothers would be proud ofhim.

The air began to warm up as the sun's rays started to gain momentum. Zarrar was breathing heavily and she could feel the tined ends of exhaled breath. Any moment now, she expected to see a head surface from the staircase and Zarrar would run a volley of bullets down the front and turn that person into a mesh. She would sit there helplessly, watch him go down. She couldn't let it happen to her knight. When on the floors below, he had ensured the safety of each one under his wing, without a furrow on his forehead. They had been hauled down from the balcony of a high floor by the fire-fighting squad.

Hansa would have been out of danger too, had Zarrar not sealed their escape with a grenade. Her hero, with an injured shoulder and thigh, had leapt like a puma through the fire and landed her on safe ground. In the flash of the fire, their eyes had engaged for a few seconds and allowed communication that would otherwise be considered inappropriate.

She had wanted to say, "Why are you doing this? No job could be worth more than your life." She didn't.

He had wanted to say, "Damn!" He didn't.

As the smoke hurled itself upwards, they had come into Zarrar's full range of view and fire. Hansa had stood up, shielding her MARCO, inviting the wrath of the terrorist upon herself.

"So, you are going to die for a rat? Is a coward worth such a beautiful life?"

"It's easy for a coward to aim his gun at unarmed people. If you're the lion that you think you are, drop your gun and then do the talking!"

Zarrar flared his nostrils and contrary to her expectation, emptied a round of bullets. Alpha Tango dropped to the floor with her. She felt a tremor run down her body as he enveloped her.

"Can you please, not say anything?" He quipped softly. The terrorist laughed boisterously.

"You want a test of bravery? Yes! Yes! I'm a coward? Yes?

Another one? Here it is!"

And another round followed, chasing two people entwined on the floor, but not touching them. Laughter punctuated the firing yet again.

When the pause was long enough, they raised their heads and steadied themselves. Hansa now felt no hesitation in clinging to her knight in dark armour, reeking with blood and sweat. This one was for real.

Alpha Tango stepped forward, moving Hansa behind him.

"Do what you came here to do. Speech is clearly not your skill."

Alpha Tango knew conversation was his only bet to stall his shooting.

"And man to man combat isn't yours. Send her across and I'll let you go."

"You can use your gun and still have her. What are you waiting for?"

"Your wish shall be granted. *Allah* be with you!"

And another deafening flare filled up the room. When it died, Alpha Tango was on the floor and Hansa was glued to the wall with large tears precipitating on her cheeks.

As Alpha Tango had moved her out of his way, he had whispered in her ear:

"Don't give up!"

Zarrar walked towards Hansa who made no effort to move.

He removed his veil and in a jerky, unexpected movement, embraced her; and then released her in the same manner. He then, tied her hands and clamped her mouth shut with the black veil.

*****

Zarrar would wait till eternity if he had to. He was not going to let anything change the equation. The gora tyrant had to come up the stairs and eat his bullets. Meanwhile, Alpha Tango was running down the steps, cutting through the smoke, to get to the ground floor. Each floor was in a different stage of burning out. He had decided not to head towards the rooftop. It took him less than five minutes to reach the base and run out of the hotel building. His team was ready with the climbing gear.

In less than a minute, three men were crawling up the south-west face of the Taj Towers, towards the roof top on the 22nd floor.

*****

The helicopter rose into view once again. It drifted towards the rooftop where the MARCOS clung to the parapet, ready to jump in. They were waiting for their cue. A second's distraction was enough. A bag fell with a thud from the chopper on to the terrace. It looked heavy and its presence was disturbing. Tiny wisps of smoke arose from it. Zarrar eyed it for a while with his gun aimed at it. It would be foolish to walk towards it. After a few minutes passed by without a movement, he decided to risk gunning it down. Even if it was a bomb, he didn't have much to lose. His rifle fired away at the gunny bag. A reaction was all they had needed to ascertain his position.

The MARCOS jumped on to the roof and rolled on to three sides. The only exit available to him now was the sheer drop down the building. One of them, fired next to the nook where Zarrar was positioned, drawing him out of hiding. A bullet ate into his hand and made him drop his weapon. He stepped out like a wounded lion with Hansa still dangling by his side like a stunned doe.

"Give up! There's no escape. Surrender is the only way to save your life."

Zarrar laughed out loud. "Surrender?" He continued to laugh, and then mumbled something under his breath. "Rohilla Suleimany shall not submit to fear. Like a mountain he stands and like so, shall he fall!"

The chopper was getting closer. The MARCOS perked up their vigil by a notch. They did not allow their vision, the slightest flicker. Zarrar stood on the parapet with Hansa. A deathly pallor had descended upon his veil-less face. The crescent had now blended into the colourless skin. He looked at the dome of the Taj. The slide was ready. Smoke rose in pretty spirals drilling holes into the blue sky, which closed in after them. The chopper hovered dangerously low over the rooftop.

"I won't let you go, this time. You'll always be safe by my side, Husna," he whispered as he gave her a long, melancholic look.

Saying this he leapt off the parapet with Hansa's arm tucked firmly in his iron-grip. Hansa screamed. Gunfire tittered at Zarrar and his grip loosened. Blood spouted from his back as he started his free fall to the ground below, where a team was waiting with two large safety nets. At the same split second, a figure zoomed down from the chopper and swooped upon Hansa like an eagle upon its game and held her securely around her waist. It was Alpha Tango, with bullets still embedded in his vest and blood coagulating on his thigh and shoulder. That was the longest, clearest look that she got of her proverbial knight.

In daylight, he looked even more endearing. The face was still covered with a cap. A high forehead without a hint of a line was what had caught her attention. He didn't smell of any expensive perfumes or after-shaves, only raw manhood. Exhaustion and trust connived and played their part well; and Hansa rested her fatigued head on the square chest.

"Can't say thank-you! Words aren't enough," she muttered. "What you said, are words enough!", he replied.

Soon, the chopper zoomed back towards the Gateway of India after having airlifted two people from the terrace. A lady in black over-sized clothes clung to a daredevil in black uniform as they cut through the grey air.

The vast expanse of the Arabian Sea below them swelled up with the tide. A mountain was shelled as it fell to its end; and she wasn't alone.

A part of him was to remain with her as the waters of the Arabian Sea crashed against the buttresses. She had finally made it out of there alive; but, would life ever remain the same? Who did she owe her breath to the inordinate killer who shot his own to keep her safe, or the mysterious MARCO, who para-dropped into her life, when she had lost hope in her husband?

Questions were far too many. She rested her exhausted head on his shoulder, and decided to let life find its own course, like unbridled water, gushing away from the lap of a mountain. The white fire on Taj's dome was beginning to get subdued as water rose up from it in jets of black steam.

PART—III
MARCO—THE COLOUR OF WATER

Fourteen

"Let's go!" Rajeev put his arm around her. She felt a shiver run through. Perhaps, there was a chill in the air. The reporters were already beginning to swarm around them and the local police looked irritated with their presence on the scene.

"Raj, where's Pa? Is he not in town?" she asked.

"You'll meet him soon. He's around. Ma returned from Chennai today. Both should be at home."

"What happened to the other people inside? Where's Ginny?"

"Most people have been evacuated. A few couldn't be. Ginny got a new lease of life. He has been rescued and is in the hospital now. Poor guy lost his right arm. We'll go and look him up in a day or two."

She sighed and walked towards the vehicle waiting to take her home. Just before getting in, she turned and threw a parting glance towards the Taj. The last three days had been a life-changing experience for her. It would be easier to take many decisions now.

"What happened to that terrorist, who jumped off the terrace? I want to see him once."

Rajeev looked at her questioningly.

"I want to see the face of the man who took me to hell and back and yet, killed one of his own to protect me. I want to know who he is and why he spared me."

"Hansa, I know you've been through the most harrowing experience but it's over now. There's no need to linger over here and extend the pain any further. Let's just go home."

"Rajeev, it's only when you've had a close brush with death, you do realise what each moment of living breath means. I can't explain why but I feel the need to know."

"He's gone, baby. He fell through the air in a stream of blood. They are probably putting his pieces together right now, or maybe they've wrapped him up and taken him away. Get real. You need rest. Plenty of it! Let's just get out of here."

Hansa turned to look at the Taj once more, hoping to get a glimpse of the man she actually wanted to see. She was gently whisked away by her husband.

"Raj, I need to tell you something," she said getting into the car, "This is not the way I'd thought of telling you but I can't wait."

"What is it, baby?"

"I'm pregnant again."

*****

It was yet another shocking revelation. In the past three days, he had made many silent promises, to the power that the world believed in, about giving Hansa the joys that she wished for but now that she was safe and by his side, Rajeev felt a little uneasy at the prospect.

"Are you sure? When did you find out?"

"26th morning. However, I had thought of telling you after that day's shoot got over. I wanted us to celebrate the moment this time."

Rajeev hugged her.

"We'll visit the doctor, once you've gained some energy."

She stepped into the car.

Rajeev had not reacted in the same manner as earlier. However, he did not express much joy either. He continued to make and receive calls on his two phones as he got in beside her.

"That man didn't want to kill me," she wanted to tell Raj everything.

"Ya ... just a minute ... I want Mom and Dad to know that you're with me."

A minute was too long a wait.

Hansa's eyes closed involuntarily and soon she was drifting in a sea of mooning faces. It was unusually hot and she was sweating, despite the draught of cool air being exhaled by the air con. Images of a veiled face, contorted laughter, slit throats and blond hair floated about in her mind. A pair of eyes with sepulchral depth refused to set her free. The more they stayed with her, the more she wanted to know the identity of the bearer. She twitched and sweated even more.

At the same time, it was the image of one man in aviators and a *balaclava*, who swung into her delta-rhythms and put her at ease. It gave her a sense of inviolability hitherto unknown to her. It was different from the way Raj had held her on the bobbing boat in Lake Thun. Or perhaps, she had forgotten that feeling altogether. In that protective stance, she had felt like a woman instead of a much-coveted trophy. In her imaginative promenade, she removed the aviators and peered into his eyes. He had tried to keep his gaze averted. But she was sure he had stolen a glance at her fleetingly during that silent tête-à-tête.

She had barely dozed off when she felt something trickle down the nape of her neck. She opened her eyes to see Rajeev wiping her cheeks with a wet towel. They had reached home. She had slept dreamlessly. Or something that seemed like that.

Hansa sighed. It had been the most excruciating sixty hours of her life both emotionally and physically. She had been married to Raj for four years, after one year of courtship.

Since the past one year, she had felt the need to take connubial bliss to the next level. Children are natural adhesives, fostering relationships that are likely to fray with time otherwise. But Raj wasn't too keen. She had tried to put the miscarriage behind her and did not allow it to dampen her spirit. She had been charmingly persistent and he had always brought home a gift, as retribution for the allure but not the idea. But with time, this little game had begun to lose its tempo and Rajeev still hadn't started to look her way. However, it was on the morning of 26th November when she had discovered that there was a new life waiting for welcoming arms, yet again. The conception had been accidental and she hadn't known how to react. Rajeev had been away on a night shoot and was to arrive only later in the morning.

This was something she couldn't have disclosed over the phone. Her maternal instincts battled with the thought of Rajeev's response. She had gone for her shoot at the Taj, trying to embody Ruttie Jinnah's emotional turmoil. Her state of mind had made it easier for her to relate to an enigmatic life from yore. To top that, each time she looked at the dangerously quiet waves, she saw her mother's face appearing on the surface and then melting into the darkness. The melancholy had established itself effortlessly. Perhaps, if Ruttiebai had children, she may have lived longer. Perhaps if her mother had a husband, she would have still been alive. Perhaps if she didn't get married to Rajeev, life would've been on a different trail. Perhaps, perhaps! Who knows? It was a sensitive issue so she had decided to tell Rajeev in person when she met him later that evening. She knew he wouldn't be too pleased and she would have to work very hard at making him see the joy that it would bring to their relationship.

After the harrowing hours spent inside the Taj, she could not keep it to herself any longer, waiting for the right moment. Sometimes, life doesn't offer too much time for planning. Incidentally, her unceremonious disclosure had done little to make the day any worse or special than it already was. She wondered if it was a sense of losing her, the golden goose, forever that had prevented Raj from giving a ballistic response this time. Trying to weave incomprehensible patterns on intertwined looms, she rested her head against his shoulder. He looked at her dotingly.

"You need to rest, my pretty," mopping the beads of sweat from her brow with a two-ply. "You can go, shower and change and then catch some sleep. Someone from the police station will come in the evening to record your statement. Or if you don't feel up to it, we can have them come in tomorrow."

"Raj…I…" Before she could finish, there was a sound of chanting in chorus that greeted them. Amidst a group of pundits and well-wishers; there stood her mother-in-law. Always poised and in control, today Gargi rushed towards the car with impatient steps. Hansa stepped out and hugged her. Emotions ran loose. Wiping her tears, Gargi led Hansa in. Fresh orange juice went down her parched throat like water. Close family members waited to hug Hansa, and to hear her story. Gargi led her through the crowd and instructed the servants to bring food to Hansa's room upstairs. There was much to be talked about, but later.

*****

Hansa stepped into the shower. The numbness of the disaster had eased a bit and thoughts and feelings were retaining form. The water was welcoming yet foreboding at the same time. She stepped out quickly and dropped into bed. She had no clue how long she slept but when she woke up, she noticed that food by her bedside had gone cold and the clock in the hall downstairs was striking nine. She rang the bell for her servant to clear the table. Her hand landed on the newspaper. The date was 29th. She picked it up to glance at it but then, driven by another thought, picked up the TV's remote control. She flicked through the channels abuzz with activity. Each channel had the same bytes to offer. The Taj had now been completely sanitised. The face with the crescent that had commandeered the entire operation now lay lifeless and contorted, as the neck was twisted at an inhuman angle. As the camera swept a glance over the bullet-ridden form, it hovered over an inked scrawl on the arm. The reporter spoke in a high-pitched voice:

"It is finally over. The ordeal and the blood bath that overtook the glory of the Taj in Mumbai came to a just end as the last terrorist was gunned down by the heroes of the most-elite force of the Indian Navy. Right now, all that is known about the identity of this terrorist is the tattoo in Pashto on his arm, which reads as Ibn-e-Zain, meaning son of Zain. The Indian intelligence has tracked the links to Islamic terror outfits

Lashkar-e-Toiba, which was in close association with *Al-Qaeda* for this operation…"

The reporter went on in a single breath. Hansa felt uneasy with the declaration of that man's sub-identity. Was this some kind of *Karmic* humour that gave her and the killer, fathers by the same name? Or was this the reason that she had been protected throughout by the ruthless anarchist? Could it be a coincidence or destiny's foul play? What was going on in his mind and by what measure? The only person, who could clear the clouds, lay dead on the television screen. Answers grappled with each other as she tried to find a clear winner. As she sauntered around a few news channels, her mother-in-law walked in with someone carrying fresh steaming food for her. The servant was dismissed soon after he had placed the trolley by her bedside.

"Feeling better, darling?" She nodded.

"Where's Raj?"

"He's meeting someone in the office downstairs. I'll send him a message that you're up."

Hansa didn't know what to say or do. She wasn't sure if Rajeev had told Gargi about her pregnancy. "Ma, did you get the news?" Gargi looked uncomfortable.

"I heard. Life is full of surprises, Hansa. In the three decades of my marriage, I have learnt that love is more than just sprouting new hopes and living new aspirations. It also means destroying the old and reconstructing all over again."

Hansa knew Gargi as a woman of few but deep words. She could make several statements with the littlest detail. Social activism and high-profile parties had provided her all that is required to strike a balance between reality and propaganda and she had processed every piece of information in her life, rather intelligently.

"Ma, I don't know what it means to Raj or you and Pa. I don't even know what it means to me anymore. I need time to absorb this fact. We need to let the thought incubate and find its own life before we can acknowledge it. For all you know, it just might fall off-course and find its end."

"Don't fret, darling! You don't have to worry about anything. This is between Sri and me and I promise you that it won't affect you or Raj. Zarine may have walked into our lives unannounced but she'll always remain a guest and no more."

Hansa was taken by surprise. Her mother-in-law and she had been talking about two different issues. And yet, the conversation had manifested itself as one. Raj walked in the door and sat by her side. He held her hand.

"You can't imagine what I went through in the past three days. It was like a horrible nightmare that refused to end." Raj had commented about his state of mind. Perhaps that was what his thoughts always comprised of. People were only props in that setting. Not once had he asked her anything about the sixty hours that she had endured.

"Yes, it must've been terrible for you," she replied.

Hansa was distracted by the news channel reporting the role of the MARCOS in the entire operation. A couple of uniformed men with covered faces were surrounded by the team and media persons, briefing them on the sequence of events inside the hotel. Words came through quite laboriously and in a languorous manner. She couldn't spot the deep-set eyes that she was looking for. And the voice she heard was certainly not the one she wanted to hear.

"Ok. So, enough of this! I'd rather hear it from you." And Rajeev switched off the telly.

Hansa looked at him and started to narrate the episode while she slowly consumed the spread that lay before her. The delicious warmth and aroma felt tasteless and odourless as she spoke. Her husband and mother-in-law listened intently. She tried her best not to let her emotions overpower facts, and she carefully evaded the brief delusional moments when she had allowed a stranger to command her emotions.

Fifteen

Hansa hadn't met her father-in-law yet. She had expected him to be among the first people to greet her. Waking up to a sun-kissed morning, in the comfort of her ploh-furnished bed, had never felt like such a privilege before. Rajeev lay on his belly, snoring softly, with the comforter on the floor. She stood by the large bay-window that overlooked the sea on one side. While sipping her coffee, she decided to get dressed and go and meet Pa. Before she could finish her coffee, Raj opened his eyes.

"Good morning, babes!"

Hansa smiled.

"Come here."

Forcing herself to retain the smile, she walked towards him. He pulled her towards him and rolled over in bed. The romantic gestures were the same and the man was the same. Hansa was not. She cringed at his touch even though he didn't notice it. He snuggled his nose in her hair as they fell open.

"I'll never let go off you again."

She found the statement quite juvenile and contradictory to his nature.

"I need to see a doc."

"We'll call one home in the evening. Till then at least, let's make up for lost time."

It was disgusting to see Raj seeking carnal pleasures even before the dust had settled.

"Raj, there's too much on my mind right now. Why don't you get dressed, so we can have breakfast with *Ma* and *Pa*?"

"Rajeev sat up. You seem to have everything and everyone on your mind except me. Why don't you go ahead for breakfast? I'll take some time. And by the way, Ma has taken time-out. She left for Delhi this morning."

"Delhi? Why? That was sudden."

"No, it wasn't. She had decided yesterday, after the news broke out. Her decision was fomented by Pa's refusal to deny anything that was reported."

"Where is he?"

"I don't know. I haven't seen him since yesterday."

"What do you mean? You haven't talked to your father, when he is going through such a crisis?"

"He doesn't deserve the luxury of a sympathetic conversation, after what he made my mother go through."

"Raj, I can't believe what you are saying. What's his crime? That he had a strong relationship going outside his marriage? Do people give up the right to have friends and confidantes the day they get married? It sounds palatable coming from a small-town nitwit but from you, it sounds despicable."

"What's come over you, Hansa? You are talking like you visited another planet. Can you even hear yourself talk? Marriage is sacrosanct. A relationship outside of it, especially without the knowledge of your spouse, is called cheating, in case you have forgotten. And cheating amounts to emotional torment. If that's okay, then killing someone should also be okay."

"You are overreacting, Rajeev. People create bonds on several planes. If one shakes a bit, the other vectors bring the equation back into place. You should have stopped Ma from going away to Delhi."

"I think she did the right thing. *Pa* must apologise to her and give up on that adulteress, if he really loves my mother and wants her back in his life."

"Who told you that this is adultery? The media? You seriously have paid heed to these stories, have you? Have you even spoken to your father about this? But I'm sure, you wouldn't understand even if you did."

"Oh, so are you trying to tell me that I'm too dumb to understand that my father had been cheating on my mother for the past thirty years and I'm supposed to be considerate and let the land lay the way it does? If that's called an intelligent approach to things, I'd rather not grow an intellect. Besides, how maturely would you handle the situation, if you found out the same thing about me after being married to me for that long?"

"Heck! No! All I'm saying is that you should give Pa some space to be able to explain his side of the story. We must try to build bridges instead of burning them. And yes, I'd definitely handle it better than you would, if we were in the same situation. Besides, I think we should just let your parents deal with this than fight over it ourselves."

And she stepped into the dressing-room, in an attempt to put out the fire, little realising she had only just ignited one.

*****

Scribes had started to call his office for appointments. Some of the anti-establishment sorts had even started to hang around the compound wall of the famous bungalow. The brighter ones bribed his P.R.O. with offers he hated to refuse. Srijann Walia stayed holed up in his office on the ground floor of his expansive home. He had a reasonable discussion with Gargi over the issue. Even though, she believed Sri when he said that Zarine was not his bed-mate, Gargi still felt cheated at having been robbed of the number one slot in his life. In this case, she felt like the other woman. It had been heartbreaking for her to hear Srijann validate the story. The decision had been amicable. She had wanted to stay away from the limelight and had thus told Srijann about her desire to take time-out and move to Delhi for a while. She would come back once she had a more objective view of the situation and some calm had started to wash over the disturbed sands.

Hansa walked into the office and found Srijee puffing away at a cigar. It was unusual to find him lighting up and it was a tell-tale sign of stress getting a bit too daunting to handle. He put it away as soon as she entered. Somehow, she knew that he knew that she knew.

"*Pa*, I'm sorry about all that is happening. It was so unexpected."

"Never say sorry with such ease, Hansa. And why should you be, when I'm not?"

"Can't we bring Mom home? It feels really odd not to have her around in the house."

"Don't worry. She'll come. I want her to stay away for some time, too."

"Sometimes, distances may not better the situation. On the contrary, your disinterest in bringing her back may plant new doubts in her mind."

"What makes you think I'm disinterested? There's a lot to be sorted and she can do without all the mess. Have you looked at the newspaper today?"

He placed the Bollywood supplement of the morning daily in front of her. Pictures of Kuber and Hansa in a passionate lip-lock covered the front page. The heading read in bold: (S)EXPOSED!

*****

Rajeev stared at the newspaper, while still in bed. His nightmare wasn't over yet. Hansa couldn't be cheating on him. He needed to talk to her immediately. He rang the bell, once, twice, thrice and then without waiting for a response, stormed out of his room, straight into his father's office.

His father expected to see him. Hansa was dialling a number.

"If you are calling Kuber, forget it. He won't answer your phone." Srijann Walia then looked up at his son.

"So Mrs. Walia, is this the reason why you were defending my father's extra-marital affair? So, how am I supposed to react to this? Like a husband or like a mature man?"

“Raj . . . .” Hansa started to explain but Srijee interrupted.

“Rajeev, it would help if you calmed down a bit and heard her patiently. And in case you can't, then you may please carry your confrontation to another part of the house. I won't sit here watching the two of you letting your tongues loose.”

“I'm sure, Dad! I believe that's another way of disowning your own guilt!”

“Shut up, Raj! There's no need to vent your frustrations on Pa. It's better if we go to our room and talk.”

“What are we going to talk about? How you managed to get so up, close and personal with that bastard? Or are you going to make me try and see something platonic in this photograph?”

Srijann sat in his swivel chair, absorbing his son's ire.

“Raj, can we discuss this later? We need to visit the hospital first.”

“Yes, we need to go sooner than quickly. Coz now I'm desperate to get a paternity test.”

“Shut up, Raj! You are insulting my presence here,” retorted Mr. Walia. “You better get a grip on yourself. Get out of here and we'll talk once you have regained your balance.” Srijee had never been, and was not ready now to be a witness to any kind of disgraceful or demeaning talk towards the ladies of the house. Hansa shuddered at the prospect of having to talk with Rajeev without her father-in-law to intercept aggressive outpourings.

Rajeev stormed out of the room leaving behind a cloud of doubt, disgust and dissent.

*****

Hansa sat in the recliner, mulling over her experiences. A new copy of Ruttie Jinnah's story rested on her belly, as she looked far away at the horizon. The sky meeting the earth was a virtual occurrence and yet, so real to the discerning eye. Just like her meeting with Alpha Tango. Rajeev had once again, shown his insensitivity and lack of rationale. Her pregnancy had yet again anchored itself in the middle of a brewing storm. Knowing Rajeev, it wouldn't settle without causing much damage. Her visit to the hospital had been emotionally charged because of Raj's absence and her father-in-law's presence. Mr. Walia had waited outside the room while the gynaecologist tried to conceal a grim expression as she conducting the sonography.

"Is everything well? You look a bit concerned."

"Hansa, I'm not going to beat about the bush. I'm sorry to say this but you have an ectopic pregnancy."

Another blow but this time it didn't hurt as much. Hansa wanted some time alone as the doctor explained the dangers of the condition to Mr. Walia. Flushing out the foetus was inevitable and unavoidable. She had been asked to take a few tests and adequate rest. An appointment was fixed for the next day and they had returned home without exchanging many words on the way.

Now, sitting by the window, Hansa found solace in Rattanbai's life. It was cold and she pulled her wrap tightly across her shoulders. The sound of a chopper distracted her. As it buzzed past at a distance from her window, she felt warmed by the thought of a man in a balaclava and aviators.

She didn't hear Rajeev come into the room. "How are you?"

She turned, a bit startled, and a tad red-faced at having been caught with thoughts of another man.

"Um, okay. I didn't expect you to be home."

"You went to the doctor with Pa?"

"Yes, he insisted to come along."

"I heard about the condition. I'm sorry," he held her hand and drew her close.

"Sorry about what? About my luck? Or about lost parenthood? Or about the fact that you didn't get to have your DNA verified?"

"Oh, Hansa! Can you please make this a little easy? This is not the only thing that I'm dealing with right now, y'know?"

"Yes, I know. We are all going through this together. The only difference is that your sails are always set in a direction away from reason. And you don't even care about the distance it creates; because your life and its decisions are only and always about you and not the people around you."

She didn't understand why she felt so bitter towards him now when he was trying to patch things up.

"Look! I don't know why you are over-reacting when I should be the one confronting you about those photographs and their appearance in the newspaper. There's Dad with a few skeletons tumbling out of his cupboard and before I can find a way out of that slush, you throw a mud-ball in my face. How do you think, can anyone think straight?"

"It's alright, Raj. I don't expect that of you anymore."

*****

Her appointment with the doctor was scheduled for the next morning. She woke up to find a note by the bedside.

"Off to Delhi to be with *Ma*. Take *Pa* with you to the doc."

Her heart turned itself into a knot and unwound itself. The creases had deepened. Languorously, she got dressed and readied herself for the laparoscopy. The drive to the hospital was quiet and uneventful, with her father-in-law holding her hand, as she looked out of the tinted window-glass, hiding her tears.

*****

The procedure did not take very long and she was wheeled out of the O.T. within a few hours. The surgery had gone through without any complications, under general anaesthesia. She opened her eyes in the recovery room after what had seemed like a lifetime. Zarine Nawaaz sat beside her.

"You're a very brave girl, darling." Srijee walked in with the surgeon.

“Ma'am, you've responded positively to the surgery. The foetus has been removed and you are in the safe zone.”

Hansa wanted to stop the tears from slipping out of the corners of her eyes. Zarine did that for her. The surgeon left after informing them about the private room where the patient was to stay for two days. Soon, she was wheeled into the room, with Zarine in attendance.

The nurses placed everything in order, turned on the TV set it on mute and left. Hansa asked, "Did Raj call?”

Zarine pursed her lips.

“He's a really lucky man to have you; and a fool of the lowest order, to not have valued you enough.”

“It doesn't matter.”

“So, tell me sweetie! How did you manage to spend so many hours inside that place and come out so calm and unshaken?”

“I guess, someone up there is watching over me. I felt protected all the time.”

“It must have been horrific to have witnessed that kind of disaster!”

“It was, and yet, I feel I've come out, a new person. There is something that has changed within me but I can't seem to put a finger on it. I may look calm but am shaken to my core. And then all this mess with photographs and all…the hours inside weren't really as ruthless as they seem now!”

A picture on screen caught her attention. Three MARCOS had been caught on camera during the last few hours of the encounter at Taj. Her eyes strained to identify the man with the strongest arms in the world. He was there. Her MARCO was there. She didn't know how she could tell him apart in the darkness, and among uniformly dressed men with uniform heights and stature. But she was sure, it was him. She watched him move as quietly as a spider; his movements akin to that of the arthropod. He touched his hand lightly to his head and flashed a finger. He looked as if he was preparing to enter the door further down the corridor. Once again he raised his hand to his head and flashed a finger. This time, Hansa understood that it was meant to be a signal.

Zarine was about to change the channel to avert Hansa's attention, but she stopped her. Her gaze stayed fixed on him. Suddenly the door opened. The spider fell to the floor and just as lightly, rolled to the side and plastered himself against the niche created by the door of another room. The terrorist leader eyed the length of the corridor suspiciously. In the darkness, the range of visibility was extremely short. He turned to go back in but then turned around again and rolled a tear-gas shell towards the area where the MARCO was standing against the door. Smoke started to fill up the area. He stood there without moving a muscle. His eyes started to fill up with water but he remained unflustered. The terrorist had expected a gasping, spluttering man to fall to the floor but none of that happened. So, he put his doubts at rest and walked back inside. As smoothly as before, her MARCO traced back his steps to the position where he was earlier and raised his hand one last time, before he turned and ran towards the other end of the corridor. The CCTV captured a blank corridor for some time before the terrorist leader came back outside. Before he could go back in, there was a round of fire from somewhere in the darkness. It kept the man engaged for nearly ten minutes. The footage at the bottom of the screen showed the time to be 21:57.

She wanted to meet him even more now.

"Where were you at this time?" Zarine got into her thoughts as she tried to read them.

"Inside that room, behind that door, where the terrorist stood," she replied, "He was the man who saved me. He put everything at stake to get me out safely."

"Well, at the risk of sounding insensitive, I'd say, he was only doing his job, honey!"

"No, I don't think so. His job was done when he rescued the entire group to safety and I was gone. I could have been just another number eliminated in the chaos. But he kept coming back for me. I have never seen so many people die like ants, getting crushed below one giant foot, for no reason at all."

Zarine sighed. "Yes, sometimes we don't know the reason why certain things happen. While we may not be able to understand why people die without a reason; we can surely understand the reason why we are allowed to live. Ma Cherie, there must be a reason why you have come out of this alive. You are yet to better something in this lifetime. Nobody can go before they've done their job. Like they say, "*coz Karma* is a bitch"."And she chuckled.

Hansa closed her eyes. Zarine's words almost always silenced her mental chatter and provided some gusto to her dying spirit.

"What if Pa decided to leave you and move on with his family life? Don't you ever feel scared of the void that it would leave in your life?"

"*Umm*, wary, yes! Scared, no! I have a very diabolical view of life. From the day we set foot in this world, we're actually slaves to the devil in exchange of material and non-material comforts. Things that we use or emotions that we exhaust are all rationed and we draw from a pre-determined quota. Some things are of a high value, some of less and a few others, indeterminate. The day our share of one consumable is over, we lose it and it is replaced by something else. People die and pass on and we learn to come to terms with it simply because we have to. So, if my quota of love from Srijann is exhausted and needs closure; then, so be it. I'll think of him fondly and his memories would warm up my heart on cold winter nights. Even though, I'd be acutely envious of Gargi. But she can't have what I had. She has to take from her own rations. And who says, there isn't love beyond love?"

Zarine looked at Hansa who seemed to be far, far away, in a somnambulant state.

"How about a nap, darling and I'll catch you when you've sorted the loose ends in your head?" Zarine had an uncanny ability to encroach upon one's space without disturbing anything. She looked at the TV screen for some time, and then switched it off. Hansa muttered something that sounded like 'fango'. Lightly, she picked up her bag and tip-toed her way out of the room.

*****

Later in the evening, her mother-in-law called. She didn't feel like answering the phone but did. It was Rajeev on the other end.

"How are you, babes?" "Still alive!"

"Angry?"

"Oh please, Raj. This sounds very childish now. Of course, I'm upset but that shouldn't bother you."

"Look, I'm sorry, I left so abruptly but I needed to clear my head and Ma needed me too. I was at ease because I knew *Pa* is there for you."

"Yes, he's there always, filling up your shoes, Raj. But the good news is that I don't miss your presence anymore." And she cut the call short.

She then made another call. The network played truant. Was it alright to do this or should she follow her heart? After many aborted attempts, she heard the phone ring at the other end.

"Hello!"

"Hi. It's me. I need your help. Where are you?"

*****

Ginny stood with folded hands, if a single hand held across the chest and hooked to the other arm is considered so. His head hung low, he mumbled an apology to Mr. Walia.

"The hyena that thinks it can hoodwink the lion and get away with fresh meat, is getting ready to become meat," boomed Mr. Walia's voice in his office. "You've axed your foot to check the edge of the blade, Ganpat."

"Srijee, please, please, please forgive me. Where will I go? I've been with Hansa madam for so many years now. I made a mistake, Sir. I will do anything you say but please don't throw me in!"

"I'm surprised you actually thought this was so easy and escapable. You thought you'd tell me that you saw Kuber giving Sheona a package and I'd believe you? One must never stretch their luck and imagination beyond their capability. Get going now. Your arrest warrant is out already."

"Sir, my family! Please, Sir!"

"Don't worry! I will look after your family the way I've looked after you all these years. Despite the fact that you've back- stabbed me! It's time you enjoyed the benefits of your vile act."

Ginny fell at his employer's feet. Srijann Walia walked out of his office.

*****

Two days later, Hansa arrived home with a heavy heart and a firm resolve. Without wasting any time, she went to meet her father-in-law. She saw him walk out of his office in a huff.

"Pa! I need to talk to you."

An intense conversation followed in the bungalow's study. It didn't go in any way that she had intended it to. However, by the end of it, her shoulders had lost their stoop and her breath felt lighter. Srijann Walia had refused to see eye to eye with his doting daughter-in-law. He had asked her to reevaluate her decision because it would put her on a path from where there would be no turning back and possibly a dead-end ahead. She didn't waver.

She needed to meet a few people immediately. Ruttie's biography lay on the small console by the bedside. She flipped through it and removed her Japanese, handcrafted bookmark in soft gold. Then opening page 132, she placed the bookmark between the leaves. She then picked up her lime-coloured highlighter, and with lime-flavoured feelings, marked the words:

S.S. Rajputana, Marseilles 5 October, 1928 "………

Darling I love you, I love you – and had I loved you just a little less, I might have remained with you only. After one has created a very beautiful blossom one does not drag it through the mire. The higher you set your ideal the lower it falls.

I have loved you my darling as it is given to few men to be loved. I only beseech you that the tragedy which commenced in love should also end with it.

………"

She hoped that Rajeev would read and understand it. That was the only parting gift she could leave for him. Eighty years is a very long time, indeed and yet, too short for lives to change. She then, walked out of the room for the last time, just like the Flower of Bombay.

Sixteen

The pain had started to surface now. He looked at the front page of the newspaper with Hansa and Kuber's story on it. It distracted him from the throbbing, burning sensations that were waxing and waning in his shoulder, thigh and hand. The picture carried such allure that he couldn't resist staring at it. To him, Kuber was merely an object. And then there was the pain. He kept the newspaper aside and looked at the fan whirling and its blades turning into a unified force, as they cut through the air. He wanted to keep looking at the picture and would have, had the nurse not entered the room rather boisterously, trying to enliven the air with her sterilised enthusiasm.

"So, my hero! Have you eaten your meal or do you like to eat bullets only?"

"Sister, your sexy voice can make a man, marooned on an island, want to run away from food and water."

"Ah! So you do accept that I'm the best thing to happen to this place. And to where would the marooned man run?"

"To you, of course, Lady Bond!"

The nurse gave off a hearty laughter and dismissed his raillery like a bad penny, quite unperturbed by its unbridled frequency. She wasn't much of a James Bond fan herself but took the allusion with a pinch of sugar and spice.

The doctor walked in soon after the nurse had performed the necessary drill.

"How're you doing, officer?" "Fighting fit, Sir! Ready for action!"

"Oh yes? Your enthusiasm is infectious but your ignorance is not."

The doctor propped up his leg in an inverted V. He then flashed a light at his wound. The light tunnelled through it and shone right through the thigh. The patient, however, remained unfazed.

"You still think you are ready for action? In that case, I could also show you the state of your shoulder."

"So then, for how long do you intend to keep a good man pinned down?"

"Till the time the good man behaves and stays good. After that, I'll have to knock him out."

The doctor left him as the nurse started to dress his wounds in fresh packaging. Admitted in the ICU of INHS Aswini, MARCO A.T. was recuperating under the best medical supervision of the Indian Navy. He had been brought in to the Command Hospital in Colaba in a critical state with severe blood loss, and infection that had begun to spread due to prolonged exposure of the wounds in the shoulder and thigh. While professionally, he had received many accolades for his heroic stint at the Taj; personally, he had suffered a severe setback as he had to be operated upon and was now bed-ridden for a minimum period of six weeks. Restraining someone like him to bed, for such duration, was equivalent to punishing him for his bravery. He had never been scared of death but a life of inactivity was his greatest nightmare.

He lay on bed planning how to spend his time, productively. In eight years of service with the most elite force of the Indian Navy, he had never ever wasted any time on dreamy-eyed raptures to the future or bleary-eyed dribbling of the past. He needed to keep his body and mind occupied at all times, and focussed on the present. But right now, that seemed particularly challenging as he tried to distract himself from the photograph in the newspaper. He was too much of a man to nurse silly crushes and sigh at moments gone by. He picked up his Sudoku puzzle book and started to write the numbers in the grid. It was too easy and thus, could not keep him engrossed for a long time. He looked at the clock. It was nearly 1700 hrs. The date was 2nd December 2008.

Birthdays didn't really matter to him or his kind. But this was one occasion when he couldn't help reminiscing about the ordeal that his mother had gone through thirty years ago, to deliver a premature baby with partial paralysis of the legs. The only thing he was thankful to God was for giving her a set of strong, nurturing hands. Thereafter, had begun a long andodious journey of challenges, in which solutions had posed even bigger challenges. However, his parents, both of who, were educationists of an intense nature, never let anything or anyone deter them from their one-point agendum in life; which was to be able to see Arjun stand up on his own two feet.

The path was long, arduous and often dark; with schools rejecting admission and the social infrastructure making his recovery least pliable. It was the unfailing belief of his mother and the persevering spirit of his father that had led to his miraculous recovery on his fifteenth birthday. His home-schooling had proven to be a better educational institution than any other in the country and he had earned a score in the matriculation examination that made his parents proud and the neighbourhood to sit up and take notice. Thereafter, he had not known defeat. From completing his graduation with distinction to completing his training as a sea cadet in the SCC at INS Jawahar, he had learnt to live with a do and never-say-die attitude. His single-minded focus on the task to be completed and hunger for perfection made him the blue-eyed boy in the training circuit. Today as he sat with his limbs propped up in bandages, he had yet again, proven his worthiness for the red badge on the sleeve of his uniform.

"Life is all about the right decisions taken in the right combinations," his father had always told him, "but without an emotional bias. A man who can manage that balance with finesse stands next to God." He had often wondered about people like Hitler, Gandhi and Lincoln, who created history with their extraordinary traits, whether positive or negative.

He looked at the book by his bedside. Blink by Malcolm Gladwell was his current favourite. He liked to read literature that helped him gain an insight to human psychology and thus, made him a better warrior in action. It was the third time he was reading this one.

"Hey! What's up, buddy?"

A trig-looking friend walked in.

"Are you alive? Leave app. dismissed?" Arjun asked.

"No and yes. How do you know? I just got out of the admin-office."

"Our bodies speak louder than our words, my friend. Anyway, I'm glad we'll have your painful company for Navy Day. Found a date, yet?"

"Finding a date is not a problem. It's the mate that's a headache. She has the potential to kill me over the phone."

And they both guffawed and then engaged themselves in a discussion about their next boot camp for new recruits. It was during their prattle that the colleague caught sight of the newspaper on the side-table.

"A bomb with a buddhu! It's amazing how a girl with such an innocent-looking face can make such a Charlie out of a super-stud like Kuber!" remarked the trig-looking colleague.

"You seem to know a lot about her."

"Who doesn't? She enjoyed his lavish attention for a good time but then the lure of the Walia surname was so strong that she decided to latch on to that bugger, Rajeev! I always thought he was quite a lucky dog till I read the Bombay supplement today!"

"What about it?"

"She's walked out on him. Nobody knows why. My guess would be she's found someone else. But who could be bigger and better than the Walias here?"

"Mate, you are ready to write a biographic epic on her. First, go and sort out your soul-mate who's going to eat you alive when she finds out you won't be home for the next two months."

"Oh, heckling harpoons! Gossip makes the road of life so much easier. At least it takes your mind off the bloody potholes."

Arjun didn't want to think about Hansa after his friend left, so he stashed away the newspaper inside the cabinet. Operation Tornado was over and it was all in a day's work, as always.

The Western Naval Command had sent instructions to tone down the scale of the Navy Day celebrations on 4th December. It was something that all young officers always looked forward to as not only was it a prestigious day for the Indian Navy but was also a highly sophisticated social event for singles to mingle. This year would be different as the fun and the frolic had been attenuated by the devastation caused in the city.

"It would be worthwhile to focus on the training programme to be organised in January," he told himself, "I hope I get out of this blooper by then!" It was only obvious then; for want of anything better to do; to float past the present and think of the days when he had arrived for the selection tests in the Indian Navy as a MARCO.

*****

The selection process to become an infallible Marine Commando had been a gruelling routine stretched over six weeks. It was his target to get through and he had not allowed any doubts to cross his mind even once. He cleared the aptitude tests and physical parameters without a hitch. This was followed by a strenuous one and a half-month routine that allowed them less than four hours of sleep per day. Six weeks went by like six hours and one batch of short listed brave-hearts stood before their trainer in black overalls.

"Boys, job well done!"

"Thank you, Sir!" The response came in orchestrated unison. "Time to take a break! Camp holiday for three days! Leaving at 0500 hours tomorrow! Destination unknown! Any questions?"

"Right, Sir! No, Sir!"

And they had come back to their dormitory as excited as schoolboys. It seemed like they had all made it to the mark. After a couple of hours of relaxed chatter that was earned in lieu of six weeks of a back-tweaking, sweat-breaking, mechanised routine, they all crashed out into a dreamless state to awaken to a quiet dawn, surreptiously creeping up on the darkness.

Nobody had dared to ask about the destination, and the air of mystery around it added to the adrenaline rush. Thirty two men in the age band of twenty-two to twenty-three years were on the high road to adventure. It had been five hours since they had started and the bus wound its way through a serpentine road in an ogre-like stretch of mountains. Intermittently, they caught glimpses of the sea peeping from behind the jagged peaks that gradually disappeared as they travelled along. The landscape was quite unfamiliar but soon became welcoming. In the month of September, the mountains in the Western Ghats are at their verdant best after a generous monsoon spell.

Their vehicle came to an abrupt halt and in a crackling second, there was a shattering sound, followed by smoke that started to eat up space inside the bus. All but one of the trainees remained seated, glued to his seat. The rest were flat on their bellies on the floor of the bus. Their trainer entered, looked around and summoned the lone passenger on the seat.

"You may alight and leave for home, cadet. There's a vehicle waiting for you outside. Any questions?"

No questions were raised and the bus proceeded on its course with thirty-five men.

It was late in the evening when they reached their destination. They filed out of the bus and tried to take stock of their surroundings. The only visible thing was a small bonfire which would last for a little over half-an-hour. Other than that, there was no visible sign of any habitable lodging.

The men were beginning to get an inkling of what they were up for.

"Ok boys. Now that you all have enjoyed a rather comfortable time in the bus; enjoying the lush landscape, I've reason to believe that you all are well-rested. It's time to go and get your dinner. We meet here again at 2100 hours." And he walked off. This time there was no prompt for questions. Clearly, they weren't meant to ask any.

For a few minutes, they all looked at each other.

"We've got to go and hunt our dinner, buggers!" Arjun cleared all doubt and suspicion which was beginning to fog their heads. "And we better find it before this fire burns out or we'll have to eat it in the 'still-mooing' state. Let's get going. Three of you, you stay put and ensure that this fire keeps going till we're back. There's no way to guess who we might have for company, so keep your gut-instinct ready. And remember, the place is new and dark. Avoid any fruit from the trees!"

He assembled the men in four teams. They pooled in their resources. There was a small collection of pocket-knives, a couple of pencil-torches and many able hands. In twenty minutes, the men had put together an assortment of a rabbit, two frogs, an owl and a snake. It was a quiet dinner around the bonfire, as five men refused to eat and the others tried their best to disguise their disgust. It was not long before, their instructor stood behind them, declaring the time.

"You need to become one with your surroundings, boys. Strongest are the ones who ride their circumstance. You, young men," he said, looking at the five hungry faces, "are not ready to ride yet. You may come with me. The others may call it a day. No more than two men together. Snooze well, boys! You have a long day ahead tomorrow."

Sleep crept up cautiously along the ageing timber of sal, *mahua* and bael trees.

*****

Next morning, the wake-up call was given by laughing thrushes, minivets, songbirds and warblers. Many others added to the synchronised orchestra in the backdrop. For the first time in his life, Arjun had experienced sleeping with dilated pupils. At least that's what it felt like. He awoke to the twitter of the birds and the sun drawing out long and lazy arms from the mountain folds. He, along with a team mate, had taken refuge in the thick canopy layer, at the risk of running into tree-frogs and consequently, tree snakes. However, it was better than having to deal with wild monkeys and eagles further up and jaguars and leopards in the under-storey. They had an arrangement such that one man slept and the other stayed up to guard.

Dewdrops had trickled down his ear and stirred his sleep. As he took a good look around, for a few minutes he was smitten by the thick layer of impregnable green all around him. His mate had decided to climb down. He now needed to get his bearings right. He crawled up the intricate network of branches and vines and reached the emergent layer, nearly hundred feet from the forest floor. The trees loomed large and magnificent and rose majestically into the skyline. His senses took in the richness of the air and he drank it all up greedily. In front of him lay a stretch of raw, pristine beauty that stretched for miles through ravines and gorges. His watch indicated that it was ten past five. The sun glistened off the precipitate on the leaves leading it to slow, unnoticed evaporation. After taking a photographic view of the lay of the land, he climbed down like a jaguar himself.

The rest of the team was getting together too, with some of the men dropping out of trees and a few others working out their muscles. Together, they spent nearly forty-five minutes, prepping their body and mind for what awaited them in the next twenty hours. Their instructor didn't keep them waiting for long. Nobody knew where he had slept. The sound of a four-wheel drive was heartening as it was likely to be carrying breakfast. The hungry men were not disappointed this time. The aroma of fresh bread, eggs and milk tickled their appetite.

"Good morning, my good men! Are you ready for a hearty meal?"

"Yes, Sir!" came the reply, loud and clear.

"Alright, fellows! The one, who burns it, earns it. About two kilometres N.E., the way the crow flies, is a waterfall. Get there, take a dip and get back here in two hours. One man today will lose his meal, if he doesn't lose his life on the way."

"Word of caution: think before you drink." "All understood?"

"Yes, Sir!"

"On your heels, and off you go."

The group set off without a grudge or a whimper.

"This way, guys!" Arjun had volunteered to lead. The day had started on an exciting note. However, the only thought that gripped each mind was—'who would be the one to lose the meal, and did that mean, going home?' It spurred them on and everyone was quiet for the first five minutes. There's nothing more frightening in a forest than silence hovering over one's back. It was a startling moment when someone disturbed the stillness.

"I say, buggers, did anyone remember to bring a mosquito repellent?"

"Oh sonny boy, maybe we should have asked for the area to be fogged before we stepped in!" someone replied.

"Damn, these suckers need flogging, not fogging!"

The trek, thereafter, was much easier. Witty one-liners were interspersed with the sound of fauna in the vicinity. There weren't many dry twigs, weeds or brambles in the undergrowth and yet there were things that crackled underfoot. They could not feel the heat but the increasing humidity in the air was suggestive of a fully-charged sun that day, and a water-body nearby.

Soon they reached a clearing in their path. It seemed like an open auditorium for the jungle inmates. Like all crossroads, the place offered several options. Arjun observed the ground carefully. Before he could turn and caution everyone about the size of the pugmarks, he was down on the ground as the roar of a tiger made everyone and everything; including the leaves that let the breeze whistle through them; come to a stunned halt.

After seconds, that seemed like minutes or maybe longer, Arjun raised his head a bit to peep through his hands. From the corner of his eye, he could see three of his buddies with their bellies flat on the ground. Others, he hoped were behind him. Before he could send out a bird-call to his group, he felt warm fuzz brushing against the nape of his neck. It stopped for a few seconds and then, started again! It was an animal exhaling down his neck, and he could safely assume that it was a tiger. A heavy paw thumped upon the body that lay motionless, trying to ascertain the freshness and flavour of the meat.

Any movement now would definitely be his last one.

A twig cracked in the shrubbery nearby; and the tiger looked askance and snorted in suspicion. Arjun could only see him from the corner of his left eye. He needed him to come around and face him in order to have a strategic advantage, if he had to fight the glorious animal. Another twig cracked and held the tiger's attention. Like a Ninja, Arjun used the power of his forearms to throw his body up in the air, performed a double flip and landed on his feet. He now stood in front of the tiger, face to face and eye to eye, with five feet of distance between them. By now, the tiger had taken offence and came towards its meal with a vicious snarl. It was not possible for Arjun to tackle this enemy with his physicality as it had a clear advantage. He needed to fight a tiger like a tiger. The tiger's leap covered a good six to eight feet, as Arjun rolled across to the other side from underneath the beast. One thing was now evident. The animal was past its prime. A young one with good vision would have made a precise leap and an instant kill. A pocket-knife came zipping through the air, somewhere from the bushes, and struck at the hind leg of the animal, causing a sensational roar that could have travelled a couple of kilometres. Enraged, the cat came charging at him once again. Arjun now needed a leap of faith. It was a do-and-never-say-die moment. The moment the cat retracted its hinds to jump, he leapt to one side, clutching and hanging on to the lowest branch of the nearest tree. The tiger missed its target once again and a heavy paw came crashing at his right calf. It provided the necessary impetus to the swing he intended, along with a stinging pain. Then like a trapeze artist, he somersaulted his way to a higher branch. The animal roared again and lashed at the trunk with its forelimbs off the ground. The tiger glared at its prey up on the tree, went around its circumference and decided to wait for it to climb down. It was easier to wait for this one than to chase another.

Arjun hung from the branch and made a few quick calculations for a way out. His companions were nowhere to be seen. The one who had aimed his pocket knife at the tiger was the bravest of them all and now, without any weapon on him, was probably keeping himself out of harm's way. Arjun needed to get out as fast as possible. The tiger was now getting restless. It would get up now and then, strut about the open space and mark its territory. Old age is capable of bringing a sense of insecurity to any species. It was now time for action. He needed to swing from one tree to another with the finesse of an arboreal dweller.

His luck ran out in the very first attempt. As he was on the upswing, the bough snapped and Arjun landed on the ground, with the tiger eyeing him rather villainously. Without wasting any time, it moved towards its prey and pounced upon him. His leap was precise this time. Man and beast grappled with each other for survival, as they rolled on the forest floor. The knife on the tiger's leg, fell out in the process causing it greater pain and thus, fuelling its fury. With Arjun pinned to the ground by one and a half quintal of muscle, the tiger found its moment and dug its incisors into his throat.

Simultaneously, a group of young men came charging towards the duo, with flaming torches in their hands. One of the guys was good at rubbing stones to light a fire and they had put together a bunch of bramble and boughs as soon as they had gotten over their stupor. Blinded by the light, the tiger lost focus as well as his control over its prospective meal and retracted. Without delay, Arjun grabbed the knife and flicked it into the tiger's belly, several times. The weapon was small and needed several jabs to put an end to the royal beast's agony and old age.

Nobody spoke a word for a minute as they tried to soak in the reality of the moment. The mesmerising life form of golden yellow coat with dark stripes and topaz eyes now lay lifeless on the ground. A king needed a farewell it deserves. They ripped off boughs and roots from the trees around them and decided to carry the old monarch back to the camp.

The party started for the waterfall once again. As the men trudged along, cutting through the undergrowth; the roots of the trees, hung from the branches, growing thicker and longer as they approached the water body. The tiger weighed anywhere between 125-150 kilos. The walk wouldn't have been so arduous had it not been for the extra baggage that they were carrying. Arjun limped ahead, keeping his mind focussed on the sense of directional alignment that he had put himself in at the break of dawn. Time and again, he would try and assess the alignment of shadows, of whatever little was made.

It took them a little over an hour before they heard the sound of gushing water. It was an open-sesame experience when they stepped through the tangles of vines and roots to witness one of the most stupendous sights that nature could foster.

Nestled in the womb of the forest was a nook that seemed to be the heavenly abode for flora and fauna alike. Frothy, milky water ran down from the top of a jagged cliff, creating many more along the way. It fell with child-like abandon on the pool of still water; that had grown old sitting there; dimpling its surface. In one pocket of the water-hole, a herd of *chital* was lapping up some water. As they saw the men emerge from the thicket, some of them unleashed themselves from the group and bounded off, only to stop and gaze back from a short distance further up, their ears twitching anxiously. The rest of them just stood transfixed at the sight of a tiger being carried upside down. On the other side, a parade of elephants was arriving at the hole and a host of little birds had started to gather to groom them. The water played noisily off the little rocks in the centre. Higher up, the moss and the lush foliage on the chiselled face of the mountain provided a shield against the direct rays of the sun. The refracted light, however, drove through the prismatic drops of water in suspended motion, thus creating numerous rainbows in the air.

The tired men were forced to overcome their awe at Arjun's call. He was leading them away from the water, further up into the jungle. One of the team members, who had been shouldering the heavy package, was too thirsty to pass fresh, drinking water by. He lay down by the edge of the pool, where little mouldy patches were floating on the surface. He removed his handkerchief and placed it on the mould. Clear water surfaced on the cloth. He cupped his hands to scoop the water, when the handkerchief rose up unexpectedly, with the rocky surface. At the same time, his legs were yanked back, several feet away from the edge. All men took cover in the thicket, bringing all movement to a halt. A crocodile senses even better than it sees. The reptile had probably not warmed its body enough to go chasing food in the first half of the day. It stayed submerged for a few seconds and then disappeared quietly underwater.

"Man, are you crazy? You've got to use a bit of common sense … going to get eaten up like that? Bugger, you'd have all those mad lizards chasing us through the forest! We've just barely got that jumbo—kitty off our behind. I'd rather eat shit than run around like a nut," the man flummoxed by mosquitoes hissed at his friend, who was now breathing heavily. Divine intervention made something whitish brown, squishy and warm land on the tip of his nose and lips.

Arjun shushed him and asked them to wait. After, the surface of the water had stopped stirring, he turned to address the little storm that was brewing up in the group, and said:

"My friend, you must not take this guy's loose remarks seriously. He's afflicted by a serious disorder, which even the doctors can't treat."

There was a sympathetic silence. Everyone looked at the mosquito-man, who was now wiping the bird-dropping off his lips.

"It's called the foot-in-mouth disorder, and he can't even 'poop' it wrong!"

Rancorous laughter pierced the air. The quietude of the place stretched itself to make room for alien sounds.

*****

Finally, the group got to drink some water at another stream that was meandering off the waterfall. Arjun had observed the rocks carefully in the watering hole and had drawn the right inferences. He had also noticed a part of the waterfall disappear behind the trees and thus, was sure that there was a safer place for a drink.

Soon, they started their trek back to the spot from where they had started, with the tiger still tucked safely between two men at all times.

"What if that croc' really got you dude? Imagine, right now you might have been floating in pieces somewhere there!" remarked one of the boys.

"Why? Wouldn't you have tried to save me, mate?"

"Are you nuts? I'd love to be a hero but there's a good difference between bravery and stupidity, man? How on earth do you think, anyone could have saved you in those croc-infested waters?"

"I would have and you may step out!" said a voice from behind them. It was their instructor and guide. Nobody had expected to see him.

"Yes, mate. Step out. You are not fit for this training yet."

"Sir, I'm sorry, Sir! This was just light-hearted banter, Sir. I didn't know you were around. Of course, I would have helped him out, Sir."

"You want to become a MARCO, sonny boy? Remember, heroism comes from a balance between word and action. And extraordinary heroism needs extraordinary balance. One outweighs the other, and you are nothing more than an infected machine. You, my boy, need to debug your system before you can think of being a MARCO. Step out. Your vehicle is waiting."

In the middle of the forest, another one of the team-mates had been disqualified for training. The mood was now sombre and each brain was cautious and alert over the use and abuse of words. The camping holiday was actually an elimination process. The chaff had already been sifted from the grain. This process was to determine the quality of the produce. The steps became quicker and the group reached the starting-point, sooner than they had expected. The number was now down to twenty-five and was expected to go down even further. Over the next two days, the trainees-to-be were given tasks of varying difficulty to assess individual strengths and weaknesses and their application in solitary and team situations. By the end of the third day, the number of trainees had trickled down to eight. They were now ready to go back and start their formal training as MARCOS.

*****

The Naval Special Warfare Tactical Training Centre, located near Mumbai, was an institute on which Arjun Tandon had his sight set ever since he had heard about it as a teenager. His basic training at INS Abhimanyu, followed by specialised knowledge of handling advanced weapons of warfare, chalked out a life for him that he had aspired for from a tender age. Travelling to the cities of Sirsawa, Agra and Cochin, the basic skills of paragliding, deep-sea diving, techniques in ninja-combat and martial arts came naturally and flawlessly to him as he had involved himself avidly in physical training and adaptation as well as meditative mind-control since the age of twelve. The first six months of acquiring the basic expertise of a general duty-combatant was therefore less stringent for him as compared to the rest. As expected, he scaled all benchmarks, exceeding expectation. Certain specialised skills like sky-diving and operating submersible crafts always set his pulse racing. The highest form of dare-deviltry came when they were taken for free-fall training. While each man had made futile efforts to disguise his fear, their body language had given them away. He had kept his pulse under control and therefore, had jumped without any thought in his head.

A thoughtless mind is the most powerful agent of cosmic design, that makes the impossible possible. Consequently, he was among the minimal few who were chosen to learn to operate the COSMOS CE-2F/X100 two-man submarines. Cocooned in a streamlined tube-like vehicle and submerging to a depth of hundred metres, with air-supply that would last only four hours, was a feat he had never consciously planned to achieve. That was yet another commendable milestone that he had crossed and felt that he had been compensated well for the absence of a normal childhood.

His performance was also spurred by the keen desire to become a part of the Prahari Bal and get involved in anti- terrorist operations. An investment of two years made him feel like the richest man in the world; a man with mind, body and spirit functioning cohesively at the optimum human capacity. All in all, it was the life that Arjun Tandon had always dreamed of and lived for. There was nothing now that could take away the MARCO in him.

*****

Each day spent in the hospital was causing him more pain than the bullets in his body; and the inactivity was making it very difficult to keep his mind off that beautiful face that had looked at him with the most incomprehensible expressions fleeting across it. There's no training module in the world; not even the Intelligence gathering, insertion methods and communication skills taught to the most elite forces; that can equip a man to read the multi-hued messages off the eyes of a woman. For centuries it has remained a mystery and for all to come, it shall probably remain so.

He opened the cabinet to bring out the previous day's newspaper that he had stashed away. His hand met empty, cold metal. It was not possible for him to move with the machinery propped up around him. He rang the bell for the attendant. The nurse walked in.

“Sister, I'd kept a newspaper here. Could you bring it back for me please?”

"Sure. What date was it?"

"Umm, not sure about that! It had…." He paused to think and said, "…never mind. You may go."

He hadn't wanted to reveal his thoughts to anyone, and especially not to the hospital staff. "You need the one for 30th, is it?"

Arjun looked at her, trying to read her intent behind being inquisitive.

"Oh c'mon man, you've been staring at Ms. Hansa Noorie's photograph all day yesterday. You think I didn't notice. Too shy to admit it, hanh? Don't worry, I'll get it for you but you will have to take me out on a date as a reward for the effort."

"I'd rather die of gun-shots than take you out," is what Arjun had wanted to say. Instead he said, "I'd take a charmer like you out anyway, with or without the newspaper." His response was in sync with his training in social behaviour. An officer is not an officer if he's not a gentleman first.

The newspaper arrived with the ward-boy. Arjun opened it eagerly and removed the city supplement. There she was, kissing another man and yet, he wanted to look closely.

In a blink, as Malcolm Gladwell puts it, there was a come-and-go of thoughts and inferences were drawn which suggested that something in that photograph was out of place.

*****

Day after day, the gossip columns doled out morsels of Hansa's personal life, even though the size of the columns kept diminishing each day. The last bit that he read about her said that she had moved into her lover's apartment in Bandra. Her husband's family was not available for comment and Rajeev had gone ahead to say that nothing was wrong between them and that she was simply spending some time in her maternal home.

Arjun had never followed Bollywood news so closely, ever in his life. This was his first brush with the world of glamour and he was already feeling a bit enchanted. He had forbidden everyone from informing his parents of his state. They did not deserve any more stress in their lives than they had already endured for him. The doctors had shushed him over his requests for an early release.

"You are lucky that your wounds didn't develop gangrene. Probably because of your aseptic life-style, your body coped well. But if you disturb anything now, you'll be in big trouble, son! Immunity is down to such a state and you can't take chances," he'd said.

His friend visited him everyday and made lively conversation. One day, while taking out a tetra-pack of juice from the cabinet, he asked:

"Hey, what's with these Bombay-News editions lined up here, buddy? You seemed to have fallen prey to the gossip-mongers!"

"Just curious, bugger!"

"Since when did curiosity start getting the better of you?" "Ever since I rescued a Greek goddess from the devil!"

"What? You mean, seriously? She was the one who kept you hanging about that place? C'mon man, don't tell me! You lucky son-of-a-gun! Now, now, there goes another good ship down the surface!"

"You wouldn't say this had you been there. She was more than just a pretty face. I mean, with cheeks smeared with soot, with some random, bloody outfit on her and light leaving her eyes, just how dazzling could she look? And yet, each time she looked at me with those transparent eyes, something within me stirred. I've never felt like this before. There was something so child-like, so angelic about her!"

"So the country's best combatant has been captured. And thus, he lays down his heart in the line of duty."

"Shut up, bugger!"

And they laughed and chatted till the visiting hours were over.

*****

Night arrived with a bit of flutter. A whacky journalist had discovered that MARCO Arjun Tandon was admitted in the room. He had somehow managed to worm his way through the corridors and past the many reception desks and doors. Night staff on duty had apprehended him and now there was some commotion in the corridor outside his room. He hated not being able to command the situation. It was a security risk for a nosey reporter to have discovered his room without being intercepted and to have made it this far without being noticed. It usually wasn't that easy for the Press to reach out to the world of MARCOS. Something was not in place and he sensed something augural in the air.

After the commotion died down, the attendants came in. "Sir, we have orders to move you to another room."

"I need to speak with the medical officer on duty." "Sure, Sir. He'll meet you in your new room."

"I need to speak to the doctor, NOW!"

"Very well, Sir. I'll send a message right away."

The doctor didn't take too long to arrive. He looked prepared with his answers.

"Doctor, what is the current status of my health? When do I get to join duty again?"

"Son, the news is to be broken to you officially."

"I have the right to know the status of my health, doctor. I need to know right now!"

The doctor paused for a few seconds and then continued in the same tone, "I don't know about the official status but as a doctor I can say that parts of your limbs have been damaged beyond repair. While you are lucky to still have them in use, any strenuous activity may be detrimental to your health. I'm afraid you may not be medically fit to continue your work as a MARCO any longer."

His world came crashing down. Not in his wildest dreams had he contemplated being in a state akin to his childhood, ever again. It may be rare but combatants do get injured in the line of duty and rejoin their Prahari Bal post-recovery. He had a sense of foreboding when he realised that security to his whereabouts had been eased and access compromised. He wanted to break free and run to the officer who he reported to. But at this point, it was important to control his pulse as well as his impulse. He breathed in heavily as his mind jostled against the problem and started scrabbling away at plausible solutions. It was not possible to take away the MARCO from within him.

Seventeen

Hansa sat in the living room of her mother's apartment. The walls were still of the same colour as she had left them. The moisture and the emptiness had failed to take away the cheer from the sunflowers on it. She hadn't wanted to reorganise anything. It would be nice to go back to the way things were four years back. The most refreshing change sometimes comes from the tasks that one has been performing day-in and day-out without making a routine out of it. She took out a duster and started to wipe everything clean. From vases to Turkish lamps, from brass urns to candelabra; she wanted to collect every speck of dust. It had to be shiny and glossy once again, just like it used to be when her mother was alive. Then on second thoughts, she left it like it was. She really didn't want it shiny and glossy anymore. She had not put up Noorie's photograph on the wall. It hadn't seemed to be a befitting place for her. Instead, she had her name engraved on a piece of raw wood and hung it on the birdhouse that her mother had lovingly put up in the small terrace-garden of her apartment. She felt at peace watching the birds visit the little wooden box and peck at the grains.

The following morning she woke up in her mother's bed to a whiff of a feathery stroke in her hair. It was not startling at all; in fact it was mildly pleasing. She opened her eyes and found a little sparrow chirping and twittering in her room. It had flown in from the window to the terrace garden that she had left ajar for the morning sea-breeze to drift in. She kept lying in bed, noticing the bird hop from object to object, memory to memory. It was trying to speak to her. She wasn't sure what the short twitters meant but she felt happy and free and a sense of belonging enveloped her. The feeling was short-lived. Rajeev had a way to shroud her feelings and give them a different form.

His name flashed on her phone. Today, she had the courage to make him wait. She picked up her diary and started to scribble in it:

"Today,

The morning is different from night, There is light,

As a sun becomes the Sun, And the dove's flight

Has wings of courage

Today,

the breeze

seeks an identity

stronger than the wind

a name more memorable a life more forceful

a turn, more eventful and is thus,

softer, lighter, gentler…

trying to be surreal, by being… just real…"

She had wanted to continue but the phone's beep distracted her again. It was a message from Rajeev.

"Come back home. Can't go on without you!"

She read what she had written, once again. Then looking at the message one last time, she deleted it before following the twittering guest to the terrace. The bird-house had already welcomed its new occupant.

*****

It was a good thing not to have a newspaper in the house. It can make a perfectly glorious morning appear menacing and dreadful. She had spent nearly two hours on the terrace, soaking in the ambience and tending to the potted plants in the little garden. There were quite a few flowers that were blooming; the pretty ones with thorns, the dainty ones with their nettle-like stems, a few with leaves that draped them completely and a few others, totally wild and unabashed and growing in clusters. She had so many such people in her life. There was no room for weeds; the plants occupied all the space, with their thorns and nettle and mystery and myrtle.

She needed a cup of coffee to invigorate her senses. As she turned to go inside, a tray of coffee sailed into the room; and the person carrying it was none other than her husband. It was his usual style to breeze in unexpectedly and turn the winds in his favour; but despite the old habit, she was startled and for a moment, her sense of cheer and belonging, left her. She felt the equanimity of the place being skewed by Rajeev's presence.

"What are you doing here, Raj? I'm not coming home with you!"

"Oh c'mon, babes! You can't be serious. A small lover's tiff and you leave home and come here? What am I going to do without you? Go on and grab your bag. Let's take a little break and fly off to somewhere. Just like old times!"

"No, Raj. I am serious about what I want this time and I'm not going anywhere with you. Nothing is like old times any more and it never will be. So, save your breath for something more productive."

"Oh well! I see two problems there. One, it's going to be incredibly difficult to hold my breath and have an argument with you and two, what could be more productive than winning an argument which I already know I'm going to win, breath or no breath!"

"Shut up Rajeev. Your sense of humour needs a health-plan, seriously!"

"Hansa, nobody tells Rajeev Walia to shut up. Stop acting so stiff now. You've already got more attention than you need. You needn't take it to this level. Let's go home and sort out the issues that you have!"

"Raj, while you may sort out the issues in your head, you will never be able to sort out the knots that have tightened slowly because of your insensitivity. Each time I needed you to understand my grief, my joy, my fears, you fastened a knot. You may sort everything and put it all in labelled compartments in your head but you will never be able to undo anything!"

"Listen, is this about your..."

"I've stepped away from the plane of discussion, Raj!"

Hansa walked away from him and opened the door for him to leave.

*****

It was later in the afternoon that she received a message: "Have dinner with me tonight. Meet you at M at 8:00 pm."

*****

It took her some time to decide if she really wanted to accept the invitation. After investing an entire day mulling over the conversation that might take place; she decided to get dressed. The little black dress always worked for all moods and occasions. Teaming it with a cashmere wrap, she stepped out for the first time in days.

She reached the hotel fifteen minutes later than she was expected. The delay was neither deliberate nor was there any concerted effort to avoid it. Lack of precision and perfection, didn't ruffle her up so much any more. Passivity made life so much more bearable.

Not many heads turned this time, as she walked past the reception lounge and through the hotel lobby. It was not so difficult to spot him. Handsome as handsome can be, with the fine trimmings of a life well-lived. Lounging by the pool-side, he had a drink and Zarine for company. Even though she had not expected to see the diva, she was not too surprised to see her with her father-in-law even if it was meant to be a private, family discussion. She had actually expected to and hoped not to see Gargi there. She would feel awkward discussing Rajeev with his mother.

The greetings were polite, cordial and in keeping with social protocol.

A round of drinks was ordered. "Finished shooting for Ruttie?"

"Yes, some dubbing work is pending. I think I should be able to wind it up in a couple of weeks."

"And when does the next project start?" "Not in the near future."

"But you had three projects lined up after Ruttiebai!" "I'm done, Pa. I don't belong here anymore."

"Hansa, I've never seen you behave so feebly. Don't you think you sounded like a pathetic destitute right now? I'd appreciate if you took your words back. The Walia name is still alive and you are very much a part of it."

"Pa, I'm sorry. That's not what I meant. I feel I don't belong to the world of glitz and glamour anymore. It's all beautiful and glossy on the outside, but you scrabble under the skin a bit, and all you find is molten lead, ready to consume everything that settles on it. For the first time today, I felt free. Free from all commitment and thus, free from all fear. I liked it and I think I'm going to keep it that way."

"Ah, the first sign of disillusionment and you turn your back to all the beautiful gems you picked up on the way. What makes you think that any other sphere of life is not going to offer you similar challenges? There will always be a Kuber lurking around the corner to get you!"

"Papa, it's not Kuber that I'm running from. Not even Rajeev. I simply want to touch base with myself. I don't even know who I am anymore."

Zarine had been listening patiently all along.

"My darling, that's a very brave step you're taking ahead. I'm not going to judge you on this one. You only get one chance to live so you might as well do it your way. However, do make sure that in the process of finding yourself, you don't end up losing those who love you the most."

"Ms. Nawaaz, did you think of all of this when you took some important decisions of your life?"

"Hansa, this conversation is not about her," Mr. Walia quipped.

"Wait Jaan," interrupted Zarine, "I think I can answer that."

Then turning to Hansa she said, "Sweetheart, if you are keeping me as the benchmark and marching ahead, you're on the wrong road. You'll never get to your destination because you haven't planned your own trip. Besides, when I set out, I was led by the heart, towards the happiness I desired. You are being led away from it!"

“Pa, I'm sure you all have formed your own perspective for whatever is happening. All I know is that I don't want to pretend anymore. I don't want to pretend to smile when I'm sad, I don't want to pretend to be a happy wife when I'm not, I don't want to pretend to look good when I'm not feeling it, or pretend to be anybody else, on-screen or off it. I just want to be me; and I want to believe that it's alright to be me.”

“Can you hear yourself, Hansa?” said Mr. Walia, “In trying to sound unpretentious, you sound like an emotionally charged on-screen character. Life doesn't fit into a 70 mm frame, my girl!”

“Perhaps! And that's the reason why, I don't want to live in the quagmire anymore. The sooner I start to shed the garb, the faster I shall find myself.”

“But Hansa,” Zarine said, "this road can get pretty solitary ahead.”

“But who knows how far ahead one will go, Ms. Nawaaz?”

Mr. Walia added, "I can understand you wanting to give up your career but wanting to give up on Rajeev is inexplicable. Every couple goes through the doldrums. You just can't bolt out of a relationship like this! ”

“Pa, you should be the last one I should have to explain the biddings of the heart to, and the first one to make room for it.”

“Look Hansa, I've taken you more as a daughter than a daughter-in-law. And in doing so, I think, it's my responsibility to tell you that what you're doing is not the right thing by any perspective. Problems don't get solved if you run away from them. Confrontation is the only way to get them out of your way. But if your intent is the run-a-gate, then there's no point having a discussion at all. Let's just enjoy our dinner and allow the evening to roll on melodiously.”

Hansa remained quiet and looked far away towards the sea where a yacht named Hansa sailed towards an imaginary horizon.

*****

A week had gone by since he had been admitted to the hospital. Six days had gone by dealing with boredom and fanciful thoughts but the seventh day had served an incapacitating blow to his morale. He had requested for a special meeting with his senior officer, who had told him in non-condescending terms that he had performed his duties well and would be recommended for recognition. However, his term with the Combat Force would have to come to an end due to physical parameters having been compromised. However, he was being considered for an administrative position in the Indian Navy, which would be well-suited to his qualification.

Meditation came to his rescue again as he closed his eyes and focussed on the seven centres of energy, the *chakras*, in his body. The restlessness, he believed, was due to something blocking the flow of natural thought. He carried his consciousness to his breathing and followed its course through his body. He remained in a tranquil state till the path of his breath reached his wounded thigh and the throbbing came back. He started all over again, breaking his journey at the sites of injury. It was in his sixth attempt that he reached the sixth circle of energy placed between the eyes when her face appeared like a mirage in a mystic's bowl of altruistic water. It wavered, beckoned and slowly faded away into ripples.

He opened his eyes to meet the nurse's.

“Hey gorgeous, bring me a phone, will you?”

“You keep asking for favours, handsome, without ever returning them. How do you intend to make up for all the good I'm doing you?”

“Oh come now! What good is a bed-ridden man to you? Get me up and about, and see what a roller-coaster ride I can take you on!”

“Hah! Take me for a ride, you will, you sexy apple! You'll get your phone and I'll hold you to your promise!”

Despite the freckled skin and buck-teeth, her presence was always pleasing and made the stay in the hospital, less of a torment. She kept her promise and brought him what he desired. Thinking of the mesmerizing face, he dialled his mother's number.

*****

With lilting bamboo flute music cutting across the sombre mood, Hansa poured some fine red wine into two glasses. As they clanked the crystal and settled down in the terrace garden, Hansa and Zarine felt the atmosphere weaving a connection between them. After dinner they had decided to stop by at Hansa's apartment for some light banter, while Srijann left for home.

The music flowed in concentric circles of penetrating silence. After a few sips of the velvety wine, the sky; that had initially looked down upon them with a dark, furrowed gaze; now appeared iridescent.

"So, if not the movies, then what?"

"Umm, haven't thought about it. I guess nothing for a while. Perhaps do things that I love to do?"

"Which is?"

"Forgotten facts! That's what I need to discover now!"

"But why give up on your marriage for that? You can still do all of that."

"Zarine, when I came back to this house, I tried to do everything to take it back by four years. But even in standing still and gathering dust, these objects had moved ahead in time and space. They can never go back to being what they were in the past. The sixty hours that I spent in Taj, were like a bridge that took me to another level in time and space. It's not possible to come back, even if I tried."

"Hansa, I can understand the pain but I can't understand the decision. The Taj experience is something that can make a better person of you but you need not carry it on your back for the rest of your life. Archive it and move on."

"No, I don't want to archive it. For the first time in my life, I felt my existence. I want to hold on to it and use it as a compass to guide me through each living moment. I could have been one among the many dead. But I was given to live. And I shall."

The glasses clinked again and the conversation continued through the night.

In a few hours, erubescent light peeped through the crack of dawn. The conversation was still on.

"…despite the hostile environment, and without even touching me, he anchored himself into my being. I have never prayed to Divinity but he certainly seemed like an answered prayer. He made me want to live. I owe my existence to that moment of realisation, and perhaps in some immoral way, to him."

Zarine noticed the faraway look in her eyes. She put her hand over hers and silently expressed that she understood that feeling.

"So, do you plan to meet him? And how? I guess it's not too easy to hunt down a MARCO."

"I don't know yet. I certainly want to see him. I don't know his name or what he looks like; yet, I know for sure that I'll recognise him in a blink if I see him anywhere. And I also know that whoever or whatever has sent him into my life, will lead me to him too."

Zarine smiled. She was beginning to see traces of herself in Hansa's personality. No wonder she had been drawn to her by some invisible cord, since the first time she had met her.

"Darling, I love people who pursue love without doubt, condition or the fear of loss. They are the most beautiful masterpieces of nature. And at the risk of stirring a hornet's nest; by which I mean my handsome beau Srijann Walia; I am going to help you get across to your knight-in-shining-armour, or shall we say knight-in-shining-amour!"

And sweet, love-struck giggles trickled into the glasses, making the dawn a wee-bit brighter and the air, a wee-bit headier.

*****

Ginny had been let out on bail. Hansa's lawyers had made him sign a few papers after explaining her terms of re-employment to him. He had signed eagerly, happily and unconditionally. He wasn't sure if it was the Walia clan or Hansa alone who had bailed him out; but whoever it was, was certainly at the receiving end of his plans that had gone through a gestation period while in the lock-up. He needed to meet a few people urgently. The first amongst them was Sheona, followed by *Baaboo bhai*. He fixed a couple of meetings before he started for Hansa's apartment. He had kept himself updated on all the developments in the Walia household.

In a couple of hours, he stood before Hansa with his only hand across his chest.

"Ginny, I'm not going to ask you why you did this. But what I do want to know is that what made you wait for so long to sell those photos?"

"Madam, I have no words to tell you how ashamed I…" "Cut the crap, Ginny. Give me the facts!"

"Ma'am there is a lot more to this story than you know." "Such as?"

"Such as, the fact that it was Kuber who shot your mother on the yacht that night."

"What? And you knew this all these years? And, why my mother?"

"Yes, Ma'am. He was drunk and had sailed in on his boat, close to where you were celebrating. I came to know from his secretary later that he was actually gunning for Rajeev and not your mother. But he was so sloshed that his target was way off the mark. I was with a photographer friend who was checking out a new camera that he had bought that day. It was Kuber's bad luck that his act got caught in a few convincing frames on our camera. Not too professional but a lot of damage could be done with that evidence."

"So, you blackmailed him?"

"That's just one side of the picture. Even though, I was tempted to draw some hard cash out of him; there was always something within me that kept me concerned about your well-being. And that's the reason why my blackmail demand to Kuber was, to not to release those photographs to the press, of which he had several copies. Till the time I had evidence against him, your reputation was safe."

"But the photos did get released and his didn't; and he is still out there, safe and free!"

"Ma'am, the photos were what kept him away from you for two years. He did make a few offers to me but I kept drifting from plan to plan. Then on the morning of 26th, I learnt that Kuber was going to meet you that evening and confess to his act. I even saw him at the Taj. I don't know what was going through his head but I felt insecure and in a way, outsmarted. Other than taking away my winning spot, he would probably destroy me in every conceivable way. It was one petty moment in which my fear and greed overpowered me completely and without much thought, I made a very lucrative deal with Sheona. I thought if your photos appeared first, the obvious suspect would be him and that would take away the factor of sympathy that he was trying to gain by confessing. But believe me Madam; I have regretted it for every moment that has followed."

"It's okay, Ginny. I have forgiven you. I guess it was your right hand that you received that money in."

*****

Hansa instructed Ginny to perform a few tasks that needed immediate attention. After he left, Zarine walked in talking to Hansa as she stepped out of the adjoining room, fresh as a breeze.

"This must be really overwhelming for you!"

"It's strange how truth unfolds on several planes. At this point, I'm unable to decide as to who is the greater criminal in my life, Kuber, Ginny or Rajeev. And much that I believe that every wrong must be brought to justice; I don't feel vindictive at all. I feel sorry for them. I think I'm going crazy. This is not normal behaviour. I should go visit a psychiatrist or perhaps go off to a holistic wellness centre for a few days," Hansa sounded as if she was thinking aloud, beady-eyed and oblivious of Zarine's presence in the room.

"My dear, it's alright; and it's alright to be feeling the way you do right now. All you need is some tender, loving care and rich, dark chocolate with strawberries and cream."

Hansa received a hug. It was warm and comforting; and it made the beads roll down without making much noise. The rich, dark chocolate with strawberries and cream tasted unusually delicious, as they watched, on an old television, Laurel and Hardy going through thick and thin together.

Eighteen

Her mind was made and the path had been chosen. She needed to set out for a new destination. She wasn't sure if she would get there but the journey was something she was looking forward to with hope and determination. She was surprised when, in retrospect, she observed that she had never really concerned herself with the lives of so many 'twitter' followers that she had. And it was also very amusing to note that every insignificant post by her, almost always drew out prompt, inane and equally insignificant retweets by many people. The world was better-connected by meaningless involvement and less by purposeful critique.

Hansa looked at the screen and decided to post. It could have irrevocably damaging repercussions but for once, she wanted to immerse herself in the emotion of the moment.

Leaving my world behind to find another.

It was less than three minutes when someone retweeted.

Are you leaving us? Please don't go; Oh, we love you so.

And another,

We'll follow you wherever you go, Mary.

And within the next half an hour, the screen-page was inundated by comments, pleas, questions and philosophies.

Where? Why? How?

Call the world and it'll come to you.

You're the goddess.

Why did you build it if you had to leave it behind?

Leaving the known for the unknown, are you?

There are so many wanting to fill the void you'll create. Don't undervalue what you have!

She got tired reading and mulling over them after the first few. Among the first two dozen, she hadn't come across even one that encouraged her to be foot-loose and fancy-free. Each 'tweet' configured a perspective into a previous statement but no one thought afresh. While doubt looked for lodging in the inner recesses, belief jostled against it for occupancy.

She called Ginny.

"Ask Sheona to get in touch with me ASAP. Or rather, don't. Just try and find out if she has access to the list of NSG Commandos and MARCOS that were present at Taj during the rescue operations. She shouldn't know that I've asked for this information."

"Ok Ma'am. I'll give it a shot. But really, it is practically impossible to get her to even share her exhaled breath without a price."

"Ginny, when will you give up your old ways?"

"As soon as I can find a new one that works", and he tried to chuckle but Hansa's glare nearly reduced it to a splutter.

*****

Ginny, in his effort to appease his generous employer, procured the list sooner than expected. However, while it carried the names of the NSG guards, the only name that the MARCOS' list had was that of the commando who had lost his life in the line of duty. It was disappointing but she was prepared for them. Besides, she had afterthoughts about the authenticity of information dispersed by Sheona.

There were a very few people who she knew outside the film industry. It was now, that she realised that despite the stature of the profession she was in, her existence was still that of a frog in a well. There were three friends whose fathers held senior positions in the Indian Navy. But it did not seem to be the right route to take either. Friends may have helped, had the reason been more palatable. Besides, it was an underlined fact that any official of the Indian Navy would not make the identity of a MARCO, accessible to a civilian. Despite initial refusals by the naval authorities, she did not give up trying every possible route to her desired destination. She prepared a list of her contacts in the Indian Navy as well as the army and started to call them all one by one.

She knew that it would not be a difficult task for her father-in-law to procure the names but she felt apprehensive calling him. If she knew him well, he would ask her to return home in lieu of fulfilling her request, without any questions asked. The only person who could coax and pursue him to do the needful was Zarine Nawaaz. She was treading the fine line between relationships. She wondered if she would be labelled manipulative and selfish if she tried that route. It didn't take her more than a minute to decide that any step towards her destination was worth the adjectives she would garner along the way.

*****

She looked at her wrists. There were tell-tale marks and the red was changing colour. She ran her fingers over it. It did not hurt any more and yet, there was residual pain. She remembered Simone's face distinctly. But every shudder that accompanied the thought of 26/11 was tailed by a strangely delicate feeling of warmth. She tried to shoo it away while trying to convince herself that it was nothing more than a dubious moment's playfulness. But the feeling lingered, rather shamelessly.

Each day that passed made the urge to meet him stronger. Days were spent in completing the dubbing for her movie. The promos for Ruttiebai were gaining visibility in the city. Luck has strange plans for a chosen few. The photographs, that were intended to smear the Walia clan's reputation and tear Ruttiebai's business to shreds, helped to build an air of intrigue around Hansa's forthcoming film, thus making her even more popular among her fans. Parallels were being drawn around Hansa and the Flower of Bombay which led to a build-up of mystique and mysticism around their respective lives. People in the business of crystal-gazing and past-life regression found this to be an opportunity to further their profits, as people started to fall for the marketing campaign that her PR agency had floated. For once, critics packed their scepticism and belted out positive reviews for the film. The teaser-trailers had done their job well and were being received kindly by the cine-awards jury.

Amidst all the attention and public glare, it was becoming increasingly difficult for Hansa to proceed with her desire and intent to find her MARCO. Phone-calls were not roping in the desired result and none of her attempts had taken her any closer to him. Even though, she cared little about the outcome of the film, she felt responsible and committed towards the investors' money. Her public appearances and statements had to be carefully designed and meticulously delivered. In such a scenario, it seemed impossible to make a public declaration to reach out to the man she wanted to meet. Her efforts were forced to be clandestine and low-profile. Ginny had started to become nosey about her interest in the MARCOS list and he had his way of putting two and two together. He had been at his inquisitive best when she asked him to get her an appointment at the office of the Western Naval Command.

She wasn't sure if he asked a gazillion questions for the purpose of application or personal interest. Old habits die hard and for Ginny, he was sure to call it a day before the habits did.

"Ginny, prepare the application. I will go personally to Naval

Office in Colaba to present my request."

"Hansa madam, if you only let me know the nature of this urgency; I will be able to draft the letter accordingly."

"Ganpat, why can't you just focus on the amount of information fed to you? Just let them know that I am a relative of one of the victims of the Taj tragedy and am fulfilling a wish of the deceased."

"But madam, we have already tried that route and it hasn't worked. I can work out a plan if I know who it is you want to meet and why? Besides, if you go there yourself, people will recognise you and any kind of gossip and wild speculation will affect the business of your film!" "Ginny, you are not being of much use. You were better off behind bars."

*****

The hype around her movie was building up. A promotional event brought her on the same stage with Zarine. Pleasantries were exchanged and the ladies decided to meet later over a cup of coffee.

"I have news for you, honey!"

Hansa looked at her with excited hope.

"Your father-in-law has come to know that you are trying to get access to the Naval Warfare College. Don't ask me how, it wasn't me."

"So?"

"So, he has pulled out a list of the names that were deployed in the rescue operation that night."

"There has to be a reason why he did it and yet another reason why he has told you all this."

"Yes; and the reason is your greatest apprehension. He'll give you the list and access to the person you want to meet, if you come back home to Rajeev."

"This is weird. Pa stills wants me to be with his son, when he knows I'm thinking of someone else!"

"Well, while he is aware of your intent to meet your saviour, he is obviously not aware of your feelings. Love can be complicated. It's your love for your MARCO that's taking you away from a loving family and it is Srijann's love for his son that is drawing him to you. We're all on a very fine balance in life and no matter which way the scales tip, it is love that wins!"

Zarine looked at her intently as Hansa stirred her coffee over and over again.

"I'm going to visit a senior faculty member at Kiranje. Let's see if I get lucky."

"I admire your courage and initiative, Hansa but if you were to take some free advice from me, I'd say, there's no harm in taking Srijann's help in this. You can explain your case to him later."

"Are you suggesting that I take advantage of his Pa's concern for his family and cheat on him to get my work done?"

"No, all I'm saying is that when you've set your mind to achieve something, you must leave no stone unturned to find it. In desperate situations, good and bad are merely perceptions."

*****

The next day Hansa was on her way to Kiranje, a quiet hamlet on the outskirts of Mumbai. The place had a low-profile identity, made noticeable only by the presence of the Naval Warfare College, where MARCOS received their training.

Her meeting with her contact, that had been established after various pleas to friends, their fathers and the Vice-Admiral of the Western Naval Command, turned out to be a damp squib. He was, or rather appeared to be, least informed about the internal logistics of Operation Black Tornado. To Hansa, it did not seem to be an impossible task for him to at least tell her the names of the MARCOS that were injured that night. However, he seemed bent on bringing the discussion to a dead-end. After several pleas and strands of futile discussions; she left the place. The only piece of information that she had picked up was that injured personnel are almost always admitted in the Command Hospital in Colaba. It was enough of a lead for her, and that was where he was likely to be, too.

*****

It was a three-hour drive back to Mumbai. She did not want to waste any more time. She called up the hospital and enquired about the visiting hours. She was just in time. On her way, she made nine calls to various people she knew, who could possibly help her through the systems and procedures. Ginny, sat in the front seat, trying to dissuade her at regular intervals from making drastic public appearances.

They reached the hospital. Ginny managed to get to the reception while Hansa waited in the car. He had suggested that he would try and get as much information as he possibly could and had asked Hansa to wait as her presence in the hospital might upset the normal flow of things. She waited like an obedient child thinking that while her presence could urge people to leave their work to catch a glimpse of her; the same aura was proving to be ineffective and almost a deterrent in getting her own work done.

Ginny came back after half an hour looking as defeated as a hen-pecked rooster. He sat in the car and asked the driver to proceed towards home.

"Wait! First tell me what happened in there!"

Ginny turned around and said, "Madam jee, I have never found any circle as impenetrable as this one. The minute you mention the word MARCO, everyone clams up. Till now, I didn't know it was so much of a secret society. Anyway, I haggled as much as I could with the staff at the reception, trying to cull information but it was quite useless. I even offered incentives but was told off. I would have taken the stakes higher had I not seen a poor reporter being hauled out of the place for having entered forbidden areas." "A reporter? How do you know he was one?"

"Well, he was shouting that he was there with prior permission and that they'd better not mess with the Press!"

"Where was he? Did you get to see him?"

"I left before they took me up after him. This MARCO business seems to be even more unapproachable than the underworld."

"Shut up Ginny. Catch hold of that reporter. He's our man. Go quickly, before we lose him!" And she pushed him out of the car again.

*****

It was not a long time before Ginny was seen walking out with a young man with his general demeanour in a state of disarray. He seemed a bit intimidated by Ginny who had his arm around his catch. He was asked to climb into the SUV.

He slid himself on the seat next to Hansa. There was a small yelp of astonishment from him as he recognised her.

"Hi!" Hansa smiled.

"Oh, my God. I can't believe this is happening to me. Am I sitting next to a screen-goddess?"

"Yes, you are and this goddess is about to treat you to dinner? Would you accept her invitation?"

"Ma'am, most people, including me, would give an arm and a leg to be with you."

He then looked at Ginny, realising that he may have placed his language skills inappropriately. As expected the look was not returned very kindly by Ginny.

They drove to Taj Lands End and went straight to Ming Yang, the Chinese restaurant on the first floor. Ginny's services had been dismissed for the night.

The two of them were seated in a private-dining area, where there would be minimal interruptions. The reporter tried hard to conceal his fascination and behave as scribes are expected to. His questions, therefore, bordered on the intimate to the weird but Hansa tossed them around playfully, thus, keeping him engaged and interested.

As soon as they sat down, Hansa broached the subject,

"So, why were you being hauled out of that place so ruthlessly?"

"Ma'am, we are used to being thrown out of places. But what I can't understand is your interest in me. What is it that I have and you need?"

"Well, there's nothing as of now but who knows, there could be!"

"Like?"

"For instance, the reason why you were there! It may or may not be of any use to me but if it is, then you are much to gain from it."

"What is it that you want to know?" "Everything!"

"I was just there to interview an injured soldier." "And?"

"And I was told, I couldn't."

He didn't seem to be in a hurry to part with information, if he had any.

Hansa prompted him patiently. "And why couldn't you?"

"I'd have fought had I known. I have no idea." He was beginning to get her goat.

"Look, if that's all you have to share, you may as well leave right now."

"Oh no Ma'am, please don't misunderstand. I just don't want the evening to get over too quickly, please. This is like a dream to me."

A month ago, Hansa would probably have smiled at the comment. But this guy was irritating. She wrapped up her annoyance in a lettuce leaf and chewed on it.

"I'm listening."

"Ma'am, I had received a cue that the commandos injured in Operation Black Tornado at Taj were being de-listed from the *Prahari Bal*. With great difficulty I managed to acquire information on these men. I could manage to get the details of only one of them. He's admitted in the Command Hospital in Colaba and I was trying to sneak my way to him and have an interview. But I got intercepted just when I was about to enter his room and was escorted out."

Hansa's heart began to race. Was this the man, who would take her a step closer to her destination? She picked up a glass of water and before putting it to her lips, asked:

"Who was this man you were going to meet?" "Ma'am, this is classified information."

"I know, and you will be compensated well to part with it."

"His name is Anwar Tariq and he is admitted in room number 401."

"Alpha Tango," she thought.

"How can I believe that you are not leading me on?"

He pulled out a diary and showed her the page on which he had scribbled the details the previous day.

She gave him Ginny's number and asked him to get in touch with him the next day. It was a hasty fifteen minutes at dinner, thereafter and all she remembered was nodding her head quietly through it. The name and the room number was what preoccupied her head all the time. Later, after she left from the hotel, it occurred to her that she hadn't even tried to know the name of the person who had come as a blessing in disguise.

*****

The next day, Hansa reached the hospital half-an-hour before the start of the visiting hours. This time she did not want Ginny to stand up for her. With her head covered with a dupatta and glares shielding her eyes, it was the best camouflage she could put on in order to avoid the media gaze.

The staff at the reception maintained their poise on seeing her. She wasn't sure if they recognised her, and if they did, they maintained a professional straight-face. She liked the discipline of uniformed men.

"I've come to visit Mr. Anwar Tariq in room number 401." The man at the counter checked his records.

"Sorry Ma'am, there's no one by that name in that room."

"Please check again, Mr. Anwar Tariq. Is there a possibility of him having moved or checked-out yesterday?"

After getting this far, she was not going to give up so easily. "No Ma'am, there's nobody by that name registered with us."

"There's surely some error. The person has sent me a message himself that he is admitted here. He is injured on his thigh and shoulder. Might have undergone surgery, but I'm not too sure."

"Can you tell me on which date he was admitted?" "Perhaps on the 29th of November!"

Hansa tried to make an intelligent guess.

"Sorry Ma'am, there's nobody by that name in the in-patients' list."

Frustration was starting to show up on her face.

"Can you tell me the names of all those who were admitted on that day?"

"Sorry Ma'am, that's confidential information. I cannot give away patient details to anyone."

"Listen, it's important for me to meet this person. Just look again! Check with the nursing staff! Check in your patient database. I'm sure you'll find his name somewhere. This is…." Hansa checked herself. She was beginning to lose her composure.

The receptionist seemed a little moved by her plea. He started to check his records again.

"Ma'am, I'd have helped you if I could. I can send someone with you to the Emergency Centre. Maybe they have more detailed records of the patient with the kind of injuries you described."

Hansa was escorted to the Emergency Centre. She pushed her request yet again, to a rather stern-looking nurse. She checked her papers and stated in a stone-cold manner.

"No Anwar Tariq here. Only one person brought to emergency on 29th by the name of Arjun Tandon. Serious injury on shoulder, thigh and hand."

Hansa's heart skipped a beat. Arjun Tandon, Alpha Tango. She didn't want to waste time on thinking about Anwar Tariq.

"Which room is he in?"

"Sorry Miss. You need special permission to meet him."

"Oh please, I am Hansa Noorie Walia. You can verify my credentials if you like, keep a document for security. I can leave my passport with you, if you want." She couldn't care much about composure now. It was imperative for her to get past this hurdle.

"Ma'am, I am not supposed to give you this information also but I did. I might get into trouble over this. I wish I could help you further, but I can't."

Hansa's heart sank. Every effort seemed to be leading to a dead-end. But she wasn't ready to turn back from here. She took out her phone and called her father-in-law. The call went unanswered. She then called Zarine and swallowed the lump in her throat as she spoke.

"Ms. Nawaaz, I need your help. Please ask Pa to help me get through this."

"What's the matter, Hansa? Are you O.K.?"

"No, I'm not. I'm going crazy and I can't see any door opening up for me."

And she told Zarine about her journey so far, who asked her to wait where she was. Zarine promised to call back. Hansa waited in the hospital lobby. She soon started to feel a bit awkward as an irregular crowd started to build up around the area where she was waiting. Her guards were readying themselves to escort her out of that place, any minute now.

Her wait lasted for about forty minutes. Then, as if driven by a divine force, a doctor made his way through the crowd and approached her. The guards closed in.

"Ma'am, this way please."

Hansa didn't feel the need to ask him any questions. She followed him quietly, despite the guards' disapproval. The doctor led them through lobbies and up a few flights of stairs. She tried to keep pace with the doctor's steps and her own heartbeat. Then as they approached another nurses' station, the doctor picked up the intercom and spoke into it. He then handed over the phone to Hansa. Her hand was a bit shaky as she took the receiver and drew it to her ear. Then, drawing in her breath, she said:

"Hello!"

She could hear someone breathing into the phone on the other end.

"Alpha Tango!"

"Alpha Tango, Ma'am. I thought I had brought you out safely from the danger zone. What brings you back in it?"

The rasp in that voice was something she could feel against her skin. There was no mistaking it. She had felt it several times in the course of sixty hours. She closed her eyes for a second, and then realising that she had people around her, spoke again,

"How are you? Can I come and see you?"

"Never felt as alive as I'm doing right now. I wish I had the 'liberty' to say 'yes' to your second question. But would you really wait for a 'yes'?"

Hansa's heart had nearly stopped beating now. Now that she could sense his slow and intense breath in her ear, she didn't know what to say.

"I've covered a long distance to meet you and I'm not turning back now."

Nineteen

A pause lingered on for too long. They drifted in the rhythm of each other's breath for an indeterminate duration. For those stealing glances at Hansa; it was a few seconds. Then he broke the silence.

"I'm trying to believe this. Have you really come to meet me? Why?"

"Can I tell you that in person? By the way, are you Arjun or Anwar?"

"Can I tell you that in person?"

Hansa smiled. There was no reason but she felt her cheeks getting slightly flushed.

"I'd like to come and see you."

"I'd like that more than you do but it's my tough luck that I can't say 'yes' to that." "Why?"

"Ma'am, a combatant doesn't have the luxury to submit to desire."

"Please call me Hansa."

Silence hung around idly, yet again.

This time, it was she who picked up the loose end. "When can I see you, then?"

"The docs say six weeks but I'm confident of being wheeled out of here by Christmas. I don't make a very patient patient."

The doctor interrupted, suggesting that talk-time was limited and she must close the conversation.

"And where would I find you? Reaching out to you here has been more of a task than I had expected it to be."

"You think I'd let a swan waddle through the muck yet again? I've been getting updates on how a gorgeous young lady has been raising hell and high water to meet me. I'm too much of a good man to let that happen twice. I'll call you, first thing after I'm let off."

"Do you have my number?"

"I have the intent. It gets me everything."

"I've never waited for Christmas. This year, I shall. Bye."

She placed the receiver back on its cradle, relieved and confident. There was a stoic promise in his speech, which she wanted to believe; and it was comforting.

*****

On her way back home, the conversation looped itself inside her head and kept playing over and over again. His breath rasping against her skin gave her gooseflesh. She caressed her bare arms. She needed to talk to someone to stop her heart from spilling over. She had barely pressed the speed- dial, when the phone buzzed.

"Hi!"

"I can sense from the chirp in your voice that you have been able to talk to him."

"I don't know how to thank you. How about a cup of coffee?"

"Is that all he's worth? A cup of coffee?"

And they laughed like teenagers smitten by the idea of being in love.

*****

"I'm happy for you, sweetheart. But it's time now that you took a reality-check. Where do you think this obsession is taking you?"

"Zarine, you are the only person who, I hope, will be able to understand me. I don't know why but nothing feels more right than this. Moreover, I don't even know if he feels the same way as I do. Yet, I want to let him know. I want to make him feel what I feel. And I do so want to tell him how he has changed my perspective of life and living."

"Well, by your conversation, it seems, he's as smitten as you! And who wouldn't be? You are any man's dream come true!"

"I hope there's more to it than plain fascination."

"Ah, now that's too much to ask for from a man." And Zarine winked at her. But Hansa knew that she understood; both, her feelings and men; better than anyone she had ever known.

She then floated through an idle conversation with the dreamy-eyed look that suggested that she, once again, had drifted to the astral world of Ruttie Jinnah.

*****

The days that followed her first conversation with her MARCO, were filled with anticipation, excitement and bouts of nervous anxiety. Her movie was to release in a few days and she had remained busy with promotional parties and events. The Friday that was to come would be another milestone in her life. She hoped that her exit from the world of glamour would be as grand as her entry.

The night of the premiere arrived. This time she had not wanted to be accompanied by a battery of followers. For the first time, a sense of isolation had not given way to a sense of loneliness and she had made up her mind to reach the venue of the premiere by herself. However, Zarine had insisted to accompany her and thus, they reached on time, just like the way Hansa had always done in the past. She had expected Ginny to be waiting with a bunch of staff and unit members. However, to her utter surprise, she was greeted by Srijann Walia and Rajeev. On reflection, she noted that she hadn't thought of Rajeev even once ever since she had spent the night talking to Zarine. She greeted the two politely. Rajeev stepped forward and gave her a peck on the cheek. Two weeks ago, she would have cringed at his touch but today, she was calm and poised as Hansa, the star, was always known to be. Courteously, she sat down beside them. Rajeev looked at her as she stared ahead, bracing herself for the conversation that was to follow.

"Missing you, baby," he whispered.

"Raj, this is not the place for a private conversation," she replied. For a moment, she felt guilty for returning his love without much favour. In a split second, she recovered from her emotional wavering and planted herself on firm ground.

"Why are you making such a big deal of this? Okay, I promise to be your bonded slave for life. Just come home," Rajeev tried again.

The white screen ran up a burst of colour, in many hues. The screening had started. He slid his hand into hers. She looked askance at their hands and then, without showing any sign of resistance, kept her eyes fixed on the screen. It didn't matter to her if Rajeev took it as a sign of submission.

On screen, the camera zoomed into Hansa's face. She was perched atop a yacht called Hansa with the night breeze flicking her hair and gently tossing the waves. The Grand Dame gazed resplendently at her as the silent waters hushed the breeze. The golden reflection in the water flickered and disappeared for a moment. It was in that flickering moment that a few men had crossed the metal detectors placed at the entrance of the Taj Mahal hotel.

Hansa relived the recent past with Rajeev's hand in hers. As the movie proceeded towards the protagonist's flashback; she tried to skim over her possible future. With Rajeev, it would be near-perfect, with a husband smitten as a kitten, a doting father-in-law and a nurturing mother-in-law. Fame and fortune had become everyday consumables and had outgrown their title as the 'objects of desire'. She could even see Rajeev conceding to her desire to start a family. Yet, there was a missing piece in the emotional jigsaw.

As her thoughts tuned in to her convalescing MARCO, she could see none of that but only the missing piece, shining brilliantly. Her heart felt an instant rush of endorphins, crawling through her entire being. Her mind felt as light as the first beam of dawn or the last strand of light at dusk, putting the endless chatter at rest. A slap, on screen, resounded in the Dolby surround-sound system. She was shaken out of her reverie. It was 'Ruttie's' father, on-screen, forbidding her to fall in love outside the social dictum of the Parsi community, with the man that the world knew as Mohammad Ali Jinnah; who was 24 years older than her, married previously and a devout Muslim. The odds stood against the match like miasmic rock. But Rattanbai Petit was undeterred and unmoved. It was strange that Hansa had started to understand her in several, non-linear ways now than when she was embodying the character for the camera. There seemed to be enough pointers coming her way about the validity of her current emotions.

Yet, Hansa felt uneasy and then, as if to prevent her thoughts from getting siphoned into Rajeev's mind, pulled her hand out of his. Rajeev continued to gaze at the screen, totally transfixed by her virtual aura and oblivious of her physical presence next to him.

The movie kept the select audience captivated and ended to a thunderous applause. The verdict of the critics as well as the focus-group was in. It was destined to be a blockbuster. Rajeev couldn't stop beaming at the grandiose applause and received congratulatory handshakes with the pride of an owner. Srijann Walia and Zarine maintained a dignified distance from each other as they were surrounded by their own set of admirers and well-wishers. Hansa was tired of maintaining a crisp, public smile and wanted to make an exit. Before she could turn around and walk through the web of expectant faces, Rajeev chaperoned her out of the hall and towards his car. Staff followed suit. He gesticulated to them to leave in another car. Hansa did not want to put up a resistance and feed the gaping cameras, being pushed around by newsmen. She allowed him to usher her to his car as he got behind the wheel, with Hansa beside him.

"Raj, please stop! Where are you taking me?"

"Relax cupcake! It is no crime to steal your wife from public glare and go looking for some privacy, or is it? For the next one hour, just forget about everything that happened and relish the moments that are to follow!"

"Raj, I'm not interested and please don't try so hard. I …"

"Why? Fear that your heart will melt and you'll come crashing into my arms again, hahn?"

Hansa sighed. "If only you were to accept the fact that the whole world doesn't revolve around you and your plans, Rajeev; you'd make a much better husband, son or perhaps even a father!"

"You can go ahead and say what you like. I'm damn excited tonight. Imagine, your movie is going to take off with a blast tomorrow and here we are, drawing my character-sketch. Who cares what kind of a man I am; I am the famous Hansa Noorie Walia's husband."

It wasn't evident earlier but Rajeev sounded a bit intoxicated now. She had been so preoccupied with her thoughts that she hadn't noticed the totter in his step when he had returned to his seat during the interval.

He slipped out the bottle and took a sip.

Hansa wasn't too pleased with this hackneyed act of amorous drunkenness. She had seen it once too often on screen.

"Raj, I don't know where you are headed but this is certainly not the direction that I want to take."

"Our directions are the same, honey and so are our destinations. Hell, or high water, we go together."

She knew that look in his eyes. It seemed that he had learnt about her pursuance. Rajeev's smile had turned into a blank stare at the road, which seemed to be getting darker as they sped along. The lights on the Western Express Highway had left them a long way back and the road had now turned into an average city road with broken or dimming lights at large intervals.

"So what, do you have planned for me? Hell or high water? It wouldn't be an understatement if I said, I've experienced both with you!"

"Sugar, you'll find out soon. Death comes easily after the heavenly experiences Rajeev Walia creates!"

Hansa shuddered. She was aware of Raj's whimsical nature but she had never heard him sound so cold. However, she did not get much time to ponder over the thought any more. The car came to an abrupt halt. He stepped out and came around to open the door for her.

"Raj, I've never been to this place and I am beginning to feel scared."

"Ssshh," and he took out a silk scarf and started to tie it around her eyes.

"Baby, don't even try to put up a fight. Here, you can neither run nor hide; therefore, it would be best if you just played along."

She knew he was right and she knew that he meant what he said this time.

The scarf was firmly in place. She took a few steps forward and was about to trip over her gown, when he lifted her in his arms. She didn't know his motive behind it but it failed to generate a spark. He walked for a couple of minutes before he put her down again. Her stilettos had been meticulously removed without her knowledge. As her feet touched cool and damp sands, water trickled in between her toes. The scarf fell down beside her. She opened her eyes to a dark and quiet beach, with the only light coming from above. Rajeev had prepared, a four-poster arrangement with flowers, vines and fairy-lights that provided a star-lit cover. She had seen elaborate sets but the simplicity and quiet appeal of this one managed to touch her heart.

Rajeev drew a string and curtains fell down on the four sides around them. It was like a honeymoon suite in the middle of nowhere. He drew her closer to him and whispered hoarsely:

"I want to make love to you right now."

*****

Arjun had not had a good night's rest. For the first time in the past ten years, something had been able to dislodge him from his state of equilibrium. His chi had been sliced into and had started to realign itself. It was disquieting, and yet the flutter seemed to bring breezy solace. Given his condition, he couldn't even toss and turn much in bed, so he lay motionless trying to confront his thoughts with good-humoured banter directed to his own self.

"Don't be stupid! She's probably just fascinated. It's just a glorified response of a famous damsel-in-distress."

"But leaving her husband and starting a search for a stranger is something which is outside the realm of ordinary feeling."

"What makes you think, she left her husband for you? It could have been a separation waiting to happen since a long time."

"But boy, the timing might have been perfect. Perhaps, you made an entry in the same chapter of her life in which she was planning to move away from that bugger!"

"Get real commando! There's no such thing as destined coincidences in life. Everything is a consequence of a planned thought or action. Besides, since when did you start believing in marvellous play?"

"Ever since I set sight on a marvel myself! What can I call a meeting which happened despite my best effort to not be in that situation? My consistent efforts to take a few days off were being turned down for the past two months. I was not even supposed to be on this team. A last-minute flip and there I was! It was a fateful meeting, meant to happen."

His internal duel continued and before he realised, sleep caught up with the game and overpowered it. In his sleep, he dreamt of drifting through the November sky with a scruffy head resting on his chest. He gazed at it and resisted the urge to smooth down the curls with his face.

*****

"Raj, behave! What's come over you? This is insane!" Hansa tried to wriggle out of his grip. It wasn't going to be easy.

"Yes! This is insanity and you've driven me to it. I've never had to try so hard for anything in my life and here, my wife wants to fill up my life with every conceivable difficulty."

"Rajeev Walia, you have no business saying this. I should be the one complaining but I'm not. Just let me go!"

Rajeev allowed her to struggle to break free. After a few frantic attempts, she got tired and stopped. It was then that Rajeev brought his hand behind her head and thrust his face on to hers. It was a forceful, prolonged kiss and Hansa felt disgusted with his probing tongue. She tried pushing him away but it was futile.

When his anger subsided, he broke free rather jerkily.

"I don't make very persistent apologies, Hansa but I broke my rule for you. This was my last one. C'mon, I'll drop you home."

It was difficult to ascertain if it was the pain of a biting truth or the humiliation that she felt at Rajeev's excesses but Hansa quietly wiped away her tears while looking out the window, on their way back to her apartment.

*****

Thereafter, began a delirious wait for Christmas. Since there wasn't much work that she had taken on, it was becoming increasingly difficult for her to stop looking at the clock and waiting for time to tick faster. Bandra had already started to look like fairyland. Christmas lights, confetti and glitter made the wait even more agonising.

On 25th December, her patience gave way and she couldn't hold her restraint any longer. She picked up the phone and dialled the hospital's number. She asked for the extension to the special-care unit. A nurse answered sweetly.

"I'd like to speak to Mr. Arjun Tandon, please." "Please, hold on."

There was a brief pause.

"Sorry, Ma'am. There's no patient by that name admitted here."

"Oh, maybe he's checked in by the name of Anwar Tariq. Could you check again?"

The pause was a little longer now. The rhythm of her pulse increased.

"Ma'am, Mr. Anwar Tariq was checked out of the hospital on 20th December."

*****

She had not prepared herself for this news.

"Is there a contact address or phone number?"

"Sorry, Ma'am! We've been instructed not to give out any details."

Hansa put down the phone. It couldn't be true. She had been certain that he would keep his promise. Her mind chided her for chasing a dream which was bound to end in a nightmare but her heart told her otherwise. The sobs, that she had kept under check so far, broke loose and came out in torrents. She dampened her mother's pillow with the deluge and slept off like a primrose battered by the rain.

*****

Days came and went inconsequentially. There was no news from anyone. In a world full of fans, facebook friends, twitter followers and a few relatives, she found herself singularly alone. She spent her days reading but the nights went by restlessly. It was only two days to New Year's Eve now. She called Ginny.

"Book me on a flight to Cape Town for tomorrow. Keep the return open-ended."

"Ma'am, how much currency should I organise?"

"Don't bother. I won't need any. Just get me a sea-facing suite. And while I'm gone, I want the feed and water in my bird-house to be changed twice daily."

After she put down the phone, she decided to take out the canvas and the easel that had been gathering dust in one of the rooms. She wasn't a painter but a strange desire to paint came over her. She placed the easel in the terrace-garden and the canvas sat on it, waiting for the first stroke. Before she brought out the paints, she placed her favourite record on her mother's LP player. Don Mc. Lean started to sing 'starry, starry night' as she toyed with the paints, not knowing what to do with them. Then, on a whim, she took red and splashed a stroke across the stretched fabric. Before she could go further with blue, the bell on the video-phone near her door buzzed. She didn't wish to see anyone. It was strange that she hadn't received a call on the intercom about a visitor's arrival.

Half-heartedly, she went to the door and looked at the camera. She could only see the back of the visitor. She didn't wish to open the door to a stranger. The maid turned up behind her.

"Whoever it is, tell them I'm not at home." And she went back to the terrace.

The maid opened the door. She could hear her talking to someone. She then closed the door and came to the terrace with a bunch of yellow gerberas with a flaming orange bird-of-paradise in the middle.

"Madam, this for you."

Hansa received the flowers and looked at the card. It read: "One bird-of-paradise for another! A.T."

She reread it and then, as if struck by lightning, she dashed to the door, causing it to fly open as she stepped into the lift lobby. He stood akimbo, beaming at her. The forehead caught her attention, followed by the well-chiselled jaw-line, distinctly visible even through the beard that looked like a day-old stubble.

Her eyes shone and she forgot to speak.

"Ma'am, you must open the door only when you hear 'Alpha Tango'!"

Her surprise turned into a blushing giggle. The voice was unmistakable.

"What kept you waiting here? My maid did say that I wasn't at home, didn't she?"

"Well Ma'am, if your maid listens to 'starry, starry night', while you're away; then her mistress is worth the entire wait a man can make."

She laughed and the glint in her eyes gave her away.

"May I come in and offer a handkerchief for your beautiful eyes?"

She looked away, wishing for her emotions to not make her vulnerable.

They sat down in the lounge.

"It's a beautifully kept house. Does the compliment go to you or your interior decorator?"

"Actually, to my mother! She had fine taste and an impeccable sense of aesthetics."

"No wonder then, she crafted such a masterpiece!" He looked her way and then pretended to thwart his gaze in another direction.

Hansa smiled again. Her face and heart felt warmed by his presence.

"Do you live here alone?"

"For a little less than a month now! I walked out of my husband's house recently."

"I'm sorry to hear that. And I'm not going to ask 'why', unless you wish to talk about it."

"There aren't any secrets in my life. We had some differences and he was unapologetic about the way he was treating our marriage. I guess it was a disaster waiting to happen. Anyway, forget that! I thought I'd see you on Christmas. It was quite a wait."

"Well, I was busy tying up with Santa to bring me the present I wanted. I think my wish just got granted."

She felt a tremor run through her body. She could barely look into his eyes now.

"Have the injuries healed well?" "If they haven't, they will now!"

"What took you so long? I was concerned!"

"Well, to cut a long story short; I am no longer a MARCO. I put in my papers on the 19th and was out of the hospital on the 24th. A few official formalities had to be completed and some protocol to be followed, before I could step out as a civilian."

"Oh, that's news! But why did you give it up? I thought you were the bravest man around!"

"Well! The Indian Navy agrees with you on that but doesn't find me fit enough to continue in the Prahari-Bal; therefore, I was offered a zero-action administrative position, which I turned down."

"Oh, I'm sorry to hear that!"

"Okay. Can we feel sorry for each other over some drinks?"

"O yes! No, I mean…would you like some coffee or some home-made plum juice?"

"I'd prefer the juice. I'm sure it has your involvement in it." He seemed to read her like a book.

"Umm, do you intend telling me your name now, or is it going to be a well-kept secret for life?"

"That depends on exactly how much time of your life do you intend to spend with me."

She called for the juice, searching for an answer.

For a few seconds they didn't have anything to say to each other. Those were the proverbial 'moments of truth' and they sensed it as they felt a bubble enclose them within itself.

"Would you like to…" "Would you like to…"

Both of them started together. They looked at each other and then looked away.

"So, the lady gets to go first. You were saying?"

"I just thought, perhaps you'd like to sit outside. That's my favourite place in the house."

"Ah! The swan's favourite place has to be Brahma's abode. Let's go!"

"And you were saying?"

"Would you like to have me as your escort and bodyguard while you holiday in Cape Town?"

She looked at him with mixed feelings of surprise, joy and amusement.

"How did you find out that I was going to Cape Town?" she asked as she led him to the terrace.

"Well! Once a MARCO, always a MARCO. Besides, I told you I had the intent!"

Birds were chirping merrily on and about their sylvan den. The sole occupant had a visitor and sounded much happier now.

"So, you paint as well? How many different screens do you aspire to set on fire?" He looked at the splash of red and quipped.

"Oh, no! I just brought this out to distract myself. I've never painted before!"

"And what did you want to distract yourself from?" The twinkle in his eyes had turned to an intense note. She could hold his gaze for less than two seconds. The maid arrived with a tray.

"Juice!" was all she could say.

They picked up the crystal. It was about three weeks ago that she had spent the night clinking glasses with Zarine and talking about a distant dream. She now stood on the same terrace with the dream taking form.

"So, what do you plan to paint then?"

"Don't know yet. I guess it will come to me. I'm in no hurry." "With your permission, may I try my hand at it?"

"You paint, do you? That's such an unlikely hobby for a

MARCO!"

"Ah, I've never painted either but I can assure you, if you allow me to, I can paint a portrait of yours in less than an hour's time!"

"That's impossible!" "Impossible says I am possible" She laughed.

"That's a borrowed line. Totally unoriginal!" "But it works! That laughter was priceless!"

"But you need to know something about form and technique."

"I'm only interested in the subject here! Technique and form can go climb the nearest pole and holler for Mr. Hussain!"

She giggled and agreed shortly, to pose for him, on the condition that he would let her talk through the session. He ushered her to the swing chair next to the bird-house.

"You can relax completely. I am not going to ask you to sit stiff for an hour. And talk to your heart's content!"

"Ah! You sound like a seasoned painter, already!"

He started to move about his hands rather aesthetically.

"Seasoned, did you say? The only connection that I have with that word is 'seasoning'. And the thought of seasoning makes me hungry!"

"Oops, I completely forgot to offer you anything! What would you like to eat?"

"Anything, that doesn't require you to move away from here!"

She asked her maid to order some kebabs from a famous

Indian restaurant nearby.

Minutes moved forward like the dunes in a desert, swift and smooth and without leaving any disturbing traces of their presence. When he was done, he stepped back and admired his work.

"Is it done? I can't wait to see!" "All yours!"

Hansa came up eagerly to see what he had painted. She looked at it and then at him, not knowing how to react.

"What's this?"

"Exactly what you see!"

The canvas had random streaks in black, something that looked like a woman's form draped in black from head to toe with unruly hair tumbling on the forehead and grey-green eyes. The black was horizontal with the red streak making up for the background now.

"This is the Hansa Noorie that I saw for the very first time and I don't mean to forget this face in a hurry!" She looked at it again and shook her head.

"This is so unfair. You made me sit for an hour for this?"

"Ma'am, I told you I have the intent. And today, the intent was to watch you watching me for as long as I could. The helicopter ride wasn't enough for me."

Hansa hadn't smiled so much in the past few months. She fervently hoped that it wasn't really just a dream. She was enjoying every moment and if it was a dream, she did not want to wake up from it. Her wish was short-lived. The maid came out with the phone.

"Who is it?" "Zarine madam!"

She took the phone and answered into it. "Hansa, where are you?"

"At home. You sound worried. All well?"

"You aren't answering your cell. Did you get the message?" "Which message? I think my phone is in silent mode. I didn't hear it ring. What happened?"

"You have to fly to Delhi ASAP."

"Why?"

"Gargi passed away an hour ago!"

*****

It certainly had to be a dream. Reality couldn't possibly be so mercurial, so as to give and take in a matter of seconds.

"Something's not right, it seems. Want to tell me?" Colour left Hansa's face like dewdrops at sunrise. "My mother-in-law just passed away."

"I'm sorry to hear that. Was she here in Mumbai?" "In Delhi!"

"Where's your husband?" "He's in Delhi, too. I'll call!"

Hastily, she called Rajeev but there was no response. She then tried her father-in-law's phone but there was no response from him either. She then noticed a message from Pa, saying:

"Gargi gone. Forever."

"I'll have to leave immediately!" she mumbled.

"You must and if I'm not taking too much liberty; I'd like to escort you. I don't think you should travel alone in this state of mind."

Hansa was relieved that he had offered support. She didn't even try a polite refusal.

"I'll organise tickets. You can pack your bags meanwhile."

*****

The flight to Delhi was devoid of any flirtatious conversation, yet she could feel the chemistry in the comfort that his presence brought; although, she couldn't help feeling awkward over the fact, that she was going to try and comfort her husband while being accompanied by the man who, in a way, led her away from him. He tried to keep her mind away from the loss by telling her stories from the days of training and combat.

It was late in the evening when she reached Gargi's maternal home. Wading through a sea of unfamiliar faces and grieving relatives, she went past the lawns, and inside to the hall where Gargi's mort lay, shrouded in white. She touched her feet and paid her obeisance. Her eyes searched for Rajeev and spotted Srijann Walia sitting cross-legged, staring blankly at his wife's lifeless body. She was about to get up and go to him but Srijee raised his hand, gesturing her to stay where she was. Her escort was nowhere to be seen in the hall. She felt alienated in her own family-home till she saw Zarine sailing into the room with a few other women. Their visions crossed paths. Zarine, without making small talk, led her up the stairs to where Rajeev was busy making arrangements for the last rites. The people that surrounded him left the room as soon as the two ladies walked in. After checking with Rajeev if all essential arrangements were taken care of, she left the two alone.

"Raj, this was so sudden. I understand your grief."

"Thank you Ms. Noorie. You may join the other ladies downstairs."

She ignored the caustic tone. She could certainly forgive him his anger today.

"What happened? I thought she was coming back home soon."

"Why would you want to know? Does it even matter to you? You've probably enacted death-scenes several times by now. I'm sure you're deft at using the most convincing expressions and words!"

"Rajeev, I'm with you in this loss. Your mother was dear to me too. Her absence leaves a void in my life as well."

"No, Ms. Noorie! You may go and continue to chase some of your phantom dreams. The real world and real people don't really find any place in your scheme of things. We tried our best to please a goddess but she left a curse on us instead. My mother bore the brunt of it. You'll find no sympathy or forgiveness from me here."

"What have I done, Rajeev? Is it such a crime to express one's feelings? I don't want a time like this to turn into a marital altercation. I have certain duties towards her and I shall perform them, whether you like it or not."

"First, I think, you need to learn to perform your duties towards her son. Her soul might find some peace!"

"Raj, I've not come here to argue. Come here. I know your heart is breaking inside. You can let it out. I'm no stranger!"

She held his hand. Rajeev needed no prodding. He wept on her shoulder like a child. She held him closer than she had ever done before.

*****

The priests needed to perform certain rituals before Gargi was flown to her husband's house in Mumbai. According to Vedic rituals, her cremation was to take place in her marital home. Hansa entered the house where her mother-in-law had received her lovingly when she had returned from the traumatic experience at Taj. Tears welled up in her eyes as she recalled her own mother's sudden exit from her life. Srijee lovingly embraced his daughter-in-law as they shared their grief. Without prolonging the agony, she got busy with catering to the needs of the visitors to Walia House.

She had not seen MARCO since the time he had dropped her off in Delhi. At the back of her mind, she knew that he would be around if she needed him. There was no uncertainty this time and neither did she feel any guilt while thinking about him, on their way back from the cremation ground. Thoughts nested themselves in disarray as she tried to synthesise the facts of her life and assemble them. She would certainly stay with her father-in-law and her husband for some time, till they surfaced from the deluge of sorrow; and till the time she took her next step forward.

Walia House probably needed a bird-house in the garden now.

Twenty

EPILOGUE

Two Years Later...

She could never eliminate the date from her mind, no matter how hard she tried. Perhaps two years was too little a time-span to let dust settle on certain events. 29th December always brought with it the fondest memories and a pang of loss. Even though one was irretrievable and the other, irreparable; she sometimes allowed them to ripple her present.

It had been an exhausting day, with a birthday celebration teamed with holiday preparations. She was waiting for him to reach home, so they could leave for Cape Town. The holiday that had been thought of impulsively, two years ago, would materialise now, but in a threesome instead of two. Like an able homemaker, she had packed things and struck them off her list. There was a fulfilling pleasure in putting things together in a box. It was like picket-fencing a garden, drawing a boundary around things; and boundaries, she realised, had a more comforting effect now than some time ago when she felt caved in by them.

The passports and bags were ready. The tickets were with Ginny who would meet them at the airport. She had a few hours before they left from home. All she needed now was to soak up some of her favourite scents in a hot-water bath. The house was quiet and there were no pressing needs, crying for attention. She stepped into her white and green tiled bathroom. A myriad-hued huddle of palm, rubber-plant and ferns in the corner added to the wild ambience of the bathroom. The jacuzzi had soft wisps of steam rising from it as jets of hot water met the cold. She dropped in a blob of bubble-bath that was labelled Forest 'sense. Within minutes, big and small spheres surfaced, glinting gently in the soft white light. 'Starry, starry night' played once more. This time it was Chloe Agnew's lilting voice that settled on the ambience like snowflakes.

She stepped out of her kaftan and into the bath. As she slid in, the spray of water met her with such gusto that it had a spasmodic effect. A shiver ran down her spine and she closed her eyes and let her body loose. The water played around her, running across, over and under in Lilliputian streams. She drifted in the rivulets for some time while the singer's voice drifted over her.

Something soft fell in trickles on her lips. She fluttered her lids as she curled in her lip to taste it. It was him. Looking at her, he bent forward to taste the honey on her lips. He did not need to be invited. Dropping his robe, he climbed in and settled himself behind her. His hands reached across her girth and rested above her navel. The hot and cold feeling seeped into her pores as she felt his arousal against the small of her back. Tenderly, he bit her shoulder and made his way towards the nape of her neck. His fingers circled around her navel, generating within her, the desire to hold them and guide them up to her breasts. Perfect communion requires no words for communication. His hands glided up her torso and circled around the contours.

Her breath was beginning to freeze and her skin starting to melt. He brought his feet up to touch hers. She loved the feel of his feet. It was soft, like baby-skin. As they travelled up her leg, she slowly rubbed her back against his chest. She could feel his nipples stiffening on his square chest. The bubbles now enveloped them together like a cosmic wrap.

He scooped up some water and poured it on her face. As the drops trickled down her cheek, he kissed them off softly. She felt his stubble against her delicate skin and felt an urge to draw him in. Sensing it, he held her hands and pinned down her legs with his feet, preventing her from turning around and thus, prolonging the wait. She hated it! She loved it! She needed him to slide over her and douse her passion. Guiding his hands, she led him to the V. It was his controlled volition that made desire flame through her body like an unchecked river in the rains.

As the fire began to grow, he released her legs. Then, placing his arm under them, he swung her around to face him. She experienced a new buoyant feeling. Before he could bring her around completely, she was kneeling before him. Knotting her fingers in his wavy hair, she brought his head forward to nestle between her breasts. There were still some traces of honey on her white skin. He licked them as his breath started to get sharper and shorter. She slid down slowly for her lips to meet his in a long engagement. It felt like an eternity before they released each other, eyes locked in half-open, half-closed tangles.

She moved away. He pulled her closer. Like a fish, she wriggled. It was now his turn to burn. Mischief carried them away from the bath to their plush bedroom. There was no light except the beams breaking loose from the tiny holes in the filigreed vase-lamp. As he pulled away the towel that draped her, she rolled into her bed with the scents on her body uncovering themselves. He climbed in by her side, gazing at her and outlining her form with feathery strokes. Her lips were beginning to get dry with his hot breath.

As his hand slid downwards, she parted her legs and felt his fingers run between them. She wanted to hold his hand but he locked them in his stately palms, planted firmly above her head. He kissed the hollow of her armpits. She heaved, wanting desperately to meet him. With the grace of a unicorn, he slid himself into her and stayed there, feeling the heat as she felt the throbbing. Then, in synchronised rhythms they moved, scaling peaks together, there bodies fusing into one being. Hands still clasped and restrained groans let out in unison, they floated and drowned in ecstasy before drowning in a tidal, soulful orgasm.

*****

It may have been ten minutes or it may have been an hour. There was no existent sense of time or space when they opened their eyes from the therapeutic slumber. Their legs were still entwined. Her head rested on his shoulder. She felt his shoulder, imagining the marks of a bullet wound and surgical stitches. There were none.

Opening her eyes, she whispered,

"Raj, it's time to leave. Any later, and we'll miss our flight." He mumbled something in his sleep.

"I'm going to get the baby ready. Will you come downstairs in fifteen minutes?"

He nodded. She knew she had to set off an alarm for him. Without it, there was no chance of him, keeping the promised time. She placed the cuckoo alarm next to him, kissed him on the forehead and got dressed. Makeup was an absolute non-requirement, as she glowed in the aura of motherhood and the attention of a husband who had lovingly come around. She didn't try to think if it was the loss of a loving mother or the pang of brief separation from her that made him begin to understand her as a woman. As long it was a desired consequence, the cause became insignificant.

She stepped out of the room when she saw the maid walking towards her door.

"Madam, the baby has woken up."

She headed towards the nursery where her father-in-law was trying to keep the little one happy in his crib. A name-plate hung on the nursery-door with the baby's name on it - ALPHAAZ.

*****

On their flight from Mumbai to Cape Town to celebrate New Year's Eve, they settled comfortably in their seats. The baby slept snugly in the bassinet while the maid enjoyed the little frills of air-travel. Rajeev had chatted animatedly with her for half an hour after take-off and had gradually slipped into deep sleep. She fell into her favourite pastime of reminiscing and reflection.

*****

29th December 2008

She felt cold. He requested the cabin crew to bring her a blanket. He had been talking incessantly for some time now and she wondered if he would ever get tired. As she pulled the blanket over her, she wished secretly to have his arm go around her shoulders to provide the warmth she needed.

To distract herself, she started another conversation.

"So, what do you like to do other than fighting terrorists?"

"I read noses."

"What?"

"Yes, I read noses. Just like some people read palms, tarot and even coffee-cups. I read noses."

"You're funny!"

"No, seriously! No kidding. Like I can read your nose for you right now and I don't even need any fancy headgear for it!"

She'd be breaking the daughter-in-law code if she smiled right now, so she suppressed it.

"There's something sitting on your nose," he whispered to her.

She crossed her brows as she tried to wipe off whatever it was.

"You can't wipe it off. It's here to stay. It's called a crush and shows up as a little pimple."

She felt embarrassed at his sudden and uninhibited disclosure of what she was feeling inside. She wished that he hadn't labelled it as just an infatuation.

"Ok. Look, I'll read that air-hostess's nose for you. She's got vile humour sitting on her nose right now. Within the next half-hour, she will get into an argument with someone. Let's just pray it's not the pilot who she manages to spite."

"You're crazy!" and she let out a giggle, despite her best effort not to.

Both of them kept looking at the air-hostess who was oblivious of their observation. She then got up to respond to a passenger's call. She walked past them as their gaze followed her from lowered eye-lids. Soon enough, they heard a sharp retort, followed by her speedy exit from the aisle. They could see that she had a drink spilled on her uniform.

"O my God! I don't believe this! Are you serious?"

"Well, I'm usually not but this time coincidence took me seriously."

And they laughed a muffled laughter together.

"But Hansa, there's one thing I'm serious about in my life." "Which is?"

"My pride; which comes from my belief in certain principles, which, people nowadays, find old-fashioned and unexciting."

"Everybody has some principles to live by. Don't they?"

"Yes, perhaps. But if your principles fail to create harmony in your immediate environment, it may be a good idea to rephrase them."

"Oh, you philosophise as well!"

"I only polarise…to do the right thing."

"And what are you trying to polarise me to do?" she asked innocently.

For a moment, he wanted to cup her face in his hands and kiss her. But he never allowed momentary distractions to shape the course of his life.

"I am distracted to death by you."

She raised her face, not expecting his confession to come around like this, at this time.

"I know you find this ill-timed and inappropriate but I believe in diffusing a bomb before it causes an explosion."

"I can't understand what you're trying to say."

"Hansa, look at me and tell me how you feel about me." She was unable to. There was a lump in her throat.

He lifted her chin with his forefinger and looked intently in her eyes.

"I think I'm falling in love with you," she murmured.

*****

An intense silence lurked in the space between them. Then he spoke with unpretentious concern.

"You are a man's dream-come-true, Hansa. And you know it. There won't be a guy on this planet who wouldn't feel blessed to have your attention. But …"

"Stop there. This word stifles hope."

"It's important for me to speak now before it leaves you for good. The first time that I saw you, I knew that I had been put there for a larger reason. Something even bigger than saving lives! The entire time that I spent in the hospital, I kept pondering over that reason. What could be larger than saving precious lives? It dawned on me slowly and gradually."

He paused to think. She looked at him in eager hope.

"I can sense that you are driving towards an end that I may not like."

"You will, Hansa. Just that you may take some time getting to like it! The only thing greater than saving lives from impending death is to infuse life in that of the people who love and live for us. Do you know what I mean?"

"I think I do, but don't wish to."

"I know you know. I have reason to believe that your husband loves you madly. He may have been foolish to not read you well but do you think he has not loved you enough?"

She didn't know what to say.

"Why are you talking about Raj? You don't know him at all." "Maybe I don't. But I do know that a man, who only dreams of only his wife night and day, may be forgiven his immature acts."

"How do you … wait a minute. Have you by any chance met Zarine Nawaaz?"

"You are bright."

"Gosh, she didn't' have to do this!"

"Don't get her wrong, Hansa. She's the one who told me about your feelings for me and I do admit; I couldn't wait to meet you and take you in my arms. All she did was state facts. I formed my own opinions."

"It's not fair. She has lived her life with my father-in-law and yet, she's trying to get me to conform."

"I don't know what her intent is but her argument is right. Hansa, without doubt, you are the woman I shall cherish as my first love all my life, while being unsure if there will ever be a second one. But I don't believe in the word 'never' and I certainly don't believe in stealing. You belong somewhere else and I'd love you even more if you infused life into those who love you."

Never before had she heard a man wanting to drive her towards another.

"Just pushing me towards him is not going to change my feelings or thoughts for you."

"I know but it will make you want to try. You don't have to hate or dislike me to love your husband."

"It's not possible to love two people at the same time. It amounts to infidelity."

"Does it? Was your father-in-law infidel to your mother-in- law? Don't you hold Zarine Nawaaz in high esteem today, as she unintentionally becomes your role-model? And the legal description of infidelity adheres to physical associations and not mental."

She breathed in heavily.

"Look," he continued, "love need not always be given a tangible form. It can stay inside us without getting corrupted by selfish design. If a Zarine Nawaaz can lead a glorious existence with love in her heart, so can Arjun Tandon."

"So, I finally get to know your name. Should I believe then, that you intend to become a significant part of my life?"

Hansa smiled and for the first time in his life, he felt a bit foxed. He smiled too, touching his hand to his forehead.

"Huh! That's just because I'm a bit tipsy right now. I managed some, while fixing the tickets. It's difficult for a man to talk like this to the woman he loves, with a sober head!"

*****

He had arrived for Gargi's funeral and met Hansa and Rajeev with perfect decorum. His eyes spoke of a solemn promise without dropping hints of self-pity or emotional martyrdom. She was overwhelmed with his sense of righteousness and the courage to maintain it. More than a lover, she needed him to be her best friend and mentor.

It was a month later that she invited Zarine and Arjun to her house for an informal dinner with Mr. Walia and Rajeev. When the men had resigned themselves to political discussions, the women slipped away into the garden for woman-talk.

"I can see that you and Raj are very happy together!"

"We are getting there. This is a good spot to be in life. I have rediscovered my husband's love and found a friend who has come like a genie in my life and swung everything around. Strangely, he's the one who made me look at Rajeev in an altogether different light."

"So, do you still feel the same way about Arjun as you did a few months ago?"

"Well, yes and no. My love for him has reached another dimension, which is beyond the physicality of a relationship."

"Does Rajeev know?"

"I don't know. I'm still trying to ascertain what to tell him and how to make him understand. Would he look at things like his mother, or would he look at things from my perspective, now that he understands me so much more. Would he really accept this complexity, given the fact that I wish to love and have him as my husband for the rest of my life? How can I make him understand when I myself don't comprehend it completely?"

"Hmm, if you were to take my advice, honey, I'd say, just let things be. You are not being disloyal to Raj by having a guiding light in your life. If Lord Krishna could have Radha and Mira devoted to him in different ways, why can't Hansa's devotion to two men, be considered pious and sacrosanct?"

"I wonder. Perhaps, I'll find an answer to that, soon!"

*****

Kuber's last attempt at meeting Hansa had not led him anywhere. A few acts are beyond the scope of forgiveness. Rajeev, as a worthy son-in-law, had taken it upon himself to put his mother-in-law's murderer to task. A long and intense battle ensued in the courts in which the brightest brains in the country fought over the sentence and release of Kuber Narang. The day that the case was presented in court, he was taken into judicial custody and was now tucked away in prison, waiting repentantly for life to give him another opportunity to salvage his dying career and reputation. For the first time in his life, Kuber Narang turned towards God to make peace with the inner turmoil and emptiness.

*****

In preparation of the first production by his company Wal-Arts, he had now become even more animated and hyperactive in organising things. One such night, while driving home himself and the driver sitting next to him, Rajeev had a crash that few people can survive.

Hansa was aghast on receiving the news of Rajeev being in critical care at Breach Candy Hospital. They rushed to the hospital and were greeted with the news that Rajeev needed blood immediately. His being the O-negative blood group, which was rare and limited in the bank, they needed a donor to pitch in. It was at this time that Arjun Tandon came to Hansa's rescue again. Incidentally, he had the same blood group and readily volunteered to donate. Not only did he bring life back to Hansa yet again by providing timely aid to Rajeev; he also became an inseparable member of the Walia clan, thereafter.

It was a couple of months later that Hansa broke the news of her pregnancy. This time, Rajeev was not only ready and accepting, and to her pleasant surprise, rather jubilant. He wished to have a daughter put together with the best traits from his wife and mother. Hansa was amused with his childlike responses.

In order to express his joy to the world in a typically Rajeev Walia way, he threw a party for close friends and relatives on their favourite yacht, Hansa. Leaving no stone unturned and no idea explored, he created a small Disneyland on the upper deck. The guests arrived and were greeted with the news, which was shared with them over a lavish display of fireworks and the finest champagne.

Zarine hugged Hansa and said, “I'm so happy for the two of you. You make the perfect couple together.”

Hansa held her hands. “There's such a change that has come over Rajeev. It's unimaginable and I keep praying for it to last a lifetime.”

“Yes, I think, a close brush with death has helped him gain a perspective in life.”

“Don't you think Arjun stepping in as his blood-donor was something of a karmic connection? I find all of this so surreal, and so beautiful!”

“I'm with you on that. And Hansa, forgive me for saying this, I think the baby that is arriving, technically, would have Arjun's blood flowing through his veins as well!”

Hansa's eyes widened with amazement as she pondered over Zarine's words.

*****

Srijann and Zarine continued to fortify their relationship by providing rational advice and emotional anchorage to each other. Neither of them made an attempt to provide a social sanction to their bond by filling the void that Gargi had left behind her. Rajeev became more for giving and understanding as he became the father of a healthy baby boy on 29th December 2009. They had discussed many probable names for the new member of the family but had not been able to zero-in on a suitable one.

The day that Hansa arrived home with their bundle of joy, they were welcomed by Zarine and other family members. The priests performed the puja and told Srijann Walia that the letter 'A' would make for an auspicious name for the child.

Everybody looked at him in anticipation. After some deliberation, Srijee spoke, “Since, my grandson's arrival in my life has left me speechless with joy; I would like to call him ‘Alphaaz’ which means words. He will now give form to our emotions and colour them with vibrant meaning.”

Hansa couldn't help looking askance at Zarine, who smiled and winked at her, quietly acknowledging the coincidence and validating it.

*****

The announcement by the cabin-staff brought Hansa out of her reverie and Rajeev out of his sleep. It was time to take the baby in her arms and get ready for landing. Rajeev did the needful and his son crooned happily in his arms.

The plane landed with a slight thud. At the airport, they moved towards baggage-claim. As they made their way towards the exit, a familiar hand waved out to them. Rajeev rushed out to meet Arjun and greeted him with a hug. As Hansa approached them with the baby, Arjun took Alphaaz in his arms and turned to a pretty girl standing next to him.

“Devanshi, meet Alphaaz, my little alter ego. And by the way, folks,” he said turning towards Hansa and Rajeev, “meet my fiancée Devanshi. My parents believe that she is the one for me and I happily submit to their observation.”

Devanshi smiled and shook hands with Rajeev, while Hansa gave her a hug. She was battling emotions that had not surfaced in the past one year. And she did not have Zarine for advice. They left the airport in Arjun's jeep and drove towards the resort that they were booked in. They travelled on a stretch of winding road that snaked around a mountain, looming large against a stretch of cobalt blue waters. Clouds hung loosely over the table of mountains and the view throughout the drive was mesmerising. Yet, an ill-gotten thought kept nagging Hansa.

She decided to pull herself out of the cloud of envy that had engulfed her momentarily. She chided herself for it and decided to embrace Arjun's fiancée as a friend. After all, he was responsible, to a large extent, for the current joys in her life. The least she could do to reciprocate was to enhance the magnitude of his happiness. In order to break the ice, she initiated a conversation.

"So, Devanshi, which part of India are you from? From what we know of Arjun, you're going to be a really pampered wife! He spoils people, you know!"

Devanshi looked back and smiled, and then continued to look ahead.

"When do you guys plan to get married?" Rajeev picked up the loose end of the conversation.

"In February. And before you form an opinion about her, let me tell you, Devanshi doesn't talk to anyone. She's speech-impaired."

Instantly, jealousy replaced itself with pride and certain traces of shame for having reduced her beau-ideal to a trite position. She now felt even more secure in the knowledge that in having Arjun in her life, she would know more about life and living than she had ever done before.

Rajeev had his arm around her shoulder and the baby gurgled in her lap. The sun shone mercifully and the wind played along happily over calm waters. It was a perfect world.